DEATH OF A STRANGER

JOHN PILKINGTON

B
Boldwood

First published in Great Britain in 2025 by Boldwood Books Ltd.

Copyright © John Pilkington, 2025

Cover Design by JD Smith Design Ltd

Cover Images: Shutterstock and Jerry "Woody" / Wikimedia Commons

The moral right of John Pilkington to be identified as the author of this work has been asserted in accordance with the Copyright, Designs and Patents Act 1988.

All rights reserved. No part of this book may be reproduced in any form or by any electronic or mechanical means, including information storage and retrieval systems, without written permission from the author, except for the use of brief quotations in a book review. This book is a work of fiction and, except in the case of historical fact, any resemblance to actual persons, living or dead, is purely coincidental.

Every effort has been made to obtain the necessary permissions with reference to copyright material, both illustrative and quoted. We apologise for any omissions in this respect and will be pleased to make the appropriate acknowledgements in any future edition.

A CIP catalogue record for this book is available from the British Library.

Paperback ISBN 978-1-80600-873-5

Large Print ISBN 978-1-80600-874-2

Hardback ISBN 978-1-80600-872-8

Trade Paperback ISBN 978-1-80656-060-8

Ebook ISBN 978-1-80600-875-9

Kindle ISBN 978-1-80600-876-6

Audio CD ISBN 978-1-80600-867-4

MP3 CD ISBN 978-1-80600-868-1

Digital audio download ISBN 978-1-80600-871-1

This book is printed on certified sustainable paper. Boldwood Books is dedicated to putting sustainability at the heart of our business. For more information please visit https://www.boldwoodbooks.com/about-us/sustainability/

Boldwood Books Ltd, 23 Bowerdean Street, London, SW6 3TN

www.boldwoodbooks.com

For Nicky, Sophie and Joni

1

Cutler caught the thief as he scuttled out of Hog Lane, carrying a bag containing something that clinked. Startled by the lantern's beam, the fellow gave a yelp and came to an abrupt halt.

'Night-stepping again, Ned?' Cutler eyed him sternly. 'What in God's name were you thinking?'

Ned Broad dropped to a crouch, eyes darting about. But he knew the constable, as he knew his chances of escape were slim. 'By the Christ, Master Matthew,' he breathed. 'You near frit me to death.' He wet his lips. 'See now, can't we do a little horse-trading?'

'What's in the bag?' Cutler demanded. 'Sounded like metal to me – pewter?'

But when the other made no answer – how could he? – he lowered his lantern, the two of them standing in the gloom of Bishopsgate Street. As rogues of Shoreditch went, this one was far from the worst. A scarecrow of a man with a large and unruly family, he took odd jobs when he could get them and stole when he couldn't, usually things of small worth which he sold to city dealers who asked no questions. And these days, with two years of plague barely over, there were still enough empty houses to tempt men like him. Broad had been caught twice, branded on his thumb with a T for thief, whipped at the post by St Leonard's Church and set in the stocks, yet here he was again. And this time, he could hang.

'Which house did you visit?' Cutler persisted, eying the man: his frayed woollen cap, his scuffed jerkin. He was sweating, a sheen on his brow visible in the lantern's gleam.

'Well, see now—' Ned began – but was cut short.

'No, I'm not seeing,' Cutler said. 'You're a fool to yourself, Ned. Whatever you've got in the bag, I'd swear without even looking that it amounts to more than a shilling's worth. That's grand larceny – you know the penalty.'

Broad gulped, lowering his gaze. They may have been neighbours, but just now, the gulf between them was vast. The constable not only had the power to arrest him; he had the wherewithal too. Few men dared to cross Matthew Cutler.

'I don't suppose you'd care to split the spoils?' the thief enquired, in a tone that suggested he already knew the answer. 'Or,' he added quickly, 'what if I take 'em back? I could do it easy enough.' He nodded eagerly. 'You know me, Master Matthew – I was widowed by the pestilence, same as you. I'm a poor man with seven brats to feed. What'd they do if I was took, eh? I mean, what would...'

But he stopped himself, for the constable's mind appeared to be elsewhere. In fact, Broad's offer to split the spoils had aroused suspicions he had harboured for weeks. There had been thefts in the parish this summer, yet somehow, the culprit or culprits always evaded capture – which to Cutler suggested one obvious explanation.

'That offer, Ned – have you made it before? Maybe to

someone who's not so particular about the law as I am? Who might even take a coin, for looking the other way?'

The other shook his head. 'Jesu, no... I never. It was a notion I had just now – I swear.'

But he was lying, and Cutler knew it. It was not yet dawn, and where was the watchman? Taking bribes was not unknown among unpaid and often discontented parish officials. Could this be an opportunity, he wondered, to get the matter out in the open?

'In truth, Ned, you've given me food for thought,' he said. He had relaxed somewhat, which made the house-breaker uneasy. 'Mayhap we could do a little bargaining after all.'

'We could?' Broad shifted on his feet, which produced a loud clink from his bag. Cutler pretended not to notice.

'If you gave me a name,' he said, 'say, of a man who's turned a blind eye to your forays in the past, I might choose to forget what's happened this night. Whisper it, and I'll wait here while you return whatever you stole. When I see you come back empty-handed, I'll escort you home and that'll be the end of it. More,' he added, 'none shall know who gave me that name. So – what think you?'

But as he half-expected, it was to no avail. Ned Broad risked the harshest of penalties: that of being hanged in chains, as close as possible to the scene of his crime. And yet, an informer he was not.

'I don't follow you, Master Matthew,' he mumbled, eyes on the ground. 'There's no such fellow, and I never done aught like that.'

They were both silent for a while, as a slight breeze blew across from Finsbury Fields. In spite of himself, Cutler pitied the man. He too had lost his wife to the terrible black plague that had swept the country – a loss he tried not to brood upon, usually without success. Sometimes, he believed he heard Anne's voice, gentle and with that edge of wry humour he had adored, giving him the benefit of her advice. What would it be this time, he wondered? Press this spindle-shank rogue further, or...

'Let me take the stuff back,' Ned said, breaking his thoughts. 'I'll go to work tomorrow, for the cooper. He's said he could use a man to carry for him.' He waited, glancing uneasily about the empty street. It would be dawn soon, and folk would be about. Finally, he looked up at Cutler, who let out a sigh.

'Do it, then get yourself home,' he said at last. 'But I mean to make you pay, Ned. Tomorrow, you'll do two hours in the stocks – for missing church, that is. Are we agreed?'

The other blinked, then let out a breath and nodded. With nothing further to be said, he turned and slouched back into the lane.

Cutler watched him go, then walked away. There was no need to escort the man back to his tumbledown cottage. Ned Broad was as straight as an arrow... unless there happened to be a deserted house nearby, with pewterware lying about.

* * *

He was home within the quarter hour, as the sun's first rays rose over the trees beyond the artillery yard. At least it wasn't raining, as it had been for much of this cloudy summer of 1594. It was Thursday, he remembered, which meant that the Queen's gunners would arrive for their weekly cannon practice. Cutler's house was across the street and slightly north of the yard, yet the gunnery noise was a trial to everyone in Bishopsgate Ward. Then, as some were quick to remind their neighbours, England was still at war with Spain, and with the Irish rebels too. It was only six years since the panic over the Armada, and the King of Spain was building another great fleet, it was said.

Cutler entered the hallway, snuffed the lantern's flame and set it down. He walked down the passage to the kitchen, and found Aunt Margery kneeling to kindle the fire.

'Up already,' he said. 'Trouble sleeping again?'

'Well now, I might say the same of you,' came the retort. She turned to look at him, tucking a stray lock of grey hair under her linen cap. 'Another night-time stroll, was it? Or have you taken to visiting Mistress Leake's?'

'I think you know better than that,' Cutler said, and sat down at the table.

'It'll take a while to warm the porridge,' Margery told him. 'There's beer in the jug.'

He found a mug and poured, then set himself to pulling off his boots. Meanwhile, the fire took hold, its maker fanning the flames with her apron. He watched her with affection: the spinster aunt of his late wife, who had been the family's cook, servant and home comfort since Anne's death at the height of the pestilence. At first unsure of her somewhat forbidding presence, he had long ago come to find her indispensable, as had the girls. Upon thinking of whom, he was about to make enquiry when the other anticipated him.

'Jane is at her toilet,' Aunt Margery announced. 'Her highness Mistress Katherine is yet abed.' And when he made no remark: 'It strikes me your eldest has been acting above herself, since yon popinjay Thorne started paying court. A born flatterer, that one. I see through him.'

Cutler put his boots aside, took a pull from his mug and set it down. Mention of Edward Thorne always made him uneasy. His spirited daughter Katherine was as pretty as any in Bishopsgate Ward, and could have attracted any beau she chose. The fact that she appeared to enjoy the attentions of a cocky young gallant who spent half his time at the bowling alley or the gambling house had been a source of tension for weeks.

'Mayhap you could talk to her,' he said. 'She never listens to me.'

'You think I haven't tried?' Margery stood up, dusted off her hands and faced him. 'You're too easy with her, Matthew. Anne would have made her see sense.'

'She would,' he agreed, lowering his gaze.

She watched him, then turned to busy herself with getting breakfast. There was a platter of crusty bread on the table, and he helped himself to a piece. Daylight was filling the room, while from outside came the sounds of Shoreditch rising: a dog's bark, a shouted greeting. A short while later, when Cutler's younger daughter came downstairs and trotted into the kitchen wearing her customary smile, his heart lifted as it always did.

'I see you've been playing at night watchman again,' she said. She pointed at his boots, which carried a telltale trace of mud.

Cutler put on a wry look. 'And a good morning to you, Jane.'

She came over and kissed him, then did the same for Aunt Margery while he chewed bread thoughtfully. His day had begun. One of the three constables of Bishopsgate Ward Without the Gate, he never knew what he might face. He frowned, remembering that he was supposed to put Ned Broad in the stocks, a task he had never relished. Thinking of Ned, his mind drifted to the graver matter of who might be choosing to overlook the activities of lawbreakers in the parish. One name had occurred already, and the notion troubled him.

'Porridge, Matthew.'

Margery's voice brought him out of his reverie, as she placed the steaming bowl before him. But as Jane too was sitting down, there came a loud knocking from the front door. Even as the three of them turned, the door was opened and a voice called out.

'Master Constable, are you within? I pray you, come forth!'

'Stephen, is that you?' Cutler was on his feet, stepping out into the passage in his hose. He knew the voice of Stephen Bland, watchman of Spitalfields Parish. Sunlight was showing from the street and there he stood, lantern still in hand, hatted and wearing his cape. Seeing his demeanour, Cutler was quickly alert.

'What's the coil?' He looked the portly watchman up and down, noting his agitation. He was not a young man, and having hurried, he was breathing hard. Putting a hand to the door's frame to steady himself, he shook his head.

'A fearful thing, Matthew. It's the Italian – Brisco.'

'The perfumer.' Cutler pictured him. 'What's he—'

'He's dead – cruelly slain.' The other cut him short. 'I've come now from his shop... It's a scene of butchery.' He shook his head again. 'You'd best come quick, for there's a throng gathering already.'

'I will,' Cutler said. And he would have left the house immediately, had not Jane's voice from behind stayed him.

'Hadn't you better put your boots on?' she said, holding them up.

* * *

Alessandro Brisco's shop was down Bishopsgate Street, almost on the border of Cutler's parish of Spitalfields. As he and Stephen Bland hurried, they saw that the Gate was already open. A cart rumbled past, heading into London, but it was the small knot of bystanders further down the street that caught the eye.

'I've got Josiah Madge on the door, keeping them out,' Bland said, panting a little. He named the Ward's scavenger, a bullish man whom few would dare to challenge.

'Who raised the alarm?' Cutler wanted to know.

'A customer, name of Whitney. He's frit enough to soil himself. Found the door unlocked, he says, which isn't like Brisco. That one's – I mean he *was* – a cautious man.'

Cutler's mind was busy. The Italian perfumer, one of a number of strangers with rights of denization in the Ward, had dealt mostly with wealthy clients in London and as a result was somewhat apart from the humbler tradesfolk. Yet he had been courteous and a good citizen, which made the news of his murder – for such it must be – even more troubling.

As the two men neared the shop's entrance, braced to force their way through the press of people, a voice hailed them.

'Cutler! At last!'

An unmistakeable figure separated itself from the group: Austen Kett, the constable of St Botolph's parish, which bordered theirs. Kett was unmistakeable because he was a dwarf: a little over four feet tall, though he wore thick-heeled boots to temper the effect. A scrivener by trade, he was also the nosiest man in Bishopsgate, or so it was said.

'At last, Master Kett?' Bland's hackles were rising already; it was well-known that he and Kett had never got on. 'Our constable's only just been told the news. Whereas you're quick off the mark, as always.'

'I thought you'd need some help,' came the retort. 'I know it's not my parish, but...'

'That's well, Austen. I'd welcome any aid you could give.' Cutler threw him a nod. 'Have you been inside?'

'I have.' The little man looked away. 'It's carnage... savagery. I've no other words.'

The three of them began to push forward. People fell back, talking in subdued fashion. Cutler knew most of them, and it struck him – as it often did – that when all was said and done, Bishopsgate was a village, as close-knit as any. One woman was in tears, being comforted by another. There were neighbours of Brisco's present, including the Dutch shoemaker who appeared badly shaken. At sight of the constables, he lowered his gaze and moved aside. Bland and Kett called out, ordering people to step away. Soon, the doorway was clear, blocked only by Josiah Madge, the scowling scavenger with a cudgel in his hand.

'By Jesu, here's relief!' The man was in a sweat, his shoulders taut as a bullock's. 'I swear I would've used this, if you men hadn't come.' He was brandishing his weapon fiercely, but at sight of Cutler, he lowered it. 'You'd best go inside, constable,' he muttered, bending closer. 'As for me, I've no wish to set foot in there again.'

'I thank you, Madge,' Cutler said. 'Why don't you go home, eh?'

'Gladly,' the scavenger said. He was moving off, then paused. 'The gentleman who found him is in the next house, taking a mug to steady himself. I bade him wait for you.'

Cutler let him go and turned back to his fellows. Kett was hanging back now, as if unwilling to be first inside. Bland ignored him and turned to his constable.

'Shall we tell the coroner?'

'I want to take a look first.'

They entered slowly, one at a time: a small shop, well-appointed with neat shelves of jars and bottles. Butchery was how the watchman had described the scene; Cutler had to admit that it was as good a word as any. Signor Brisco, clad in a good maroon doublet and breeches, lay on his back on the floor, which was awash with his blood. His face was composed, eyes closed. The small table on which he had always conducted business was on its side, along with several broken glass phials. As a result, the room was filled with a miasma of perfume from the spilled contents, almost enough to make the three men dizzy. But it was the victim's wounds which struck Cutler most forcibly: the stabbing had been ferocious. Moreover, it was obvious from the disarray that he had put up a fight.

'Sword-thrusts, would you say?'

Bland was breathing steadily, mastering himself. Both he and Kett had already viewed the blood-soaked body, yet further sight of it seemed to compound the shock. Kett took a pace forward to stand beside Cutler. He was holding a grimy kerchief to his nose.

'What scent is that?' he murmured. 'Lilac?'

'Storax,' Cutler said. 'They use it to perfume gloves.' To Bland, he said, 'Looks to me like a poniard was used. Whoever wielded it was in a rage.'

'But who would want to kill him?' The watchman wore a look of disbelief. 'He never did any man harm, that I knew of. Nor had a harsh word for anybody.'

There was a stir from the doorway; following Madge's departure, people were nosing in. Turning sharply, Cutler told them to stay outside.

'I'll go as doorman,' Kett said, with a glance at his fellow constable. 'This is your parish, after all.' He turned away, clearly relieved to quit the scene.

'It stinks like a whorehouse,' Bland said. 'Civet, damask-rose... storax too, if you say it is.'

Cutler moved towards the corpse and dropped to one knee. There were in fact fewer stab wounds than he had first thought, one to the heart having drawn most of the blood. A gash on Brisco's palm spoke of an attempt to ward off the assault. But his own poniard was in its sheath, seemingly untouched. On closer inspection, from the way the blood had congealed, it seemed likely that he had been killed the previous night. When Cutler touched the man's hand lightly, he found the body stone cold. Rising to his feet, he looked round.

'I'll speak to the one who found him. Whitney, wasn't that his name?' And when Bland nodded: 'There'll be an inquest of course, likely at the White Hart.'

'Then I'll go to the coroner. Seems to me you have your hands full here.'

'Do you know aught of his family?'

The watchman shook his head. 'He lived alone. I heard there was a wife, once.'

With a last look at the slain man, Cutler started towards the door. Bland went out first, heading off towards the city. The crowd had thinned now, and Bishopsgate Street was already a-bustle. Kett stood outside with a cudgel, the one formerly held by Madge.

'Is there a way to lock the shop from outside?' Cutler wondered. 'I couldn't see a key anywhere. He would have bolted up from within.'

'I could bring a couple of scantlings, nail them across the doorway,' the diminutive constable suggested. 'Will that serve for now?'

'It will. I'm obliged to you, Austen.'

They parted, Kett saying he would find someone to stand watch while he went to fetch boards and tools. Meanwhile, Cutler went to the next house, knocked on the door and was admitted. He found Master Whitney, a well-dressed gentleman in his forties, seated in the parlour with the elderly householders, and seemingly still shaken. Having exchanged words with the constable, the couple left him and the finder of the body alone. Seating himself, Cutler was about to ask him to give his account, but the other forestalled him.

'Such wickedness – such evil!' he exclaimed, with a rapid shake of his head. 'How else may a man describe it? And by the heavens, constable, I believe I know the cause!'

'You do?' Cutler blinked. 'How in the—'

'He was a stranger, was he not?' Whitney broke in, with some heat. 'You know how some feel about interlopers. Have you forgotten the broadsides set on the door of the Dutch church, back when the pestilence started? Foreigners are always blamed, for everything from stealing the bread from Englishmen's mouths to starting the plague. It's plain as a pikestaff!'

But seeing the constable's frown, he stopped himself. While there was some truth in his words, Cutler was loth to leap to conclusions. There had been immigrants here for decades, and most had been long accepted. Furthermore, Brisco's trade was an unusual one, displacing nobody. As Stephen Bland had said, the perfumer had never caused trouble.

'How well did you know Brisco, Master Whitney?' he asked, after a moment.

'I knew him to be a man of honour,' the other replied tersely. 'A kindly and diligent fellow, who prepared scented pomanders for me, most skilfully. That's why I went early today, as soon as the Bishopsgate opened. I was to collect a gift for my wife. It's her birthday...'

On a sudden, the man faltered, his anger ebbing away. He screwed his eyes shut, as if he were reliving his grisly experience. Cutler waited.

'I was unmanned by what I found,' Whitney said at last, in a softer tone. 'The door was unbolted, so I went in directly. I believe I called out, before I saw him.' Taking a breath, he eyed Cutler directly. 'You'll have seen what I did. I backed to the door, got myself outside. A passer-by called the watchman.'

'When had you last seen him, before today?' Cutler enquired. And on being told it was a week ago: 'Did he seem troubled, or distracted in any way?'

The other shook his head. 'By no means. He was affable as

always – a yeoman, yet in every other way a gentleman, almost the equal of myself.'

'Do you know aught of his family?'

The other considered. 'In truth, I do not. He comes – I should say he came – from Venice, I believe.' Upon which, Master Whitney reached for a cup which lay at his feet, lifted it and drained it before setting it down. 'Now, master constable,' he said, 'I've told you all I can. I'll to my business.'

He stood up, then on a sudden dropped his gaze. 'My wife will have to forgo her pomander for some other gift,' he murmured. 'I shan't be coming here again.'

Cutler too got to his feet, and bade farewell to the man who had unwittingly become the last customer of the slain perfumer. Walking heavily, Whitney passed out to the passage and was gone. The constable stood mulling over what had been said, as the gravity of his position weighed heavily about his shoulders.

It was the first such crime he had faced in the months since he had agreed to act as constable in lieu of the man elected. The elected man was a gunsmith, busy with his trade and content to pay another to serve in his place. His name was John Willard, Shoreditch born and bred – and he was also Cutler's father-in-law.

Just now, he thought it might help to pay him a visit.

2

Head down, Cutler walked briskly along Bishopsgate Street. The sun was up and traffic had increased on foot and on horseback, mostly moving towards the city gate. One or two people drew near as if to address him, before sensing that the time was inapt. He barrelled on, and was almost at the door of Willard's workshop when a voice hailed him. Turning, he frowned at sight of another upholder of the law in Bishopsgate Ward Without: the deputy alderman, Henry Deans. Just then, this man was one of the last he would wish to see.

'I've only now been told what's occurred,' Deans said as he approached. Cutler was unsurprised to find him at his most officious: cloaked and hatted despite the weather, and wearing a frown. Standing stiffly, he gave good morning but was cut short.

'Did you not think to inform me, constable?' the man snapped. 'From what I can tell, all of Bishopsgate knows of this catastrophe already. I demand a report!'

'News of Brisco's death has been taken to the coroner, Master Deans,' Cutler said mildly. 'I believed that to be my first duty. I would have called on you in due course.'

'What of Thomas Skinner – has he been told?' Deans countered, puffing out his chest. A bluff man with a beard trimmed to a steeple-point, he was notorious for believing himself more suited to the post of alderman of this ward than Master Skinner, a view with which few concurred.

'I pray you, be assured I'll speak to him soon,' Cutler replied. 'In the meantime, do you truly wish me to tell you all that I've seen this morning, here in the street?'

'Well, perhaps not all of it... not at this time.' Deans blew out a breath. 'But is what I've heard true? That the Italian was robbed and murdered in the night?'

'I saw no sign of robbery,' Cutler told him. 'But murdered, yes. Stabbed most cruelly. Austen Kett will board up the shop, while—'

'While you search?' the other finished. 'Indeed, the culprit must be caught quickly. And it's your place to mount the hue and cry.'

'Hue and cry?' Cutler echoed. 'What purpose would that serve, when nobody has the least idea who it is we're seeking?'

'Well – perhaps so,' Deans blustered. 'And yet, this horrid business is most inauspicious for our Ward. I stand ready to act, as must the other constables. You say Kett is aiding you?'

Curbing his impatience, Cutler nodded. He was eager to talk matters over with John Willard, who knew the district better than anyone, as he knew almost every person within it. But when Deans brought up another name, he frowned.

'Farrant? I'm loth to call upon his services. Moreover, he would mislike the notion of aiding me. He's no friend to one who went upon the stage, even if those days have passed.'

Deans bristled – but it was true, and most people knew it. Not so long ago, Cutler had been a player at the Curtain Theatre, which stood on Holywell Lane a short distance north of where they stood. By an ironic quirk of fate, both the Curtain and its neighbour the Old Theatre lay in the parish of St Leonard's, whose constable was Roger Farrant: a man of stern and somewhat Puritanical beliefs, one of them being that places of sin such as theatres should be closed down forever. He had never accepted Cutler as a fellow officer of the law, and made no secret of it.

'I say a fig for that,' Deans grunted. 'You and he must work in consort. The matter is too grave to allow for your scruples. People are most fearful – I've seen it already.'

'As have I,' Cutler told him. 'And I'll work day and night to bring them succour. Hence, I'd like to proceed as best I can – with your leave, that is?'

And while Deans eyed him, the constable strode off to Willard's, caring little what the deputy alderman thought. Once inside the door, he closed it behind him and sighed.

'You look like you need a cup of something,' a gravelly voice intoned. 'Do you care to sit?'

* * *

The gunsmith had barred the door, no customers being due for the present. He and his son-in-law sat together, bonded not only by family ties and the loss of Cutler's wife – John Willard's only daughter – but by a mutual respect. In the back of the shop, among the tools and half-finished products of Willard's mastery, the two of them shared a jug of ale. It was the first refreshment the constable had taken since a mouthful of beer in his kitchen, which already seemed hours ago. Aware of a powerful thirst, he drank while a short distance away, the small furnace burned fiercely. Willard was in his shirt, open to the waist with sleeves rolled. Cutler had removed his jerkin, and was setting his cup down on the workbench as the other spoke.

'I've heard the tidings about Brisco,' the greybeard said quietly. 'A terrible business...' He paused, then: 'By the looks of you, I'd say you've been there?'

Cutler nodded. 'Along with Bland and Kett. It's a bloody sight.'

'So, what's to be done?'

'An inquest, the verdict of which should be in little doubt. Meanwhile, a search for anyone who might have had a grudge against the man.'

'And that's why you're here,' Willard said. 'To pick my brains for such.'

'It crossed my mind,' Cutler admitted.

'So.' His father-in-law sipped from his cup and considered. 'The matter is, I didn't know the Italian well. Then again, not many people did, hereabouts. Few have the means to do business with a perfumer.'

'True enough,' came Cutler's reply. 'I spoke with the one who found the body, and...'

'And yet.' Willard eyed him. 'Were I in your place, I'd not listen to those who speak too warmly of Brisco – his kindness, and what a fine fellow he was for a foreigner. All of that.'

Cutler gave a shrug. 'You mean, he wasn't a saint? Well, what man is?'

'All I'll say,' the other went on, 'is that he was engaged in other practices than perfuming gloves and garments for ladies, or for the sort of popinjays that strut about the Court. He loaned money, for one thing.' And when his son-in-law raised an eyebrow: 'And I don't mean mere pennies, or even shillings.'

'Will you say more?' Cutler prompted.

'If you seek for names of his debtors, naturally, I cannot.'

'Of course – yet surely there would be a record of loans. If we searched his shop...'

'You could,' Willard allowed. 'Though I find it hard to imagine any man resorting to murder, simply because he owed Brisco money.'

'In truth, John, so do I.' Cutler took up his cup. 'And it was a savage attack.'

'Something darker behind it, then.' The other drank, then levelled his gaze. 'Whereupon, you should seek for other causes. And thinking on it, I'll admit that one name has already come to mind.'

'Indeed? Then I'll hear it.'

'Though it's merely a suspicion, Matthew... I'm loth to point the finger of blame,' the gunsmith said. 'I urge you to tread softly in this.'

'I will.' Cutler nodded. 'Yet I must begin somewhere.' He took a pull from his cup and frowned. 'The aldermen are in a coil already.'

'Of course, the likes of Skinner and Deans will bay for the murderer's blood,' Willard observed. 'It's the strangers here outside the Walls who will be in fear... and you know why.'

'You believe that could be reason enough?' Cutler's frown deepened. 'I saw enough of that kind of ill will, back in Canterbury. It saddens me to compass it.'

'As it does me,' came the reply. 'And I dislike to give a name, though I will.' He hesitated, then: 'It's Richard Martinhouse, up at St Leonard's.'

He lowered his gaze – but Cutler was troubled. 'The stonemason? Surely not.'

'Know him well, do you?' The other looked up. 'Have you seen him when he's drunk?'

'Not that I recall.'

'He's an angry man, Matthew – and most bitter, since the loss of his daughter in the pestilence. He's turned his grief to rage –

rage against the strangers in our midst. He rants about it some nights in the White Hart, to anyone who'll listen.'

'But murder?' Cutler was unwilling to believe it. 'Martinhouse is a churchwarden... he was even a constable, a few years back.'

'Those years of plague changed many things,' Willard said. 'People, too.'

He fell silent. Cutler pictured the burly stonemason from St Leonard's parish in Shoreditch: a taciturn man who, some said, was more comfortable among gravestones than among his fellows.

He finished his drink, and set it down beside a finely-tooled matchlock pistol with a walnut stock: a costly weapon. It occurred to him briefly that his father-in-law too served the wealthier customers of London, as had the unfortunate Alessandro Brisco.

'How fare my sweet grand-daughters?' his kinsman asked then, breaking his thoughts.

In spite of everything, Cutler managed a smile. 'Jane is my constant delight, while Katherine is my trial. Wilful, but clever – like her mother was.'

'She was.' Willard nodded.

'You must take supper with us soon.'

'I will.' The older man watched Cutler get to his feet. 'I wish I'd the time to aid you in your quest,' he added. 'I feel I should, since you carry the burden I was elected to bear.'

'You've aided me already, John.'

And they parted, each to his work. Once outside, Cutler headed northwards with a heavy heart to speak to Martinhouse, the stonemason. Despite his father-in-law's suspicions, he found the notion of the man committing murder repugnant, if not preposterous. But just now, what else was he to do? He did not know that matters were about to take a somewhat different turn, after he had walked through the Liberty of Norton Folgate into

Shoreditch. Here he would find himself at loggerheads with the man Henry Deans had spoken of as one who should aid him: the hawkish constable of this parish, Roger Farrant.

Farrant was the eyes and ears of St Leonard's, a man who prowled his patch like a watchful hound. Cutler had reached the old churchyard when his eye fell upon the stocks, reminding him on a sudden of his intention to place Ned Broad there. With all that had occurred, the business was forgotten – and now seemed of small importance. He was musing on it, when a tall figure appeared from round the corner of the church and blocked his way.

'Master Cutler. Pray, what's your business here?'

'Master Farrant.' A nodded greeting followed. 'I'm here in accord with my duty, to speak with one of your parishioners.' The constables faced each other: Cutler in his plain jerkin and breeches, the other clad from head to foot in black. Farrant fixed him with a piercing look.

'Who might that be?' And when the answer came: 'The churchwarden? Why so?'

But as Cutler began to explain, he was interrupted.

'By heaven, do you suggest that Martinhouse has some connection with that terrible event?'

'I suggest nothing. Indeed, I hope to strike the man from my—'

'Your suspicions?' Farrant frowned. 'But this is direful – an insult. He is a former constable, and a faithful servant of this parish.'

'He's also given vent to threats against strangers hereabouts,' Cutler said, calmly enough.

'As have others,' came the retort. 'And sometimes, I might say, with a degree of reason.' The man was annoyed, his chest rising.

'The perfumer was a known Papist... Does that not colour your view of his murder?'

'Until now, I confess it had not,' Cutler said, after a pause. In spite of his feelings about this man and his ways, he realised that the matter of Alessandro Brisco's religion had not been part of his deliberations. The murdered man was an Italian who mixed with others of his faith, and was believed to take mass in private when he could. It was a sobering thought.

'Then I advise you to reflect on it,' Farrant said haughtily. He was treating Cutler almost as a dimwit, which finally nettled him.

'I will, constable,' he replied. 'I'll also speak with Martinhouse, whatever your feelings on the matter. He lives close by, does he not?' And he would have turned on his heel, had the other not stayed him.

'Not without me present, you won't,' he said, raising his voice. 'This is my parish!'

'Well then, let us go together.' Cutler faced him. 'Time draws on, and justice waits for no man – not even for you.'

At which Farrant opened his mouth, then closed it and drew a breath.

'Very well,' he sighed. 'Though I'm certain it's a fool's errand – and one you may regret.'

* * *

A short time later, the two of them stood in the single downstairs room of Richard Martinhouse's small cottage. The man had been summoned from his workshop at the rear of the house by his wife. Mistress Mary was a gaunt woman who bore life's tribulations with a stoicism admired by all of Shoreditch, not least since the loss of her teenage daughter to the plague. Cutler disliked being here, though not as much as did Farrant, who began with an apology for their presence – or rather, for the presence of Cutler. Yet his words had little effect on the stonemason, who regarded them both without expression. The visitors had not been invited to sit, and the air was thick with resentment.

'Say what you wish to say, and have done with it,' Martinhouse rumbled, standing in the middle of the room in his dusty apron. 'Some of us have work that can't wait.'

Cutler was about to speak, but Farrant was quicker. 'Likely you'll have heard the news from Spitalfields, Richard,' he said. 'The murder of the Italian, Brisco?'

The stonemason indicated that he had heard.

'Well, it seems the constable here must ask questions of you. I'll leave it to him to say why.'

Martinhouse paused, glanced at his wife who was standing by the doorway, then shifted his gaze with a deliberate slowness. 'Is it so, Master Cutler?'

'It is,' Cutler said. 'Yet I hope our discourse will be brief, for I bear no ill will. I'll merely ask if you can account for your whereabouts last night, after sunset.'

'Well, now.' The stonemason appeared to ponder the matter. 'At sunset, I was with the parson and the sexton, to speak about the matter of the midsummer church ale. We talked for an hour or more, then I came home and went to my bed.' Deliberately, he turned to his wife. 'Is that not the truth, Mary?'

'It is true,' the woman said, with eyes lowered.

'Or, mayhap you'd like to hear of what we did there?' Martinhouse's tone now bordered on the contemptuous, as he faced Cutler again. 'Widowers thirst for such tales, do they not? Since they're not getting any such joy after dark themselves. Unless it be by the hand.'

Farrant, standing stiffly beside Cutler, was silent. The hostility in the room was palpable. But Cutler glanced at Mistress Mary, her troubled expression – and a suspicion flew up, that made him frown.

'I hear you're given to angry words when you're in drink, Martinhouse,' he said. 'Railing at folk for little reason – strangers from other lands that live among us, say. I wonder now if such words might lead to deeds.'

'So... it's as I thought,' the stonemason said with a nod. 'You come to accuse me.'

'I do not,' Cutler replied firmly. 'But I wish to satisfy myself of your innocence in this matter. After what's occurred, suspicions will fall like rain, and my task is—'

'Nay, save your breath,' the other broke in harshly. 'You seek a culprit, to win praise for your efforts. And so, you'll pounce on any man who's dared speak his mind about Papists and incomers – those who've no more right to dwell in England than the rats that jump ship in our harbours! I say a curse upon—'

'Richard, enough!' It was Farrant, displeased by what he heard. 'This is unchristian of you. The slain man was indeed of the Roman faith, yet there are laws to constrict such. And we speak of murder here.'

'We do,' Cutler said, more sharply than he intended. 'And whoever committed such a crime is at large to kill again.' He looked to Farrant, then back at the stonemason. 'Yet for now, I'll take my leave – and whatever you may think, I care naught for praise. What I do care about is the safekeeping of the people of this Ward.'

'Fine words, Cutler.' Martinhouse was almost sneering. 'Then, that's your skill, is it not? A jumped-up player, who lost his living when the theatres closed and snatched at the first chance of a wage, thanks to the charity of his wife's father. Now I'll to my work, and you can go—'

But at a sound from the doorway, he stopped himself. All

three men glanced round to see Mistress Mary with a hand to her mouth. Drawing a breath, Cutler started towards her as if to offer a consoling word – but he was forestalled by Farrant, who placed a hand on his shoulder.

'I think you've stirred up enough mud already,' he said.

And with that, the unpleasant encounter was over. In silence, the constables went to the door, the wife of the house standing aside. Farrant murmured a few words as he passed, to which she barely nodded. Meanwhile, her husband remained where he had stood, like a block of granite. But no sooner had Cutler and Farrant stepped outside than there came a sound of rapid footsteps. They turned to see Mistress Mary, clutching her skirts as she drew close.

'I ask your pardon, masters,' she said, somewhat hastily. 'Richard is brought low... he burns with anger, it's true – but it's against himself, more than any other. He's never dealt with our loss... our daughter Susanna, you'll recall. He sees it as his failure... and whatever he may say when he's taken drink, he wouldn't hurt a fly – I swear it, as I would on the holy book.' In near desperation, she faced Farrant. 'You know him, Master Roger. And what he says is true, about last night. He came back from the church and went at once to bed, where he slept until dawn. That too, I would swear.'

At once, Farrant nodded. 'I never thought otherwise, Mary. I pray you, be at peace.'

He looked pointedly at Cutler, and the accusation was stark – but his fellow constable seemed not to hear. He had seen something that not only troubled him: it might explain a good deal. There was a large bruise on Mary Martinhouse's cheek, which she had attempted to disguise with what looked like wheat flour. Drawing a breath, he turned away.

'I too ask your pardon, mistress,' he said. And without further word, he turned about and walked off down the street. He did not look back.

* * *

It was afternoon already, and by now, the news of the murder would be everywhere. Unable to think where else to go for the present, Cutler went to the inn: the White Hart, close to the city gate. He needed to find a corner and think – but once inside, he saw that it was impossible. The place was crowded with folk talking animatedly. As if to compound his unease, as he entered, there came an explosion of cannon-fire from the artillery yard. He had forgotten it was Thursday: the day for gunnery practice.

'Constable, over here!'

He turned to look, peering through the haze of tobacco smoke, but saw only a throng of drinkers. Then several of them parted abruptly as a short figure pushed his way through: Austen Kett, raising a hand to Cutler. They were in Kett's parish, though he had no wish to confer with the man now. His fellow constable, however, had other ideas.

'I've claimed a seat,' he called, waving him forward. 'Come, for I have tidings.'

Without enthusiasm, Cutler followed him to a table, where the two of them squeezed on to a bench. The drawer came up, and Kett called for mugs of the house ale. There was a platter with a half-eaten pie upon it, which he seemed eager to share.

'I'll take a morsel,' Cutler said. 'Though in truth, I've no great appetite.'

But he ate, relaxing somewhat, more encouraged by the other's presence than he expected. Kett was talkative, keen to speak of boarding up Brisco's shop and making enquiries. He had run into Stephen Bland, who had informed the coroner as promised. It was a while since an inquest had been held here at the White Hart – the landlord was less than pleased about it, but likely it would be good for business. Meanwhile, there was something to impart... He bent close to Cutler, lowering his voice in conspiratorial fashion.

'Meanwhile?' Cutler glanced round, but no one seemed to be eavesdropping. The drawer having returned, he took a mug from him. Turning back to his fellow constable, he waited.

'I have a suspect for you,' the little man announced softly.

On a sudden, despite the gravity of the present situation, Cutler was almost inclined to laugh. As a former player, he knew all about stage whispers. Kett, it occurred to him, had always had a touch of vanity about him. He was wasted as a scrivener, toiling at his inky trade. He could delight the crowd at the Curtain, where ribald comedy was the rage.

'A suspect, for murder?' He raised his eyebrows. 'Who might that be?'

'In truth, I'm loth to speak his name,' Kett muttered, lowering his gaze. 'For he's known to you. And yet...'

He paused as if pondering the matter – but quite quickly, Cutler was losing patience. He had acted on one man's naming a potential culprit already, and regretted it. It struck him now that others might come forward with accusations, in some cases driven by little more than dislike, or to pay off old scores. Somehow, he would have to sift the wheat from the chaff and follow his own instincts. Moreover, he saw, Master Kett wasn't loth to speak this name at all; he was holding it back with difficulty.

'Say it then, Austen,' he breathed. 'And let's waste no more time.'

'It's Nicholas Wincott,' the other said. 'One of your old trade – a player, alongside whom you performed, if I recall correctly.' And when Cutler looked startled, he added, 'The man's a master of fencing and handy with a poniard too – needed for stage fighting, as we know. Yet as one of hot temperament, I believe him capable of straying beyond fakery, into venting real anger against one he thinks has wronged him.'

Whereupon, having observed the impact of his words, Kett took up his mug. Meanwhile, the noise of the inn swirled about them. But Cutler looked away, unease settling over him. He not only knew Wincott, one of the finest players he had ever seen and a favourite at the Curtain; he deemed him a friend, if one of a choleric nature. But what was worse was that, some years ago, Wincott had fought a duel and killed a man, escaping execution by pleading self-defence and reading the neck-verse that had saved many an educated man from the gallows. Hence, he was perhaps capable of such an act – but was it possible he could have murdered Brisco?

His thoughts flying about, Cutler took up his mug and drank deeply, while from the artillery ground came the distant boom of cannon.

And Kett resumed his tale, with what sounded suspiciously like relish.

3

'They quarrelled, Wincott and the Italian – heatedly,' Austen Kett said. 'Over the cost, I'm told, of a pair of perfumed riding gloves – a gift for one of Wincott's paramours. He's known to overspend on ladies of fashion – women far above his station. He's a man of shameless and lustful appetite.'

He spoke rapidly, nodding from time to time, but Cutler was barely listening. In his mind's eye, he saw the handsome player, a companion of his when they were both with Pembroke's Men, smiling as he made his bow before a cheering crowd. Among them, in a crush before the stage, there were always wenches trying to catch Wincott's eye, but he would ignore them. Instead, his gaze would stray to the galleries, where what Kett called *ladies of fashion* fluttered their lace kerchiefs, bestowing hints that he would likely follow up later. He was a man who took risks and laughed while he did so – a quality that the younger Matthew Cutler had always liked. He had not seen Wincott in a long while, yet he doubted he had changed.

He brooded on the matter, while his companion talked on.

'Hard words were said,' Kett continued, waving his half-empty mug for emphasis. 'On Wincott's part, that is. Brisco never raised his voice in anger, you know that as well as I do. The player claimed he was being cheated – that the price had been raised without his knowledge. There was talk of the cost of the perfume, I learn, but to no avail. He left the shop in high dudgeon. So...' He paused. 'What think you now?'

'From whom did you learn this, Austen?' Cutler enquired. 'A jealous husband, perhaps?'

'No, indeed...' Taken aback by his tone, Kett hesitated. 'I admit it's little more than gossip, but there were witnesses to the coil – passers-by, who heard Wincott's harsh words as he came out of the door.'

'Not customers, then?'

'I know not...' The other frowned. 'I see you're unwilling to believe such wickedness of your fellow player. I merely thought to pass on what've heard.'

'Which you've done, plainly enough.' Cutler looked about, saw one or two men glancing at him, and sighed inwardly. He was constable of the parish where a murder had occurred, and it was his place to act. He should leave... In fact, perhaps he'd been unwise to come here.

'I thank you for the bit of pie,' he said, rising from his seat. 'The reckoning for the ale shall be mine.' Finding his purse, he drew out a coin and laid it down.

'Do you not want my aid, then?' Kett enquired, looking up at him. 'I thought—'

'I know,' Cutler said with a nod. 'Likely we'll talk again.'

He moved off, easing his way through the throng. But as he neared the door, a customer put out a hand to stay him.

'Will there be a search for the one who slew the Italian, Master Cutler?' the man enquired, somewhat sourly. 'If it were my task, I'd be tearing the place apart, not dawdling here. Or did you mean to spy on every man in Bishopsgate?'

It was an ugly moment; the fellow was tense, his voice slurred with drink. But Cutler merely looked down, until he thought better of his action and removed his hand.

A quarter hour later, the constable was walking along Holywell Lane, towards the theatres.

***

In the mid-afternoon, performances at both of the Shoreditch playhouses were in progress, the noise of large crowds audible from within the great timber structures. People drifted about: sellers of nuts and bottled ale, trulls seeking customers, boys holding horses for the better-off playgoers. Ahead and to Cutler's right was the Theatre, the first permanent playhouse in England, now almost twenty years old. To his left stood the Curtain, its slightly younger neighbour, where he himself had played almost up to the closure brought about by the plague. It was here that he hoped to find Nicholas Wincott, now with Lord Stange's company, the last he'd heard. On enquiry, however, he learned that Wincott was not upon the stage this day. The cause, it transpired, was his recent tardiness at rehearsals, which had annoyed his fellows.

'He's a law to himself, that one,' Cutler's informant said. 'Played lords and knights so often, he thinks he can strut about like one. The company thought to let him fret for a few days, before he gets a part in their next play. Teach him a lesson.'

The informant was a hired man named Gamage: a minor player Cutler remembered, one of those who took whatever roles he could get. Standing by a stall with a bottle of ale in hand, he was more than willing to exchange theatre gossip.

'Then, you know Nick Wincott well enough, Matthew,' he

said, grinning. 'You can guess at the reason he was coming in late in the mornings – whatever her name is.'

'I can,' Cutler allowed, with a wry look. 'He'll never change – nor will he marry, I suspect.' He glanced round, then asked if the other knew where he might find the man. As it happened, the answer afforded him some relief.

'Why, he's at the Theatre as we speak,' Gamage said, pointing towards it. 'Showing his defiance, if you ask me, by going to watch his company's rivals.' His grin fading, he gave a snort. 'Or more likely, he's at a loose end and can't keep away from Shoreditch.'

'Likely enough,' Cutler said, somewhat absently. He was thinking of Wincott and his weakness for well-bred ladies, which had got him into trouble in the past. And now there was Kett's tale of a heated dispute with the murdered perfumer. He was eager to speak with his friend, and to assure himself of his innocence. It was a matter of waiting by the doors of the Theatre when the performance finished, and trying to catch Wincott when he emerged from the main arena.

'So, you saw him before he went in, Gamage?' he asked. 'Did he pay his penny, to stand among the groundlings?'

'Do you jest, Matthew?' the other countered. The grin was back, as he shook his head. 'This is Gaudy Nick we speak of, who'd spend a shilling as if it were a farthing. If you wish to waylay him, you'd best stand by the stair to the galleries and see him descend in his finery. Like I said, he's played nobles so often, he thinks he's become one.'

For Cutler, however, the news was not unexpected. Bidding a farewell to the hired man, he walked off across mudded and trampled grass to the Theatre which, to judge by the din of the crowd within, was packed to the doors. The play was over now; he heard lively music, for the dancing that always concluded the afternoon's entertainment. Making his way through assorted idlers, his eye fell upon at least two men who were likely cutpurses, moving towards the gallery staircase which was guarded by a doorkeeper. There could be rich pickings among the gentlemen who came out...

But he looked away; much as he would have liked to collar one of those rogues in the act, just now, he had other business. Finding a spot which commanded a view of the stairway, he set himself to wait. Soon, the gates of the theatre swung open and a noisy throng began to pour out, while from the gallery stairs, the first of the better-off customers appeared. And a short time later, to his satisfaction, Nicholas Wincott stepped out, garishly dressed in a flame-coloured doublet and feathered hat.

At once, Cutler moved to block his way.

'Gallant Sir Nicholas?' He put on a smile. 'Well now, how long has it been?'

'Matthew Cutler – is it you?' The dandyish player's mouth fell open in mock-surprise. 'Why, I heard you'd turned precisian, and begun to shun the palaces of sin. Or have you ceased to be a pelting constable, and forsaken the law? In which case, I say let us drink to it!'

He was smiling broadly. Hurrying forward, he embraced Cutler, then stood back to view him. 'See now, were you down among the ragged mob?' he demanded. 'You should have been my guest, upstairs. Not that the play was worth the fee,' he added, with a look of distaste. 'Do you concur?'

'In truth, I was out here and never saw it,' Cutler told him. But he too was smiling. Wincott had often lifted his spirits... Why should this occasion be different?

'Wise man.' His friend nodded. 'So – my invitation holds. Shall we carouse? I sometimes take a cup at Ben Pimlico's tavern in Hoxton these days. It's the finest—'

But he stopped abruptly, his face clouding. 'Oh, God's heart.'

He faltered, putting out a hand as if to call back his words. 'Your wife died... I had forgot, Matthew. You poor fellow... I pray you, forgive my folly.'

'Nay...' Cutler shook his head. 'It's been more than a year, and I give thanks that the girls were spared. We're content enough.' He drew a breath. 'But what of you?'

'I?' Wincott gave a shrug, glancing round at people as they passed. 'I ride the waves of fortune, as always. Got myself out of London during the pestilence as you did, touring with a scratch troupe. Not that we were welcome at every town, yet it passed the time.' He stuck on another smile. 'But see now, I've a powerful thirst. Shall we away?'

'Alas, I cannot. I'm still a pelting constable, as you term it. And just now, my hours are trammelled. Or perhaps you haven't heard of the singular event in my parish, that occurred last night?'

'No, I don't believe I have.' Wincott's smile altered, to appear somewhat conspiratorial. 'In truth, I pass most nights in the city at present, in the company of a new and most pleasing acquaintance. I won't say more.'

'This acquaintance...' Cutler hesitated, then: 'Might it be the one for whom you bespoke a pair of perfumed riding gloves, quite recently?'

He was watching his friend carefully – and was relieved at his reaction. He blinked, and his eyebrows shot up. 'Jesu, how in heaven's name did you know that?'

'I'm not the only one who knows of it, Nick.' Cutler met his eye. 'And I've grim news to impart. The perfumer, Brisco, was slain in his shop. Bishopsgate is abuzz with the news.'

'Slain – you mean murdered?' Wincott seemed not to understand. 'Impossible... I saw him only days ago. This is surely some error...'

Whereupon, the penny dropped.

'Good Christ! I wrangled with him – and that's why you've sought me out! You think I killed him—'

'No!' Cutler shook his head, but too late: the damage was done.

Wincott reeled back from him, a look of horror on his face.

'You, of all people... who shared his last penny with me, more times than I could count? Who chased wenches with me... how could you?'

'Listen to me – I no more suspect you than I would one of my own family,' Cutler said urgently. 'I came only with questions, for one who did business with Brisco. I'm charged with scouring this suburb for answers – further afield too, if I must. People are afraid, and need—'

'They need someone to hang.'

The player's words came, sharp as a whipcrack. One or two passers-by looked round. Feeling wretched, Cutler was about to speak – but his friend was having none of it.

'Good Christ,' Wincott murmured again, shaking his head in disbelief. 'A man argues with a shopkeeper over the cost of a few drops of perfume – a man he's done business with before, I might add, and bickered cheerfully over prices – and is then accused of murder. Well now, I know the times are out of joint, but...' He lowered his eyes. 'You and I were firm companions, Matthew. But men change... Now you're a stalwart of the parish – a stickler for law and order. Constable Cutler.' He lifted his gaze. 'So, what's next?' he demanded, in a bitter tone. 'Am I to be questioned as to my whereabouts when this wicked deed was done, or—'

'Nick, enough!' Cutler cut him short. 'Believe me when I tell you I'm casting about for snippets, and nothing more. What you say of Brisco is true, which makes this event all the more mystifying. No man wished him ill – and I know full well you're not the one I seek. In truth, I'd never have come here if...'

But he broke off, feeling a sudden surge of anger – towards Austen Kett. The man's words came back with some force: Wincott was *one of hot temperament, capable of straying beyond fakery into venting real anger... a man of shameless and lustful appetite...*

Mastering himself, he eyed the player. 'You were accused,' he said flatly. 'And unjustly – I'm certain of it. That's why I came, for I believed I must.'

'Accused, by whom?' Wincott frowned. 'God's heart, tell me his name, and—'

But it was his turn to stop short, realising how it sounded. Not far from here, he had slain a rival in a foolish duel over a lady. It had cost him dearly, in his friends as well as in his reputation – and more, it had cost him the affections of the lady too. With a haggard look, he drew a long breath and addressed Cutler.

'You know me as well as any man, Matthew,' he said, speaking low. 'As you know my past actions – and more, that I vowed I would never draw sword again, except on the stage. Yet, it comes as small surprise that some still suspect me of shedding blood.'

After a moment, Cutler nodded. 'Mayhap they do... but not I.' He summoned a smile, and put out his hand. 'Come, forgive me for being such a clod,' he breathed. 'It would hurt me sorely to think we were no longer friends... were I constable or not.'

Their eyes met, whereupon Wincott gave a sigh, and appeared to relent. 'Of course,' he said, offering his own hand. They gripped each other firmly, then let go at the same time. But it was clear that something had passed between them – something that would not be forgotten.

'Your pardon, but I'm late for Pimlico's,' the player said, growing brisk. 'I suppose your duties call you elsewhere?'

'With regret,' Cutler said. 'But does the invitation stand, for another day?'

'It does, with all my heart,' came the swift reply.

Yet it was false; he was acting, though perhaps only a fellow player would have seen it.

Somewhat hastily, they bade each other farewell and turned away: Wincott striding towards Hoxton, and Cutler making his way back to Holywell Lane. Walking among the last of the playgoers, eyes on the path, he found a curse rising to his lips.

He was suspicious – of a fellow constable. Why, he wondered, was Kett so ready to name Wincott as a likely suspect for Brisco's murder? In fact, why had he been so eager to offer Cutler assistance, from the very start?

* * *

He was home, and it was time for supper. He entered the house to the chatter of women, which lifted his mood somewhat. In the kitchen, he was greeted by his daughters, who were engaged in setting the table. Jane smiled – but Katherine, he thought, seemed somewhat tense.

'You are tired, Father.' At once, Jane came over to kiss him. 'Sit, and I'll pour you some ale. There's a capon and a sallet, and sweet cakes.'

He nodded his approval, then looked at his elder daughter. There were times when Katherine resembled her late mother so markedly, it took his breath away. And she was most fair; everyone told him she would make a good match.

'He's been out the whole day, turning Bishopsgate upside down.' Katherine laid a platter down on their old, scrubbed table and moved towards him. 'Though with small thanks for it, I suspect.' She kissed his cheek, then stood back. 'The street is rife with gossip – wild talk, even. It's hard that you should bear this burden alone.'

'Alone?' He shook his head, and sat down. 'Nay, others are doing their part. Bland, Henry Deans... even Kett.'

'Little Austen Kett, the busybody?' Katherine wore a wry look. 'That's no surprise. He cannot bear to be left out of anything.'

Cutler said nothing, only a word of gratitude when Jane set his mug before him. Hearing the street door open and close, he turned to see Aunt Margery bustle in with a covered basket.

'I was late at the bakery,' she explained, somewhat breathlessly but with an air of triumph. 'They said they'd sold everything, but I knew different. They always keep a few loaves back, and I said I wasn't going home empty-handed.'

'I'd wager you put the fear of God in them, Aunt,' Jane said. 'Will you catch your breath?'

Meanwhile, Katherine took the basket from her.

Preparations for supper advanced, and Cutler began to relax while the women moved about, talking low. Only then did he notice that the table was set not for four people, but for five.

'Are we expecting a guest?' he enquired. And when no answer seemed to be forthcoming, he frowned. 'Katherine?'

But it was Margery who answered. 'She's invited Master Thorne to sup with us,' she announced, in a flat tone.

'Is that so?' Cutler turned to Katherine, who at first avoided his eye. Then:

'It is, Father. Edward has something he wishes to say to you. I knew that, as a fair-minded man, you would hear him out.'

At that, a silence fell, and his heart sank. He had a good idea what it was Edward Thorne wished to say – in fact, he realised, he had long expected it. On a sudden, all thoughts of his duties as constable were pushed aside.

'By heaven, Kate,' he sighed. 'You've picked a fine day for it.'

'We'd talked of it already,' Katherine said hurriedly. 'I would have told you this morning, but you were gone when I came down. Of course, I...' She swallowed, then with a touch of shame, added, 'I know the timing is poor, with what's happened since. But it was too late to alter things. Edward was in the city today, I know not where.'

Cutler refrained from replying that he could have made a guess as to where Master Thorne had been: in a gambling house, say, or at bowling. He glanced at Jane, who looked uncomfortable – had she known this was coming? But he eyed her sister, and nodded.

'Well then, let the invitation stand,' he said. 'We have ever been hospitable folk, have we not?' But when Katherine showed her relief, he looked away. It promised to be a trying evening, after what had been a most trying day.

Whereupon, as he took up his mug, there came further news that compounded it.

'Mercy... I near forgot,' Aunt Margery said. 'There was a boy came this afternoon, Matthew, with a message. You are called to attend Master Skinner in the morning. The alderman, that is. It sounded like a matter of urgency, which I suppose is to be expected?'

With another sigh, Cutler nodded and took a long drink.

And an hour later, with five of them seated cheek by jowl round the table, he was still imbibing, somewhat more liberally than was his habit. For seated opposite him was the unwelcome guest: young Master Thorne, his blond hair neatly coiffed, wearing a fine doublet slashed to show the yellow lining, along with a smile as false as any Cutler had seen.

'What times are these, eh?' Thorne shook his head. 'Murder and mayhem, almost on our doorstep? Your doorstep, I should say, master constable.' He favoured him with a nod. 'I was most shocked to hear the news... but then, here outside the Walls, such events are not so uncommon. Do I hit the mark?'

Cutler made no answer, leaving the others to fill the void.

'This was ever a lively suburb, Edward,' Jane said. 'Yet Bishopsgate folk are good-hearted, in the main. There's an appetite for justice, as strong as you'd find in Broad Street.' She named the Ward bordering Bishopsgate Within on the west, where Master Thorne shared a set of chambers with other young gallants; none knew exactly how many, not even Katherine, who had never been there.

'Well indeed – and no man is better suited to dispense it than your good father, Mistress Jane.' Thorne paused, then took up his cup of sack – a jug of which had been brought in that day by Katherine, Cutler had learned – and saluted his host. 'I've oft thought it, but not said it before: this Ward is fortunate to have one who was born a gentleman to serve them. In truth, I wonder at times how you can bear it.'

At which, Cutler was stung to respond at last.

'I can't imagine what you mean, Master Thorne,' he said, calmly enough. 'I came here first as a player, and found myself at ease among these people. I even married one of them.'

'Of course... your pardon.' Thorne assumed a look of contrition. 'I cast no aspersions...' He glanced at Katherine, who had lowered her gaze, and eyed her father again. 'Yet, I recall that you yourself are a Canterbury man, are you not?'

'I was born there, then got a scholarship to the University, then went travelling. The life of a player seemed to suit me.'

There was a lull after that. Cutler preferred not to speak of his family: his severe father, the magistrate, his silent mother and the brother who despised him for marrying the daughter of a gunsmith. He had not been back to Canterbury since his Cambridge days, and had no desire to do so.

Thorne, however, enlivened by drink, chose to plough on.

'And it's my regret that I never saw you upon the stage,' he said, assuming another smile. 'I'd wager you were among the very best, be it for tragedy or comedy.'

'You flatter me,' Cutler said. 'I was not among the best.' He fell silent, thinking of his encounter with Nicholas Wincott. The memory was raw, and would stay with him.

'Father is too modest,' Katherine said quickly. 'He was lauded as a player, as he is respected as constable.' She threw Cutler a look which he understood well enough: it said, *I know our guest displeases you, yet I beg you to humour him, for he is dear to me.* Drawing a breath, he looked down at his platter and pushed it aside. The meal was over – and whatever might follow, he was now impatient to face it.

'Do you still take tobacco, Master Thorne?' he enquired. 'I do not, you'll recall, yet you're welcome to step out into the street later and light your pipe. I'll accompany you, to pass the time before you leave us. The gate closes at sunset.'

There was an intake of breath about the table – barely audible, yet filled with portent. Aunt Margery, who had sat in silence for most of the meal, looked sharply at her kinsman. Jane lowered her gaze... but Katherine turned to the man who, everyone knew, intended to ask for her hand in marriage.

And Edward Thorne nodded and smiled – a smile that suggested to all those present that he was more than willing to talk with the man who would become his father-in-law.

What followed, however, would lead to a very different outcome.

4

They stood in Bishopsgate Street in the cooler air of the summer's evening: Thorne puffing at his pipe, Cutler standing apart. The guest wore his cloak, draped casually about his shoulders. People had passed by, some greeting the constable. Mercifully, no one had waylaid him to speak of the grim discovery of that morning.

'So, Master Thorne,' he said, after some minutes had passed. 'Katherine says you have something to tell me.'

The other gave a nod, blew out a stream of bluish smoke and lowered his pipe. 'As you please, constable. And yet, I wonder if you've already guessed what I will say?'

Cutler said nothing, but by his manner invited him to continue.

'Well then, I'll lay it forth.' He bent, knocked the smouldering ashes from his pipe and straightened himself. 'First, I expect you'll wish to be assured on the matter of money.' And without waiting for reply, he added, 'I'm uncertain how much Katherine has told you concerning my position, but you will have heard of my father: Sir Robert Thorne, of Ongar in Essex. A considerable landowner in those parts.' He turned his gaze on Cutler and frowned slightly. 'Mayhap his name is unknown to you – but no matter. The fact remains that I'm his sole heir, with a current allowance of thirty crowns each month. More than sufficient, until the day I inherit.' He paused, then: 'And more than sufficient, I need hardly add, to bespeak rooms where Katherine may reside in comfort. She would have her own servant, and whatever she needs: clothing, jewels and fripperies aplenty.' He was smiling again now. 'At the risk of sounding boastful, Constable, I could name several young women who would be envious of such an offer.'

For a moment, Cutler failed to understand. Turning slightly, he faced the man with a look of puzzlement. Later, he would excuse himself by recalling that he was tired, and had drunk more than he should have done. Then, as the meaning of Master Thorne's words struck him with full force, he stiffened.

'Rooms where she would reside in comfort?' he echoed.

'Of course.' Thorne nodded. 'In the city, not far from my chambers. I've already spied a house that would suit, although Katherine would first approve. After all, she would be mistress of the dwelling – and naturally, have choice of the furnishings.' Whereupon, in all innocence of what was to follow, he put on a sly look.

'The bed I will choose myself: the most magnificent I can find. Fit for the paramour of a duke, instead of a mere gentleman like myself. To visit her, at such times that are fitting, shall be a joy – to us both.'

Upon which he paused, and delivered the final blow to Cutler's pride: 'And of course, I intend to make a substantial settlement to yourself, for your pains. Would a sum of forty crowns be sufficient?'

Cutler stood rigid as the words rang in his head. His first reaction was to blame himself, for the fool he had been. It was followed by a pang of shame, and pity for his daughter who, in all innocence, believed Thorne wished to marry her despite her humbler station. Instead... he took a long breath, straining to contain the anger that welled up. It had been an illusion all along – how could it be other? The notion that this dandy, heir to lands and wealth – an idler who had never worked and never would – wished to marry the daughter of a parish constable who was once a player, was absurd.

His intention was that Katherine be his kept woman – his trull, in effect, there merely to satisfy his lust whenever he chose. Moreover – and here was the bitterest pill of all – he expected her father to agree readily to it, for a fee of forty crowns.

'Well now... that's how the land lies, is it?' Cutler's gaze shifted towards the distant gate; the sun was sinking, and it would soon be time for closing. It was a relief, for he was uncertain how much longer he could stand here without giving vent to his anger. 'So, Master Thorne, you would make me a pander to my own daughter,' he said at last.

The young man looked taken aback. 'I would not put it so.'

'No? How would you put it?'

'A gentleman's arrangement, between two men who know the workings of the world.' Tapping his pipe idly against his thigh, he lifted his eyebrows. 'Do I take it that my offer of forty crowns falls short?'

'Oh no, it isn't that.' Cutler turned deliberately to him – and Thorne flinched.

'Well then, what is the—'

'I'll not say what.' The sharp reply silenced him. 'In trying to answer you, and laying bare how deceived we have been – all of us, let alone Katherine – I fear I might lose all restraint, and act unbefittingly for an upholder of the law. Hence, I'll say only this, *sir*: that your course now is to walk to that gate before it closes, and never come near any of my family again. Is that plain enough?'

But at that, Thorne was dumbfounded. In truth, Cutler saw, it had not occurred to him that his offer to keep Katherine as his compliant woman would be rejected – let alone scorned. His face flushed and he drew back, his cloak falling from one shoulder as he moved.

'By heaven,' he stammered. 'What baseness is this? A man of your station, daring to insult me – more, to issue threats? Do you not think what you do?'

'I know what I do,' Cutler said, in a tone which made the other flinch again. 'As I know that if I ever see you in my parish, I'll find a way to make you regret what you call your *offer*.' And before he could help himself, he had lifted a hand to point directly at Thorne's face. 'Now get you gone from here – and swiftly!'

Taking a step backwards, Thorne opened his mouth, but saw it was fruitless. With an angry gesture, he turned away, grabbing his cloak before it fell. Whereupon, giving the garment a swirl, he strode off.

Cutler watched him go, remaining where he stood until the man was lost among folk hurrying towards the gate, before it closed for the night.

He was seething, and yet he was relieved: relieved that Katherine would be free of a man he had neither liked nor trusted. She would be hurt, of course, but it was for the best; she would never lack suitors. And she would learn from the experience, or so he hoped. Though how he might break the news – that she would not see Edward Thorne again – he did not know. He turned to go indoors... and stopped.

At first, he was unsure why he had paused, then he knew. It was a scent, and one he recognised – recognised from early that morning, when he had stood in Alessandro Brisco's shop. *Storax... they use it to perfume gloves...* the words came back, to be followed by a realisation that shook him.

The scent had come from Edward Thorne's cloak, as he fumbled with it before stalking away.

* * *

The next morning, under heavy clouds, Cutler left the house early and walked determinedly to the city gate, which had just opened. He was to attend the alderman of his Ward, Thomas Skinner, as instructed by yesterday's message. But he knew only too well why he had come out at this hour, sooner than he needed. It was to avoid having to explain how matters stood to Katherine, who had gone to bed disappointed when he told her he would talk later of what had passed. She was still abed this morning when he left, having barely spoken to a puzzled Aunt Margery. Now, as he walked, he berated himself for a coward.

They are impatient to hear, he told himself. *And I've run away rather than break news to my daughter, that will strike her heart.*

Whereupon his shame turned to anger, as that haughty young man's words came to mind again; in fact, he had lain awake half the night, reliving the conversation. But now, there was something far more troubling: the scent of storax on Thorne's cloak.

Head down, oblivious to passers-by, he turned the matter over, racking himself for an explanation. Surely the perfume was common enough, he reasoned – and surely there were other perfumers, where the man might have picked up the scent. It was a powerful and distinctive odour, and it lingered – though the garment itself was not tainted by design; he was certain of that. He had never heard of a cloak being treated in such a fashion. It had been contaminated, perhaps by being placed alongside or on top of something else... which raised other questions. But in the end, he realised, it was useless to speculate; whatever Thorne's faults – and whether or not he had ever stepped inside Brisco's shop – he was surely not a murderer. It was unthinkable.

He shook himself, striving to dismiss the jumble of unwelcome thoughts. Walking faster, he forced himself to think on what to tell Skinner, knowing he had precious little to report.

He was at the gate, passing under its arch and into the city along with others, when there came a crack of thunder, and the heavens opened. At once, the rain began to fall, great droplets that drenched his clothing within seconds.

The sunny spell was over, and the wet summer of 1594 had reverted to type.

* * *

Thomas Skinner may have been an alderman and comfortably off, but he was still a tradesman: a cloth-worker, like many others. Having been admitted to his modest house in St Helen's parish, in that half of Bishopsgate Ward which lay within London's wall, Cutler stood uncomfortably in the main chamber, drying himself before the fire. His clothes steamed, and he had removed his sodden cap which Skinner's mousy young maid had stuck on an andiron. Her master, clad in an old morning gown over his shirt and hose, stood by impatiently until the girl had gone. Cutler having arrived somewhat early, the alderman had not yet breakfasted and was in a poor humour. Nevertheless, he was prepared to get to work.

'I bid you speak first, constable,' he said, 'for I hear you were active yesterday. Henry Deans came to report the sad event. As if our Ward hasn't suffered enough, with the plague deaths.' He frowned. 'I've more to say of Deans, but let it wait. Tell me your news.'

And so, Cutler told him. Starting with Stephen Bland's hurried arrival, his viewing of Brisco's body and brief questioning of the man who found it, he moved on to speak of visiting John Martinhouse, without saying who had suggested it. He then spoke of Kett's naming of Nicholas Wincott, before stating that he had ruled both those men out of any involvement in the crime. He was intent on continuing enquiries, yet there was no disguising that whoever had murdered the perfumer was still at large. Moreover, it was hard to colour the fact that Cutler was at something of a loss.

Coming to the end of his tale, he fell silent and waited, half-expecting a reprimand. Master Skinner was a man of hard reputation who ruled his own apprentices ruthlessly, and was not unknown to take a similar line with the deputies and constables of his Ward. But instead, the alderman surprised him by taking in the news calmly, before walking to the table that served for his writing desk. Picking up a scrap of paper, he brought it over.

'Aside from Martinhouse and the player, I can tell you now that another has been accused of this terrible crime,' he said, with a look of distaste. And when Cutler frowned, he proceeded to read out the message. '"Know ye, Master Skinner, that your deputy Henry Deans slew Brisco, on account of owing him moneys he could not pay. This from one who wishes to see justice done. God save you, a citizen".'

He lowered the paper, moved to the table and threw it down. 'The missive was pushed under my front door, seemingly early this morning,' he said. 'The maid found it when she arose. It's in a crabbed hand, poorly written. My first thought was to throw it on the fire, yet I thought to tell you of it first. So, what say you?'

'I say it's a lie,' Cutler replied. 'The notion of Henry Deans—'

But he was cut short. 'Of course it's a lie – only a fool would think otherwise!' With sudden anger, the alderman took a step towards him. 'A wicked and baseless accusation. Deans is an honest man, who would no more stoop to such an act than I would. What matters is the identity of the villain who penned it – and who, it appears, is eager to throw suspicion on another. Surely that can only mean one thing? That this comes from the hand of the murderer himself!'

'Nay...' Frowning, Cutler gave a shake of his head. 'I would urge caution, alderman. There could be other reasons... someone with a grudge against Deans, say. And in truth, I've already heard of the Italian lending money. It seems a long leap from there, to make the sender of this letter his murderer.'

'Other reasons, say you?' Skinner gave a snort. 'Like Brisco being a stranger, for one? He was far from alone in that. More, he was liked and respected, from what I hear. But then again...' He checked himself. 'Since you seem to know more of him than I do, perhaps you'd care to speculate?'

His voice was heavy with sarcasm, obliging Cutler to maintain his calm. Thoughts flew up – among them the unnerving matter of Edward Thorne and his cloak with its scent of storax. That, however, he decided to keep to himself.

'I fear I cannot,' he said. 'Though I'll try my utmost to delve into the business. I had hopes that the inquest might provide some answers.'

'God above, let us hope so.' The other gave a sigh, and made an attempt to rein in his anger. For all his petulance, he was clearly troubled by what had happened. 'As for the inquest, I'm told it will take place tomorrow, in the White Hart,' Skinner added. 'You must attend, of course, along with the other officers. I...' He hesitated. 'I too would be present, had I not business at the Court of Aldermen.'

At that, Cutler felt a touch of resentment. So, Skinner wished to distance himself from the affair – but then, it was to be expected. It was no secret that he hoped to be the mayor of London one day, and the last thing he wanted was unrest in his Ward.

'Then in truth, there's little more I can tell you, alderman,' he said. 'With your leave, I'll be about my business.'

But when the other faced him, there was a warning in his gaze. 'Were it my choice, constable, I'd let Austen Kett and Roger Farrant deal with this matter,' he said blandly. 'They're good men, born and bred in Bishopsgate. Whereas you – no native of this Ward, nor even of London – do your office at the pleasure of your kinsman. A player, were you not? In the eyes of many, not far short of what the law terms *rogues and vagabonds*.' He sniffed and raised his head, every inch the petty official.

Cutler eyed him. 'I know what the law says, Master Skinner,' he answered mildly. 'And I'll do my part in trying to serve it – as must we all.'

He moved to take his cap from the andiron, and turned to leave. Like the cap, his clothes were still wet, yet just now, he had a powerful urge to be outside. The air, he thought, could hardly be chillier than it was in the alderman's house.

* * *

Mercifully, the downpour had almost ceased. Walking through crowded Bishopsgate Street, Cutler mused on his encounter with Skinner. How the man expected him to find a murderer among the teeming population of London – grown, it was said, to almost two hundred thousand souls – he did not know.

He was turning the matter over as he passed back through the gateway into St Botolph's, the parish just outside the city wall, to find himself waylaid. Coming towards him was its constable, Austen Kett.

'Cutler.' The little man came to a halt, somewhat out of breath. 'I'm glad you're here, though I have grave news. There's been another attack, on a stranger.'

'What?' Cutler stared at him. 'Is it possible?'

'The button-maker, Meunier. He's unhurt, but—'

'When was this?'

'Scarcely an hour ago, when he opened up his workshop.' Kett nodded vigorously. 'Someone threw a poniard at him, but by God's mercy, it missed.'

They stood in the middle of the street, as people passed by. A dray was rumbling towards them, the driver flailing his whip. When he called out to them to make way, Cutler drew his fellow constable aside quickly, under the eaves of a cook-shop. There, as raindrops fell from the thatch, he waited to hear more.

'You know Meunier,' Kett said, speaking fast. 'He'd no sooner unbolted his door than some villain burst in and launched the dagger. Fortunately, the Frenchman's a nimble fellow – he ducked, it flew past him and the fellow bolted. Meunier's unhurt, as I said – only scared.' He paused to catch breath, then: 'And he's not the only one. After what happened to Brisco...'

'Yes, I see it.' Cutler was still, his mind busy. He recalled the faces of the crowd outside the perfumer's shop the previous day: many of them strangers, fearing the worst. Perhaps this attack was unconnected, he thought – though he feared he was clutching at straws.

'Meunier's shop is in my parish,' Kett said. 'But mayhap we should go there together? Or...' He raised his eyebrows. 'Are you averse to us aiding one another?'

Cutler shook his head quickly.

The button-maker's small house was a short way up the street, just beyond the old mansion known as Fisher's Folly. Picking up pace, the constables hurried past Bethlehem Hospital, the asylum that was little more than a prison for those deemed insane. As they walked, Kett jerked his head towards the door of the forbidding-looking building.

'I've sometimes thought that, if one of the madmen in there could slip away by night, he could do untold mischief before he was caught,' he said with a grim look. 'And in truth, who's to say it hasn't happened?' He paused, then: 'Now I think on it, there could be a ready-made solution to our ills.'

At which, Cutler stopped walking.

'Do you jest, Austen?'

'Jest? Well, of course I do.' The other stopped too. 'I only meant—'

'I know what you meant.' Cutler gazed down at him. 'Find some poor, dull-witted fellow and accuse him of attacking strangers – have him mewed up in Bedlam, then sent to the gallows. That would clear our troubles in one swoop, would it not? Save that whoever is really to blame would still be at large.'

'By the Christ!' Kett blinked, then stepped back. 'I said it was a jest – do you think so badly of me?' His puny chest rose in anger. 'Mayhap I should attend Meunier alone, and leave you to delve into the death in your own parish.'

A moment passed, while they faced each other – and Thomas Skinner's words came back to Cutler: *I'd let Austen Kett and Roger Farrant deal with this matter... good men, born and bred in Bishopsgate, whereas you...* He sighed, and managed a look of contrition.

'Your pardon for my brittleness. I'm in a poor humour. I've only now left the house of our good friend and alderman, Thomas Skinner.'

'Ah... scorched your ears, did he?' Calming himself, Kett gave a nod. 'He's done that to me, more times than I care to remember.' He paused. 'Well then, shall we go?'

They walked up the street to the button-maker's house. To their relief, there was no jostling throng outside the door, which was closed. Kett went first, knocked and lifted the latch. But when they entered, they were surprised to find several men in the shop, eyeing them warily. A murmur arose – and there was no doubting that the mood was hostile.

'*Alors*, you come now, *messieurs*!' a voice called out. 'What do you mean to do?'

Jean Meunier – a slim, dark-haired man with a bristling moustache – came forward. He was pale and somewhat shaken, and in his hand was a hammer which he had raised as the door opened. He lowered it, glancing from Kett to Cutler and back again.

'Must I tell it all again, Master Kett?' he demanded. 'You know my tale – why do you not catch this assassin? No, let me answer: because you cannot. Which is why my friends and I will move to protect ourselves – you see?'

The constables saw, clearly enough. Looking round at the assembled company, Cutler realised that all the men present were strangers: artisans from overseas, each of whom had acquired the Patent of Denization allowing him to work and own property. There were Frenchmen and Dutchmen, including the shoemaker who had been outside Brisco's the day before, as well as the hatter from Savoy. And yet, despite his status, each of these men was classed as an alien – and never before had it struck Cutler as forcibly as it did now: that they were yet foreigners, and on the defensive.

'I pray you, good citizens, be at peace.'

Despite his stature, Kett could summon a loud voice when he needed to. Raising his hands, he took a step towards Meunier. 'I swear that I – and Matthew Cutler here, whom you know – will strain every sinew to catch whoever has assailed you,' he announced. 'If it proves possible, we'll mount a hue and cry – someone must have seen the fellow. Meanwhile...' He looked round at the group. 'Meanwhile, I beg you all to calm yourselves. Every officer of this Ward is at pains to hunt down whoever is—'

'Whoever is bent on villainy against foreigners?' someone broke in harshly. 'Who wishes to drive us back from whence we came, till only purebred Englishmen be left?'

A silence fell. The one who had spoken was an Italian, whom Cutler recalled as a maker of purses from Genoa. When Kett hesitated, he faced the man and spoke up.

'I hear you, my friend, and I cannot blame you for your words. Yet I too would urge calm, before we leap ahead so quickly. This attack looks to me very different from that upon your poor countryman – which I'm at pains to unravel. Today, I spoke with Alderman Skinner, who is as troubled as are we all. And like Master Kett, I'll not rest in this business. Tomorrow...' He paused, to eye each man in turn. 'Tomorrow, the inquest will be held at the White Hart, and we may hear all the evidence. Some of your neighbours will serve on the jury. But for now, I pray you: go back to your homes and your trades, and leave us to speak with Master Meunier. Will you do so?'

He waited, hoping his words had the desired effect. On a sudden, it almost felt as if he were back on a stage again, declaiming a speech... He glanced at Kett, who threw him a look of approval. But the final word, it seemed, lay with Meunier, who now turned to his fellows. Speaking low, he addressed them and heard their replies. There was some muttered discourse, whereupon he faced the constables again.

'Very well,' he said. 'My friends will disperse now... yet they are resolved. From this day forth, we will be armed, and set a watch upon each other's houses. For in truth, *messieurs*, what else is there? Can the watchmen of this Ward be everywhere, at every hour of the day or night? What would you do, I pray, if your own people were in fear?'

Another silence fell, but it was brief; neither Cutler nor Kett had an answer, nor was one expected. The two of them stood aside as, one by one, the company filed out of the shop. A few of them, Cutler saw, held weapons: a knife, a mattock, even a pair of shears. With a heavy heart, he lowered his gaze. They were decent men, who wished only to work and raise their families – like the Huguenot weavers he had known and liked back in Canterbury. And what indeed, as Meunier had demanded, would he do in their place?

A moment later, he and Kett were alone with the button-maker, who had calmed himself. Whereupon, at a sudden noise from the rear of the shop, both constables turned as a small, bright-eyed woman appeared.

'Are they gone now, Jean?' she enquired, with a heavy French accent. 'And shall I bring cider?'

Her husband looked round, and nodded.

5

They stood with cups of Madame Meunier's sweet cider, while the button-maker told Cutler what he had already told Kett earlier that morning. It was soon clear, however, that his account would be of little use. Meunier had barely opened the shop – somewhat late today, he admitted – when a man in a grey jerkin and breeches, with a cap pulled low, threw the door wide and hurled a dagger before hurrying off. It was done in haste, he thought, as if the fellow were frightened, and his aim was poor. His intended victim had veered aside, fortunately in the right direction, and the weapon missed him before clattering to the floor. He now produced it, frowning as he placed it on his work table. It was a plain poniard, of the sort that could be bought anywhere for a shilling. The constables regarded it briefly.

'So, you never saw his face?' Kett enquired. And when Meunier shook his head: 'And you have no notion who he might be?'

'An enemy, is who he is,' the button-maker said. 'Who meant to kill me, it seems.'

'And yet, he was poorly suited to the task, was he not?' Cutler observed, looking down at the weapon. 'Even if he'd hit his mark, there's no certainty it would have served his purpose.' He picked up the dagger and ran his thumb along its edge. 'It's blunt... That's odd.'

Meunier frowned, but Kett looked startled. 'What do you imply? That this was but a warning of some kind?'

'I cannot know,' Cutler answered, feeling the weapon's point. 'But now that I...' He stopped himself and put it down again. A notion had occurred which made him uneasy.

'Now that you what?' Kett asked, with some impatience.

'Nothing...' He shook his head. 'It merely adds weight to my notion that this man was unfit for his task. Perhaps a hired rogue, or some such petty villain.'

'Hired by whom, Master Cutler?' The Frenchman looked uneasy.

'I can't answer that.' Cutler looked away, wishing he had never started on this topic. He would not reveal what had occurred to him: that the blunted poniard was a theatre prop: the sort of weapon he himself had wielded on the stage, and which could barely have cut bread. 'I only speculate,' he added. 'Mayhap I should be on my way now, and leave you in peace?' He finished his drink and laid down the cup.

'I'll stay here a while,' Kett said. Turning to the button-maker, he added, 'You should open the shop again. Let everyone know you are uncowed by what happened.'

'Well, indeed... you are right.' Meunier nodded, and looked at Cutler. 'I will come to the inquest. I stand ready to help, if I am needed.'

Cutler gave a nod, murmured his thanks for the cider and went out.

Once in the street, he began walking again. The rain was gone, but angry clouds scudded across from the west.

Having no notion how to proceed just now, and finding himself close to John Willard's door, he thought it could do no harm to go in. When he entered, however, his father-in-law was at his workbench, busy with a customer. Willard looked up and gestured to him to tarry, whereupon he waited until the other came over.

'I've thought better on what I confided yesterday, about Martinhouse,' he said quickly. 'I was remiss... Old suspicions, that got the better of me.'

'Well, it's done with,' Cutler said, after a moment. 'I spoke with him, as did Roger Farrant. We still seek a murderer. And doubtless you'll hear soon that there's been another attack, though without blood spilled. The button-maker, Meunier. He's unhurt – only scared.'

'Is it so?' Willard frowned. 'That's grave news.'

'Yet this is no time to speak of it, for you're at your work.' Cutler glanced at the customer, who was looking in their direction. 'Come to supper tonight,' he added. 'The girls will be most glad to see you.' He could not air the notion which had arisen, which allowed him some relief: that their grandfather's presence might enable him to put off his conversation with Katherine, concerning Edward Thorne.

'I will, and gladly.' The gunsmith nodded. 'Until the evening, then.'

But as Cutler was about to leave, he was called back.

'I meant to tell you,' Willard said. 'Margaret Fisher has returned, and occupies her house again. She went to the country during the plague, as you'll recall.' He paused, raising his eyebrows. 'I thought you might like to know.'

He turned away, to return to his customer. Cutler turned too, and made his way to the door. But once outside, he stopped in his tracks.

So... Margaret had come home. He had not seen her in two years, shortly after she was widowed. An image flew up: of the handsome, auburn-haired woman in mourning clothes, dignified even in bereavement, favouring him with a smile. They had been friends, nothing more – he had always said so, especially when Aunt Margery made pointed remarks. As for Katherine and Jane... He sighed, his mind in a tangle.

What in heaven's name, he wondered, might happen next?

* * *

The afternoon passed slowly – far more slowly than he liked. Since his enquiries concerning the murder of Alessandro Brisco had led nowhere, for the present, he could do no more than walk the parish while he thought on tomorrow's inquest. Though now that he faced it, he knew it was unlikely to reveal much – rather the reverse, in fact. He had a vision of an angry chorus of Bishopsgate people, demanding justice. Nor would Thomas Skinner be there to offer support – as if he ever had. Henry Deans would, however... He thought briefly of the anonymous letter Skinner had shown him. Who could have sent it, and why?

He was still turning the matter over as the afternoon waned, standing in the street to eat an apple, when thoughts of Margaret Fisher arose again... and this time, she would not leave.

He was back in his playing days, taking his bow before a noisy crowd at the Curtain. Was Nicholas Wincott there? Probably... his memory was vague as to those who had performed with him, as indeed it was of most of the plays. What was not vague was the memory of Mistress Fisher, a regular at the theatre along with her husband before the man fell ill. She was often in the galleries above the stage, making no secret of her admiration for what Cutler had always thought of as his limited acting skills. They had spoken, if rarely: hurried conversations after the play, with people milling about. There was no opportunity, nor indeed any desire on his part, to advance matters; he had Anne and his daughters, she was married to a wool merchant, though childless. The surprising development came when, with her husband ailing at home, the lady still attended the theatre, accompanied by a servant. It was followed by an evening he now recalled with clarity, in Holywell Lane, when Margaret had confronted him. Her husband was near death, it seemed, and yet she was calm. The marriage had been a sham, she confided: an arrangement to suit others. And when the business of mourning was over, perhaps...

He was frowning, standing in Bishopsgate Street with a half-eaten apple in his hand, thinking on a woman he hadn't seen in years – ever since the pestilence had flared up in the fateful summer of 1592. Those who could escape London and its environs did so, and quickly. Margaret went to stay with a sister, he did not recall where, while he took to the road with his fellow players after sending his family away. The intervening two years seemed like a blur.

But now she was back, and Cutler too was widowed.

He threw away the apple core and started homewards.

* * *

It was a supper he had dreaded, his mind dwelling on breaking news to Katherine that would dismay her. As it happened, however, there was enough chatter at the crowded table, chiefly about the business at Meunier's, to let his unease pass unnoticed. Or so he thought, until he saw his elder daughter eying him with what he thought was an accusing look. When she spoke, however, it was on a different topic.

'Stephen Bland came by this morning, after you'd gone. He

wanted to know if there was any news about the perfumer's death.'

Cutler raised his eyebrows. 'Did he? Well, he knows as much as anyone.'

'Crafty old bird, is Master Bland,' Aunt Margery observed, stabbing at her raisin pudding. 'More to him than meets the eye, I always thought.'

'You say that about a lot of people, Aunt,' Jane said.

'Yet, she is right,' John Willard put in. Their guest had enjoyed the company, and was in convivial humour. 'I would trust Bland to call the hour, when he passes in the night. I'm unsure I would trust him further.'

'Nor I, Brother,' Margery said. 'Those that get accustomed to walking abroad by night are prey to dark thoughts.'

At that, there was some shared amusement on the part of the Cutler girls, before the conversation moved on to other topics. But Cutler was thoughtful: mention of Stephen Bland reminded him of a matter that had troubled him long before the man's arrival the day before, to report the murder. His mind flew back to Ned Broad's attempted thievery, and Cutler's suspicion that one of the watchmen was taking bribes to look elsewhere when such crimes took place. It had occurred to him that Bland – ageing, and aware that his usefulness to the parish could soon be at an end – was a likely suspect. With all that had happened of late, the matter had slipped his mind – as, he recalled again, had the business of putting Ned Broad in the stocks to teach him a lesson. With a sigh, he took up his mug and drank.

'You're frowning, Father,' Katherine said.

He met her eye; she was on edge, waiting for his account of the conversation with Edward Thorne. In fact, he knew that it had been the unspoken topic all evening, and could not be delayed further. Aware that all eyes were now upon him, he nodded.

'I must speak with you when supper is done,' he said. 'Out the back, when you're ready.'

And a short while later, in the small yard behind their house, overlooking Finsbury Fields, he seated himself on the old bench where he and Anne had often sat on summer evenings. It was cloudy still, though the rain had held off. As he knew she would, Katherine soon appeared, closed the house door behind her and sat down beside him. But before he could speak, she stayed him.

'It's not good news, is it?' she said. 'Else you would have broken it before now, and not avoided me as you have done.'

He took a breath, but found no reply.

'I know you never warmed towards Edward, Father,' she went on, rather quickly. 'Yet I carried hopes that, when all was said and sifted, you might—'

'Kate, hear me now,' he said, cutting her short. 'You're right, and I heartily mislike what I must say. Moreover, I have indeed put the matter off, and cursed myself for a coward in doing so. Yet I ask you to ready yourself.'

Beside him, he felt her tense. Staring ahead, she waited.

'Master Thorne is gone, and will not return,' he said, as gently as he could. 'His intentions were not as you hoped... and in truth, he is unworthy of you. I know no other way to say it. I can only add that, for the love I bear you and your sister, you must know I would always act as I think best.'

She was silent, gazing into the distance.

'He wished – no, I'll not speak of that,' her father said, striving to dismiss his anger. An image flew up of Thorne in his cloak: his haughtiness, his lascivious tone as he spoke of the bed he would bespeak for his intended mistress. 'Being tied to such a man would have made you unhappy, Kate,' he added, knowing how feeble it sounded. 'I can but ask you to trust me when I say that. Your happiness is dear to me.'

'I know that,' Katherine said, her voice tight. 'And yet...' She was struggling, her hands clasped before her. 'You seek to spare my feelings,' she went on, turning to him at last, 'but I would like to know what passed between you.'

'I'll not speak of it,' Cutler repeated with a shake of his head.

'Well then... I suppose that's how it must stay.'

She turned away again, breathing deeply, and his heart sank. He had sat here often with Anne, talking of the girls and what hopes they had. How thankful he would have been now, to have his wife share this burden. He sought for some words of comfort, but it was useless. His daughter rose, and left him. He heard the house door close, but did not look round.

Of course it was all to the good, he told himself – how could it be otherwise? Tears would be shed – kind-hearted Jane, when she learned the news later in the chamber they shared, would try to offer comfort. Yet in time, the grief would pass... It had to.

But he stayed seated, brooding until dusk fell. In the gloom of the gathering night, he believed he heard the distant call of the watchman... Bland, again? He tried to turn his mind to matters of business, and failed.

And yet the morning came: Saturday, the day of the inquest, and he was the constable of Spitalfields, who must act for the good of his parish.

* * *

As he had expected, the White Hart was packed to the doors, the air warm and clammy. Cutler looked round keenly as he pushed his way inside, thinking all of Bishopsgate Ward seemed to be there. Some had arrived early enough to order beer, but the inn's business was now suspended. The innkeeper stood stolidly beside the barrels in the corner, flanked by his drawers in their aprons. Close by, a table had been set aside for the coroner, who was already seated: elderly Christopher Balshaw in his black gown, white-haired and glum, fussing with his papers. Beside him, a clerk sat to record the proceedings, while to one side, the sixteen men of the jury were crammed on benches. Cutler recognised most of them, solid citizens all – if the scavenger, Josiah Madge, could be so described. Standing nearby were others he knew, like Meunier the button-maker. Since there were no seats to be had, he eased through the throng to a position facing the coroner's table – whereupon a familiar voice piped up from nearby.

'Got your report to mind?' Austen Kett enquired. 'Old Balshaw's a stickler for details.'

'I know it,' Cutler said, looking down at him. Around them was a low muttering, people waiting impatiently for the business to start. Kett, for his part, was clutching a cup which contained neither beer nor ale, but strong water; its heady reek floated up to Cutler's nostrils.

'That's to steady your nerves, is it?' he asked.

'If you like,' Kett retorted with a shrug. But he was ill at ease; Cutler saw it, and wondered why before his gaze fell on Henry Deans, the deputy alderman, and beside him Stephen Bland, who looked tired; likely the watchman had come straight from his duties without having time to rest. Deans saw him and nodded stiffly, stirring Cutler's thoughts – until his eye fell upon someone standing at the far side of the inn, by the open windows that overlooked Bishopsgate Street... and at once, he froze.

Edward Thorne, of all people, was attending the inquest,

perhaps out of passing interest, or... the thought struck him like a blow. Was he here out of sheer defiance, to show that he was not to be cowed by the father of the woman he had wanted?

He stared at Thorne, who appeared not to notice – and then he saw the bodyguard: a beetle-browed fellow in a pinked leather jerkin, surveying the room belligerently. So, Thorne had brought a hired ruffian for protection. And as if to drive the notion home, Katherine's former beau chose that moment to turn and meet Cutler's eye. *Here I am, constable*, the young man seemed to say. *And how do you propose to stop me?*

'Jesu, will you look at that?' A bystander's voice broke his thoughts, making him relieved to turn away. The man was pointing, whereupon he looked, and showed his own surprise.

'Now, who'd have thought to see her here?' The fellow said to no one in particular. 'The Queen of Bawds herself – and does she look the part!'

It was true enough. With mixed feelings – among them a scrap of admiration – Cutler regarded one of the most notorious women in Bishopsgate: Alice Leake, who kept the trugging-house up the road in Shoreditch. Defiant, almost magnificent in her brazenness, the mistress of what she claimed were the prettiest and most obliging trulls to be found anywhere in London's suburbs of sin, sat demurely upon a stool, her embroidered skirts arranged neatly about her. Behind her stood a servant: the equally notorious guardian of her person and her premises, a heavy-bearded giant who towered above everyone else. Edward Thorne, it seemed, was not the only one to bring along a protector.

Cutler was turning back to Kett when a sudden rap on a table sounded; the coroner was calling order. At once, a hush fell, and all eyes were upon him.

It began routinely enough.

His reedy voice barely audible to those at the back, Master Balshaw opened the inquest into Alessandro Brisco, perfumer, late of Spitalfields parish. Without emotion, the coroner droned on while his harassed clerk scratched away at his side. Finally, after little had been said that wasn't already known, Balshaw called Austen Kett, constable of St Botolph's, to give testimony. Cutler was unsurprised, since Kett had seen the body first. Then he remembered Whitney, the customer who had stumbled upon the scene... but Master Whitney, it seemed, had been forgotten. Kett turned and thrust his cup at Cutler.

'Hold that, will you?' he breathed, with a sickly expression.

Kett's account was brief enough, and needed little elaboration. He had been in the street, heard a commotion and hurried to the perfumer's shop. There he spoke with the watchman who had been informed by a customer who found the body, whereupon Constable Cutler was also summoned. He and Cutler had viewed the body together, and noted the stab wounds. After that, he had brought boards and nailed the shop door shut. Having said his piece, he was excused. Cutler expected to be called next – but what followed came as a surprise to everyone.

'I will hear from Niccolo Scamozzi,' the coroner announced, looking round the room. 'Sir, will you show yourself?'

To general muttering, a figure stood up, prompting heads to turn in his direction. Cutler's eyes narrowed... Had he seen this man before? Clearly, he was someone of importance. Neatly coiffed and bearded, dressed in a fine suit of dark clothes, with a jewelled earring and a sword at his side, he took a pace forward – and people fell back instinctively.

'I am Scamozzi,' he said, in a heavy Italian accent.

Master Balshaw peered at him. 'I understand the deceased

was well-known to you. Will you aid this assembly by telling us what you can?'

The witness nodded curtly and began – and soon, the company was hanging on his every word. He described himself as a merchant who resided in one of the new houses in Hoxton, though he also had premises in the city. He had known Alessandro Brisco for years, and considered him a friend. And more: the man had been his tenant. The shop in Bishopsgate Street, like others elsewhere, was owned by Scamozzi.

So... this was Brisco's landlord. Cutler eyed the man, thinking he was one who might make a dangerous enemy. Kett, who had rejoined him and recovered his cup, took a slurp and frowned. Whereupon, Signor Scamozzi spoke up again. As for why anyone would want to slay this good and honest man, he continued – it was a wicked act, carried out with no motive he could imagine save that of—

'One moment, if you please.' Master Balshaw, disconcerted by the man's tone as much as by his testimony, was frowning. 'It is for others to speculate on such matters. You have given an account of the character of the deceased, and your relations with him, and hence—'

'Signor coroner – I will be heard!'

Scamozzi's voice rang out with such authority, even Balshaw was silenced. The Italian's dark eyes swept the room, before he faced the coroner again.

'The death of a stranger – a foreigner, in the eyes of every Englishman here – might come as small surprise,' he said. 'We know what some think, since those papers were set on London walls during *la peste* – the plague, that men say was sent by God to chastise us. Some were driven to madness – even so far, I would state, to doing murder. That, I believe, was why my countryman was slain – because he was a stranger. And that is why, I tell you now, I have taken it upon myself to claim his body, and to arrange burial as befitting a man of our faith.' He stopped himself, looking around again. 'I need no aid from anyone here,' he added, 'nor would Brisco have wanted it. Matters concerning his goods and affairs will be dealt with by me and my lawyers. In the meantime, the shop will be closed.' With that, he faced the coroner once more. 'Well, sir – have I said enough?'

There was a moment, while an indignant Master Balshaw recovered himself. Beside him, the clerk sat open-mouthed, quill in hand; clearly, he had failed to record a word of what Scamozzi had said. About the room, a murmur began... Who was this foreigner, who thought he could speak in such a manner, and even take the law into his own hands?

But Cutler, somewhat to his shame, felt a sense of relief. The Italian would take the body and arrange burial, and the shop would be closed; at least that much would be settled. Whereupon a voice sounded from the middle of the room, that made every head spin round.

'What of the money that was owed to Brisco, Master Scamozzi?' Alice Leake demanded, rising to her feet. 'Will you demand repayment in his place? Or will all debts be cancelled?'

'Madam, I pray you be quiet!' The coroner banged a hand down upon the table. 'That is not a matter for this inquest.'

Mistress Leake, however, was not to be silenced so easily. 'I but ask on behalf of others, sir – friends, I could say,' she went on. 'Someone must voice it, so it may as well be me.'

At that, there came a sound, which could have been muted laughter. Cutler caught a few wry smiles, and understood: Alice Leake's concern for those she called her *friends* was purely monetary. Debts being written off meant clients with fatter purses... and on a sudden, it seemed an open secret that some people owed Brisco money. He was musing on it as the coroner faced this brazen woman sternly.

'Any further word from you, and I'll have you removed,' he wheezed, before settling his eyes upon Scamozzi again. 'And as for you, sir, I believe we've heard enough.'

The Italian returned his gaze, then nodded brusquely and stepped into the crowd. Cutler watched him leave before glancing at Mistress Leake, who had sat down, albeit unwillingly. But he turned sharply, realising his own name had been called. Master Balshaw was gesturing impatiently to him. He was on.

Mercifully for him, if to the disappointment of some who were enjoying the drama, the remainder of the business passed uneventfully. Cutler gave his testimony, as did Stephen Bland after him. Henry Deans was not called, somewhat to his chagrin. In fact, there was little more to be said, and the bald facts remained: no one knew why Alessandro Brisco had died in such a violent manner, let alone at whose hand – apart from the fact that he was an interloper in the Ward, and resented by some. Hence it was no surprise to anyone when the jury, having deliberated for barely half an hour, delivered their verdict: the perfumer had been unlawfully slain by persons unknown. God rest his soul.

So, it was over. The coroner gathered up his papers and prepared to leave, the clerk with him. As the crowd rose, Cutler made his way towards the barrels in the corner. Others followed, eager to slake their thirst; the inn had become unbearably stuffy, and stank from the press of unwashed bodies. He looked round to see Mistress Leake leaving, unbowed and dignified, her huge servant clearing a path.

'I'm buying you a mug, Master Matthew,' a voice behind him said. Cutler turned to find Bland the watchman pushing forward.

'Well, I meant to speak with Kett.' He looked round, but saw no sign of the man.

'Gone,' Bland said. 'Couldn't get out quick enough, the little weasel – and I can guess why.'

'Is that so?' Cutler eyed him. 'Do you care to say more?'

'I will,' came the reply. 'But let me order the beer while you find somewhere to sit, eh?'

Cutler hesitated, then gave a nod.

6

As it transpired, there was nowhere to sit, the inn still being full of folk clamouring to be served. Cutler and Bland took their mugs outside and stood by the open doors of the White Hart, with Bishopsgate Street abuzz. Whereupon, with a start, Cutler recalled Edward Thorne's presence – how could he forget? Along with his hired ruffian, Thorne must have left without his noticing... though that too brought some relief. With any luck, he might never have to set eyes on the man again. He drank his beer, and waited for the watchman to speak.

'Kett owed Brisco money, I'd say that's why he went off,' Bland said, somewhat carelessly. 'After Dame Leake raised the topic – no one expected that.'

Cutler frowned. 'Kett was in debt to the perfumer?'

'Of course he was – and there are plenty of others. The stonemason, for one, Martinhouse. He drinks more than he should... more than he can afford.'

This was hardly a revelation to Cutler. But he had recalled Aunt Margery's description of Bland as a *crafty old bird*. His suspicions were rising again, while the other took his silence for encouragement.

'That Brisco was a close fellow, behind his smiles,' he said between gulps of beer. 'Yet I knew naught of that landlord of his, did you?' And when Cutler shook his head: 'A gentleman down to his fancy shoes – yet to my mind, a varlet underneath. Did you not think it?'

'I formed no opinion.'

'No? Scamozzi spoke of owning other houses, did you mark that? I wonder which. Maybe Alice Leake knows – a holder of men's secrets, is that old bawd. Small wonder she asked about money owed to Brisco...'

'Which brings us back to Kett,' Cutler broke in, to change the subject. 'I've always thought him a clever little cove – not the sort to get himself into debt.'

'Yet you know his weakness,' Bland said, with a wry look. 'Never married, which folk used to say was because no one would wed such a twisty little runt. The truth is—'

'I know what the gossips say, Stephen,' his constable broke in somewhat impatiently. 'That he cleaves to men instead of women. I say it's none of my affair as long as he serves his parish well, as he's always done.'

The other made no reply, merely grunted; the constable's tolerant ways – a hangover from his player days, some said – had always seemed a mystery to men like Bland. Whereupon, somewhat against his better judgement, Cutler aired another matter.

'Talking of serving the parish,' he said, 'I'm troubled by the thieving that's gone on, from a couple of houses empty since the plague. Men you and I know – like that slippery rogue Ned Broad – have been up to their old tricks. I've been meaning to ask if you've seen anything, when you're abroad at night.'

'Me?' Bland raised his brows. 'Well now, don't you think I'd have told you, if I had?'

'Indeed, I would have thought so.'

At which, the man's expression darkened. 'What do you mean?' And when Cutler seemed to hesitate: 'You think I'm not up to my task, is that it?'

'I never said that.'

'Nay – but you think it.' His anger rising, the watchman glared. 'I've heard men say I'm too old, and should be put out to pasture – are you of the same mind?'

'Calm yourself, Stephen.' Cutler lifted a hand. 'You know Bishopsgate like it was a part of you. People know they can sleep safe in their beds with you passing and calling the hour—'

'Yet you speak of thievery,' Bland broke in, 'and by heaven, I begin to see why! You think I let it happen, for a price – do I hit the mark?'

'In truth, I'll admit it crossed my mind,' Cutler said at last, tired of being less than forthright. 'If not you, another of the watchmen—'

'By the Christ! How...' The other caught his breath. 'How can you talk of this when there's murder been done, only yards from where we stand? You, of all men... the one who everyone says is slow to judge, and treats folk fair – you pierce my heart!'

He was in a fury, the sweat starting on his brow. Passers-by turned to look, before hurrying on. Cutler was chastened – and yet, his suspicions remained. Bland's outrage was real enough, but was there fear behind it? Had he been caught out, and was trying to cover his guilt?

'I'll ask your pardon,' he began – but he was too late. The man drew back from him, raising a shaky finger.

'Shame upon you,' he said. 'I'll not drink with you again.' Whereupon he turned and stumbled back into the inn.

Cutler watched his retreating back and sighed. He barely noticed when someone emerged from the doors and came to a halt.

'Master Matthew?' Josiah Madge, the burly scavenger, was eying him. 'You look like a man in the dumps.'

'Are you in haste, Madge?' On impulse, he turned and offered his mug. 'Or will you aid me by taking this back, after finishing what's in it? It's half-full, and I'm not thirsty.'

'Well, I'll do so,' came the reply. 'Had enough of the White Hart for today, have you?'

'I believe I have,' Cutler told him. He handed the mug over, and left.

* * *

His mind in a turmoil, Cutler walked up the street, heedless of the bustle about him. He thought of what had passed at the inquest, and knew that it changed nothing. He thought of Meunier, of the failed attack on his person, and the blunted dagger. Kett also came to mind, yet he would not dwell on that. Instead, his thoughts flew to Katherine, who had stayed abed when he left the house... which raised an image of Edward Thorne, standing brazenly among the company in the inn. Why, he wondered, would the man bother to attend if not to defy him? More, did he even harbour some notion of ignoring the warning Cutler had given him, intending to see Katherine again?

Head down, he was passing the cook-shop where he had stood with Kett the day before, and the entrance to the ginnel beside it, when a voice called out, seemingly in distress.

'Constable! In here, for the love of God!'

He stopped, veered round and hurried down the alley. Was it a woman's voice? He passed barrels and boxes, peering ahead. On either side of him, walls pressed closer, as the way narrowed. Then he was in the grassy space behind, with chicken coops and a stack of firewood, yet there was no one in sight. He slowed, looking about – and was seized from behind in a grip of iron, while a voice he knew at once spoke in his ear.

'A man of your station, who would insult me... those were my words,' Edward Thorne said. 'And now I intend to pay you for your insolence.'

The next moment, he was whirled about to face the young dandy himself, standing before him with a smirk. He wore a sword, but his hands were empty. Cutler stared, but had no words.

'Or I should say, my man will pay you,' Thorne added. 'Regretfully, I have to be elsewhere, and haven't time to enjoy the spectacle.' He glanced over Cutler's shoulder at the one who held him: the rogue in the pinked jerkin, of course, who had been at the inquest. He could feel the man's hot breath on his neck. He tried to struggle, but the fellow's strength was too much.

'So, I'll bid you farewell,' his captor said. 'Only remember – constable – that the behaviour you displayed two days ago gave such affrontery, it cannot go unpunished.' He sniffed, then allowed his anger to show. 'I urge you to reflect on that... Perhaps this will help.' Upon which he raised his hand and dealt Cutler a blow across the face.

'Nobly done,' Cutler said, finding voice at last. Fixing the other with a gaze that, he hoped, would indicate how matters would fall out if he were not constrained, he might have said more – until he was spun round again, and a meaty fist slammed into his stomach. With a gasp, he doubled over.

'That was your first lesson,' Thorne snapped. 'There will be more, I promise.'

'To the devil with you,' Cutler breathed... whereupon something happened that would change matters considerably.

Seemingly from nowhere, a slight figure came running – and swinging a wooden billet. The next thing Cutler knew, the incomer had cracked Edward Thorne on the side of his head, sending him reeling. The man then turned to Cutler – which was the chance he needed. Feeling the brawny arms about him loosen, he tore himself from the hired ruffian's grip, whirled round and kicked him hard on the shin. With a spluttered oath, the rogue staggered but quickly went into a crouch – and at once, battle was drawn.

Unfortunately for the bully, however, the odds had changed dramatically.

'Ned?' Cutler swung his gaze towards his unlikely saviour: Ned Broad, club in hand, who had dropped into a crouch himself.

'Step back, Master Matthew,' he muttered. 'And draw your poniard.'

There was no time to think, for Thorne's man had already drawn his dagger. Cutler pulled his own blade from the sheath and glanced swiftly aside, to see Thorne sitting on the ground, groaning and holding his head. With no threat from that direction, he faced his foe – who leaped forward with a roar of anger.

But the man was outnumbered, and he was clumsy. When he made a grab for Ned Broad, his nimble opponent dodged aside and swung his billet again, catching him on the shoulder. He took the blow and swung his dagger – but he was wide of the mark, allowing Cutler to seize his chance. Avoiding the fellow's outflung fist, he ducked and jabbed his poniard into the hand which held the weapon. With a yell of pain, Thorne's man dropped his dagger – whereupon Ned waded in.

He was merciless; Cutler was surprised at the way he laid into their opponent, who was bleeding and cursing roundly. Wielding the club – which Cutler now saw was merely a length of timber seized from the pile of firewood – Ned beat the rogue repeatedly about the head, neck and shoulders. Roaring like a bear, his victim tried to seize the weapon, but to no avail. He was sagging, arms flailing... and quite soon, it was at an end. When Master Broad lifted his billet high before bringing it down on the man's head, he fell to the ground and lay still.

'By heaven, Ned...' Cutler turned to face him. 'I never thought I'd say this, but you have my undying thanks.'

'It's no matter, constable.' Panting, Ned managed a nod. 'I was passing, so...' He stopped, looked at the stick of wood and threw it aside. 'I didn't like what that one was doing to you.' He looked over at Thorne, still holding his head. 'Someone you've offended?'

'You might say so.' Recovering himself, Cutler sheathed his own dagger, then stepped forward and picked up the one Thorne's man had dropped. 'Here – why not take this for a reward?' he suggested. 'You could sell it for a shilling, at the least.'

Ned brightened. 'Well, so I could.' Taking the weapon from Cutler's outstretched hand, he lowered his gaze. 'Though I need no reward. I owed you, did I not?'

He meant the business of the other night, when Cutler had allowed him to return the stolen goods – which reminded him once again of forgetting to put Ned in the stocks. With a wry look, he nodded. 'Let's say that's forgotten, shall we?'

Ned grinned, then looked round briefly at the man he had knocked senseless. Shoving the dagger into his belt, he turned about to take his leave – whereupon another thought struck Cutler.

'Will you linger a while?' he asked. 'I mean to speak with our friend here...' He nodded towards Thorne, who was trying to get to his feet. 'You can stand witness.'

'Me?' Ned was uneasy. 'You mean—'

'I mean help me scare the breeches off him, nothing more. Then you can be on your way – will you do that?' Whereupon, taking the other's silence for assent, he walked over to the man who was now at his mercy, and reached out a hand. Thinking Cutler was about to help him, Thorne took hold – only to find himself lifted, then shoved back on to his rump.

'Among my limited powers,' Cutler told him, 'is one to arrest men for affray. I could do so now, and convey you to the stocks by St Leonard's. My friend there...' He jerked his thumb towards Ned. 'He is my witness.'

'By God, you wouldn't.' Thorne peered up at him. 'You cannot!'

'And in the meantime,' Cutler said, as if he hadn't heard, 'I'll ask you to surrender your sword and poniard. Or...' he bent closer, making the other blink, 'would you prefer I summon a sergeant-at-arms, and have you conveyed to a magistrate?'

A moment passed, but though it was little more than a bluff, Cutler knew that the man would yield. Shocked at the way things had gone so badly wrong for him, he put a hand to his head and winced. 'See now, there's money in my purse,' Thorne said, looking up again. 'More, I'd wager, than you make in months. Can we not settle this now like gentlemen? I gambled, as you might put it, and I lost. What say you to that?'

'I say stand up, take off your sword and hand it to me,' Cutler answered. 'Or must I and my witness take it by force?' At which point, Ned Broad came up to stand beside him, looking down with apparent concern.

'That's a nasty bump you've got, sir,' he observed. 'Best see a barber-surgeon, is my advice.'

'You blasted rogue – you struck me!' His temper flaring, Thorne scowled. 'It's I who could swear out a warrant,' he added, turning his gaze upon Cutler. 'Then we'll see who's taken to—'

'The matter is, I would lay a counter charge,' Cutler broke in. 'Assaulting a constable engaged upon his duties is a grave matter. The alderman of this Ward is most protective of his officers, and has the ear of the Lord Mayor too. So – what say *you*?'

'Good God...' The young man sagged. 'May you burn in hell!'

'I take it you will comply, then?' Cutler enquired calmly.

A moment passed, but it was clear that Thorne had given up the fight. With a groan, he got stiffly to his feet, unbuckled his sword and held it out. Cutler took it by the hilt and waited for the poniard to follow, then turned and threw both weapons towards one of the chicken coops. The startled birds squawked, while the constable leaned closer to Ned and spoke low. 'You can disappear now,' he said.

With a relieved look, Ned turned on his heel and started towards the ginnel. In seconds, he was gone. Cutler turned to Edward Thorne, with a look that subdued him at once.

'I might forget what happened here,' he said quietly. 'Providing, that is, I get some answers concerning a different matter that troubles me mightily.' And when the other frowned: 'It concerns your cloak – the one you wore when you came to supper at my house. I caught a whiff of a most particular fragrance from it – that of storax. The only man hereabouts who supplied such a perfume was murdered... so.' He paused, letting the words sink in. 'I want to know how such a scent ended up on a garment of yours – and I'm not leaving until you tell me.'

But the answer, when it finally came, proved to be something of a revelation.

* * *

'Her name is Petronella,' Thorne mumbled, avoiding Cutler's eye. 'She is much prized, and much spoiled by those who can afford her.'

They were walking in the fields behind the houses: two men strolling, seemingly in quiet conversation. Cutler, however, kept a hand on his prisoner's elbow, steering him gently. The henchman, still unconscious, had been left to lie where he fell.

'Petronella – you mean the Dutch trull, at Leake's?' And when the other made no reply: 'So – you, who speak scathingly of Bishopsgate, frequent its whorehouse.' He frowned. 'Yet for all that, you would have made my daughter your kept drab.'

Again, Thorne had no answer.

'Petronella, then... you say the perfume on your cloak came from her?'

'They all use scents,' Thorne said. 'I recall a shift perfumed with storax, in her chamber... I might have laid my cloak beside it, while—'

'While you uncased,' Cutler finished. His anger at this man had risen again, but he was thinking fast. 'And if I spoke with her, she would confirm your tale?'

'How should I know that?' the other retorted. 'Can anyone take a trull at her word?'

'The matter is, I know not whether to take you at your word either,' was his reply. 'And while I and my fellow constables seek a murderer, we're inclined to be sceptical.'

'God in heaven...' The young man looked round sharply. 'You cannot think I had aught to do with that vile business?'

'I'll reserve judgement.'

The constable stopped walking. Thorne stopped too, glancing about as if seeking support, but there was no one nearby. The noon-day heat was oppressive, with clouds louring overhead.

'We should part now,' Cutler said. 'You'd best see to your

hired man. Likely he'll want further payment, after what he's suffered. You can retrieve your sword and poniard, though I fear your friend might have lost his in the tussle.'

To which remark Thorne muttered something under his breath, his eyes on the ground.

'What's that?' Cutler enquired. But when the other merely shook his head, he removed his hand from his elbow and stepped away. 'Now I'll warn you again – and this time, the case is somewhat altered. If I ever encounter you hereabouts, I'll make things difficult. And I think you know by now that it's no bluff.'

Whereupon he turned and left Edward Thorne, standing bruised and humiliated in the middle of a field. It seemed unlikely that he would see the young man again.

A short while later, he was walking past St Leonard's church, gathering himself to enter the disreputable premises of Alice Leake, renowned bawd of Shoreditch.

* * *

He had never been inside the trugging-house; it was not his habit... and besides, to do so could invite trouble of many kinds. And it was well-known that Mistress Leake was careful to avoid conflict with the law. She ran a tidy ship, was her way of putting it: a passing reference to her sea-captain husband, long deceased. Drunkards and trouble-makers were swiftly despatched from the premises by the giant known with wry humour as Cerberus, after the watchdog at the entrance to Hades. Her trulls too, she had always maintained, were of the better sort: clean and well-mannered, at least on first impressions. Cutler was tense as he opened the gate to the garden that fronted the large house, set back from the road. Ahead of him were steps leading to a door with iron studs, which stood open – and guarded by the black-bearded fellow last seen at the inquest, now seated on a stool with a cup of something at his feet. As the constable walked up, the man rose and stood to block his way. Having given his name and stated his desire to see Mistress Leake, Cutler waited.

'My lady is most burdened with work,' the giant grunted.

'Yet she will see me, I think. I'm on lawful business, under instruction from the alderman.' He lifted his gaze to look the man in the eye. 'You were at the inquest earlier – you know what my position is.' And when the other merely stared back: 'You'd not want to hinder a constable at this time.'

The big man frowned slightly, but said nothing.

'Come now, Master Cerberus.' With a wry look, Cutler reached for his purse. 'Here's a penny for your pains, and another when I leave. Your mistress will know naught of it – and I'll overlook your thwarting of an officer discharging his duties. Can we not trade?'

'Well, we might,' the other replied. He glanced briefly over his shoulder. 'That is, if you claimed to be a customer, with shillings to spend.'

'God's heart... if I must.' Cutler sighed and handed over the coin, which disappeared at once. The giant then stood aside, nodded politely and waved him in. He walked into a dimly lit lobby, squinting in the gloom, and stopped.

'Good-day, master. How can we aid you?' a voice called out.

He turned to see none other than the mistress of the house herself, rising from a chair by the wall with a welcoming smile. Over her head hung portraits of young women, also wearing smiles. He glimpsed a table with a jug and cups, and in the corner, a staircase rising to a darkened upper floor. The house windows, he realised, were all covered.

'Mistress Leake.' Cutler nodded stiffly – at which point, he was recognised, and the woman's smile vanished.

'You're one of the constables... I saw you in the tavern.' Drawing herself to full height, she folded her arms. 'What do you want here?'

'I need to speak to one of your girls – Petronella.'

The bawd's brow creased slightly. 'Why, is something amiss?'

'I hope not,' Cutler replied. 'In truth, I want to ask after one of her... after a man who visited her. She herself is not in trouble.'

'Well now...' Mistress Leake hesitated. 'Master Cutler, is it not?' And on receiving a nod: 'I must tell you that those who enter my house do so knowing that no questions are asked. They may give whatever name they choose, or none – it's all one to me.'

'Provided they've enough money in their purse,' Cutler said, without thinking. To which, the other merely returned a hard stare. 'I mean no insult,' he added. 'Yet you will know what I'm concerned with – the death of Alessandro Brisco. I've reason to think—'

'Jesu – is it perfume that brings you, then?' On a sudden, the woman was defensive. 'My girls use only what's bought for them... by me, or by friends who visit us. I speak of rose oil, or powdered orris—'

'Or storax?'

'Civet, I was about to say,' came the swift retort. 'I don't recall storax scent here.'

'And yet, your girl Petronella has a shift perfumed with it,' Cutler said. 'I spoke with a man who will swear to it. So...' Allowing the words to strike home, he paused, then: 'Call it a whim, but I want to know whence came that shift. On receiving an answer, I'll leave her – and you – to your work.'

A brief silence followed, broken suddenly by cries of pleasure from above, which Cutler chose to ignore. Keeping his eye on Mistress Leake, he waited – then at the sound of footsteps, looked round. A man was coming down the stairs, walking quickly, but at sight of someone standing before him, he stopped in his tracks. The two of them stared at each other... and recognition followed.

'Farrant?' Cutler raised his eyebrows. 'Is it you?'

His fellow constable dropped his gaze, and wilted like a thief caught in the act.

7

There was no need for words. Cutler merely stood by while Roger Farrant, clad not in his customary black but in an old doublet of faded blue, lurched past Mistress Leake, avoiding her eye as he avoided Cutler's. So, his secret was out – Cutler was tempted to voice it, but decided to spare the man's blushes. Nor did the bawd address him, as he swept by. In a trice, Farrant was out the door, his footfalls fading as he descended the steps.

Cutler faced her again, and found a smile tugging at his mouth. 'Well, madam... it seems I'm not the only constable with business here today.' And when the woman did not answer: 'Then, this is his parish after all... does he have an arrangement with you? Private moments with your wenches, perhaps, in exchange for leaving you in peace? For a man of his persuasion, it must weigh heavy on his conscience.'

But if Mistress Leake was abashed, she was not about to let Cutler see it. 'You asked about Petronella,' she said, with an edge to her tone that would have made some men wary. 'If I were to bring her to you, and have her answer your questions, would that suffice? Or...' she raised her brows. 'Was there something else you hoped for?'

'Nothing else,' Cutler replied, matching her gaze. 'I'll tarry here.'

The bawd promptly ascended the staircase and disappeared, while faint sounds from above came to his ears: muffled voices, a peal of laughter. He glanced out through the open door, thinking it would rain again soon, then turned his mind to the business in hand: how to question the drab known as Petronella. Thorne's words came back to him: *she is much prized, and spoiled by those who can afford her...*

Whereupon there were footsteps again, and he looked round to see Mistress Leake reappear on the stairs, with someone walking down behind her. The bawd wore a look of annoyance at this disruption to her day. Maintaining a calm expression, he waited.

'Here's one of those likes to talk, and take his pleasure later,' she said tartly. 'Why don't you both sit yonder?' She indicated a bench by the far wall, wide enough to seat three people. Cutler glanced at it, while she moved back to her chair. As she went, she threw him a warning look; it was not unusual for women of her station to have powerful friends. Dismissing the notion, he faced Petronella... and blinked.

He had expected a maid of some beauty, but the one who stood eying him with a smile was stocky in build, with a flat nose – and worse, a slight squint. It struck him that she bore a passing resemblance to the famous clown and comic player Dick Tarlton, dead these past six years. He took a breath, whereupon:

'Not dumbstruck, are you, sir?' Petronella said, in a sly voice. 'Well, let us dally while you master yourself.' She moved to the bench and sat down, whisking her skirts aside as she did so. Cutler caught a glimpse of thigh, and understood: her instructions were to distract him, then tempt him to go up to her chamber. To Mistress Leake, he was merely a man with appetites like any other – and doubtless, it would profit her to have another constable as a customer. Gathering himself, he walked over and sat on the bench, leaving a space between the two of them.

'I'm not here to dally, mistress,' he said, his eyes upon her. 'I'm on Ward business, following the murder of Brisco, the perfumer.' And when Petronella raised her eyebrows: 'I'm told you own a shift perfumed with storax, which Brisco sells. Did it come from one who did business with him?'

She was taken aback. So, while she appeared to be summoning a reply, he pressed on.

'I make no accusations. Some men bestow gifts on you, do they not? Perhaps one presented you with the scented shift – a costly garment. If you know his name, I need to hear—'

'Nay... this is vile!' The maid stared at him, as if the import of his words had just struck home. 'You hunt a murderer, yet you come here asking about my clothes?' Her mouth dropped open. 'I thought—'

'Listen to me,' Cutler broke in. He threw a quick glance across the lobby to Mistress Leake, who was observing them keenly. 'I've no wish to make trouble, but you must tell me what you know.'

But with a shake of her head, she lowered her eyes. Only now did he notice how low-cut was her gown, clearly meant to draw his gaze. He looked away and waited.

'It's but a plain shift,' she said at last, speaking hesitantly. 'I know not what the perfume is called, save that it smells so pretty.' Now he caught her accent: the inflections of the Low Countries, which thus far, she had managed to conceal. So... she was frightened, which spurred him on.

'Who gave it to you?' he asked.

'Master, I pray you...' She swallowed. 'It's not as you think.

The shift was passed to me, but the giver was innocent. There was no need for you to come here.'

'Well now, I'll be the one to judge that,' Cutler began – but she looked up.

'You do not understand. The one who gave it is dead... many months since.' And when he frowned: 'More, it was none of my... of the men who come here. You should forget this—'

'Petronella.' In a voice that would brook no argument, he stayed her. 'I want to know the name of the one who gave you the shift. When I have it, I will go, so let's not dawdle. You wish to be elsewhere, and so do I.'

But again, the girl shook her head. 'I'll not say the name, for I promised.'

'What are you afraid of?' Cutler prompted, sensing he was about to learn something of importance at last. 'That you will suffer if you tell? Whoever this man was—'

'It was not a man!' Petronella retorted. 'Now, will you let it be?' And as his face clouded, she added, 'She was my friend – the shift was given to her, yet she knew she could never wear it. She bade me take it – and now she is dead!'

'Wait – what goes on here?'

The voice rang out harshly. Mistress Leake had risen from her chair, and was coming towards them with a face of thunder. Cutler got to his feet, but just then, there was a noise from the doorway. He looked round, as did the bawd, to see two young gallants enter, talking loudly. Thinking fast, he stepped towards Mistress Leake and spoke low.

'You attend to your business,' he breathed. 'I need but a few words more, then I'll go.'

She hesitated, but only briefly. Leaving him alone with Petronella, she went to deal with the customers, summoning her welcoming smile. Cutler turned and spoke quickly.

'Tell me her name, and none shall know it came from you,' he said. 'I give my word.' And when she still hesitated: 'If this woman who was your friend is dead, it cannot harm her. But it may help me to bring justice for the man who was slain.'

Another pause followed... until at last, an answer came, albeit unwillingly.

'She came to me for aid, but I failed her,' Petronella said, speaking softly. 'She was with child – whose child, I swear I do not know, yet I know he was the one who gave her the shift. I told her of remedies known to our sisterhood, but to no avail. She was broken, and afraid. She took her own life – drowned herself in the pond by Bunhill Fields.' She looked up – and to his surprise, a tear fell from her squinty eye. 'She was the sweetest of girls – a lamb, who had been ill-used. So, master... I will give you her name, in the hope she may find peace in the next world, for she had precious little in this.' And when he bent low to listen, she told him. 'It was Susanna Martinhouse, the stone-cutter's daughter.'

She stood up – and as Cutler watched her move off to join her mistress, he saw her manner change in an instant: to that of a brazen trull, ready to serve the men who regarded her with broad grins. He turned and went out through the door, without looking back.

As he came out, the black-bearded Cerberus half-rose from his stool. But if he was waiting for his second penny, he was disappointed; this was one promise Cutler decided not to keep.

***

Scarcely knowing where he walked, he crossed the street and found himself by St Leonard's church. Whereupon, he walked into the churchyard and sat down on a bench beneath a yew tree. As he did so, raindrops began to fall, though he barely noticed.

Susanna, the much-mourned daughter of Richard and Mary Martinhouse, believed lost to the plague... yet it was not the pestilence that had taken her. Instead, he realised, the matter had been concealed – there were so many deaths during those fateful years, few would question the cause of one more. Her parents must have devised it – and yet, who would blame them? A suicide was not permitted to lie in hallowed ground, yet Susanna's grave was here among the others, the headstone carved by her own father. Briefly, he wondered if the parson – or even Roger Farrant – had helped to arrange it. Knowing what he did now...

But that, he told himself firmly, was not his business. What mattered was to find a trail that led to Brisco's murderer. And though the way was yet murky, sitting there in the rain, he resolved to follow it to the end. In view of what he had learned, perhaps there were others beside the slain perfumer for whom he might bring justice.

He got up, pulled his cap down and walked out of the churchyard, readying himself to confront the stonemason. Just now, it seemed the only course of action.

And soon, he stood once more in the Martinhouse home, facing not the householder but his wife.

Her husband being elsewhere about his business, Mistress Mary was uneasy at Cutler's arrival, as he stepped out of the downpour. Knowing no gentle way to put it, he broached the topic of Susanna Martinhouse's death – only to be silenced by the reaction.

'Oh no... do not speak of that.'

She was aghast, a hand flying to her mouth. Cutler hesitated, then: 'Believe me, mistress, I've no desire to open old wounds. But there's a matter that must be laid bare. I spoke today with one who knew Susanna, and learned—'

'You learned what?' Mistress Mary asked, trying to contain herself. 'For if it's what I fear, I swear that what I told you when you last came here is true. Richard has done naught that he can be accused of.' She frowned. 'Is that not why you come?'

He regarded her, as Petronella's words rose in his mind. Susanna was pregnant... Could she truly have hidden that from her mother? It was time to throw caution aside.

'You knew Susanna was with child, did you not?'

She let out a gasp, but gave no answer.

'I say you did,' he persisted. 'Yet I promise it shall stay a secret. I only wish to have the name of the man—'

'Richard did not know – I swear on my daughter's life!' Her face was haggard, her hands working nervously. 'You must believe me. He knew naught of the child, for we dared not tell him. He thought Susanna was sick, though not of the pestilence. Had he known, he would have—'

She broke off, realising she was babbling. But Cutler's thoughts leaped. He was in no doubt that she spoke the truth; knowing Richard Martinhouse, he guessed that, had he learned of his daughter's condition, he would have forced her to tell the father's name, then gone to vent his rage on the man... even, perhaps...

'I understand, and I believe you,' he said. 'And no word of that shall be spoken, to anyone.' He paused, trying to find the words. 'You bore a terrible burden – all the heavier when your daughter died. On the manner of that, too, I'll remain silent. Yet I must know the name of the man who used her – I'll not say why, save that it may have a bearing on the murder here.'

At that, she flinched. A secret she had kept was no longer secret – and yet, the constable was a man to be trusted. Finally, to his relief, she gave a nod. 'He was a player at the theatre,' she said. 'Susanna was loth to tell me, yet I made her. She was but sixteen, and besotted – all the more when he flattered her and gave her tokens of affection. His name is—'

Nicholas Wincott.

Before she had even spoken the words, he knew it. A picture flew up of the handsome player in his feathered hat, boasting of his latest conquest. At mention of the name, his heart sank.

'You will not tell Richard – you said you would not,' Mistress Martinhouse urged. 'You know what he is like. I have put the player's name away, never to be spoken again. Now, I pray that whatever comes, you'll keep Susanna's name unsaid. I beg you, master constable – will you so swear?'

'I will, and I do,' Cutler replied, after a moment. 'And once again, I'll ask pardon, for raking over those coals. I'll not trouble you again... or your husband.'

Upon which, to his regret, she lowered her head and gave way to tears.

Without further word, he left her and went out into the rain.

* * *

Saturday was done; he had no stomach for more. As the wet afternoon passed, he went back to the churchyard and stood under the yew tree, brooding on what he had uncovered.

So... Nicholas Wincott, contrary to his usual habit of bedding ladies of means, had seen fit to seduce a humble Shoreditch girl: easy pickings, for a man like him. She would have been at the theatre, stagestruck as others were, yet prettier than most. Likely what followed was nothing more than a tumble under a hayrick – yet for Susanna Martinhouse, it was her undoing. And now, recalling his encounter with Wincott, he found himself thinking of other things: Kett's accusation, the player's recklessness – and the blunted stage dagger hurled at Jean Meunier... whereupon his spirits flagged.

It made no sense. Something, he felt, lay beyond his vision – something dark. For a moment, it even crossed his mind to go to Thomas Skinner and ask to be replaced as constable; he could speak with John Willard, and they would find another man to stand in his place. Just now, despite Skinner's desire that the Bishopsgate officers work together to hunt Brisco's murderer, he felt very alone. Kett had been of little help, Deans even less so, while Farrant... He shook his head at the memory of the man, hurrying shamefacedly out of Mistress Leake's. *Scratch a Puritan*, it was said, *and find a hypocrite beneath*.

He gave a sigh, turning his thoughts to home – and to Katherine. Yet despite a pang of regret, he took comfort from one thing: the encounter with Thorne had brought home what an escape his daughter had had.

He turned, starting to head homewards, when the church doors opened and a woman emerged, with a cloak held over her head against the rain. She saw him and paused... whereupon recognition struck them both.

'Matthew?'

Cutler halted in his tracks. With all that had occurred, Margaret Fisher's return to Bishopsgate had slipped his mind – yet here she was, regarding him with a look of mingled surprise and... was it pleasure?

'Margaret.' He took a step towards her. 'I heard you had come home...' He stopped, feeling like a tongue-tied youth; she had lost none of her beauty.

'But this is fortuitous,' she said, pushing her hood back. 'I wondered – nay, I hoped we would meet soon. I'm at sixes and sevens, finding my feet again...' She stared. 'But you are soaking wet. Will you not come to the house and get dry?'

He hesitated, but only for the briefest of moments. Just now, this was a relief.

* * *

Her house in Shoreditch was in disorder. During her long absence, rain had come in through the thatch. Men had already been engaged to repair it, but one of the upper rooms would be uninhabitable until it dried out. Meanwhile, Margaret's two servants – the only ones she had retained when the pestilence forced her to leave – were busy setting the place to rights. Yet there was a fire in her parlour, with padded chairs before it. Despite the warm and humid weather, the house was still somewhat chilly. Cutler felt it as he peeled off his wet jerkin, and accepted a welcome mug of mulled ale.

Margaret's servant having left them – the man he remembered, who used to accompany her to the theatre – they sat down together, facing the fire. Now that they were alone, neither seemed eager to be first to speak.

'I'm most glad you got clear of the infection,' he said at last. 'So many did not.'

'My feelings are the same, concerning your escape,' she said. 'You went away with your company, I heard.' And when he nodded: 'Yet you have forsaken the stage, for life as a constable. Why so?'

He gave a shrug. 'I grew tired of it. Getting too old, perhaps—'

'What nonsense,' Margaret retorted, though she was smiling. 'There are men older than you at the Curtain, doubtless ranting as we speak.'

'The girls,' he said, after a moment. 'Since Anne died, their aunt has been their guardian – almost a substitute mother. Yet I thought I should be home.'

'Ah... your daughters.' She took a silver cup from the small table at her side and raised it. 'They must be full-grown by now – are they well?'

'Quite well – but what of you? I had a notion that, following your own loss, you might want to live elsewhere. Does the house not seem large, for a woman alone?'

'It does,' Margaret agreed, and took a drink. 'As does the bed.'

He turned quickly, but she did not meet his eye. And yet, it could not be unsaid. For her, he thought, little seemed to have changed. Whereas for him...

'Do my words displease you?' she added abruptly. 'We are both bereaved, and I believe the flame that was once between us is undimmed. At least, that is my hope.' She paused, then: 'I learned something, during the pestilence: that life is as frail as a cobweb. We should seize each moment. Or...' She faced him. 'Must we grow old, and regret what might have been?'

So there it was, stated boldly and without shame. Then, she was a forthright woman; he remembered earlier times, at the Curtain. And in truth, what obstacle was there now, to prevent their growing closer? Surely, he thought briefly, Anne would have wanted him to...

'I cannot,' he said flatly. 'Or, not yet...' He fumbled for the words. 'You're right, about what passed – and I should count myself lucky. But I ask for time, to order my thoughts. Your marriage...'

She stiffened, but it had to be said.

'You told me once that your marriage was a sham,' he went on. 'Nor did you grieve for your husband – I saw it myself. But my loss was like death... a chasm inside me. I know no other way to say it. And more...' He tried a smile. 'I'm but a headborough here, with few powers. And yet the work—'

'The work fills that chasm,' Margaret finished. 'You busy yourself with parish matters to push aside your grief.'

It was true, and he knew it well enough – though as yet, no one had voiced it. Now, he could imagine Anne saying the same thing.

Meeting Margaret's steady gaze, he managed a nod.

'Well...' She gave a sigh, and took another drink. 'What then, are we to do?'

* * *

It was evening, and he was home once again. Katherine and Jane moved about the kitchen in silence, while Aunt Margery readied the meal. Cutler withdrew to the chimney corner, his mind in a turmoil. He could not forget Margaret's words. He had left her soon afterwards, finishing his drink in some haste before putting on his still-wet jerkin. Yet she had seen him to the door, and her manner was not unkind. Perhaps, in time... the invitation was plain. With an effort, he brought himself to the present – whereupon there came a knocking from outside, which startled everyone.

'I'll go,' he said, getting up at once. He walked down the passage and threw the door wide – to see the diminutive figure of Austen Kett standing before him. The rain had stopped, yet he was quite bedraggled.

'There's something you should know,' he announced.

'Is there?' Cutler frowned. 'Have you come to accuse someone else of murder, or—'

'Nay, nay...' The other waved a hand carelessly – whereupon the penny dropped. The man was somewhat drunk.

'What, then?' His fellow constable eyed him. 'I was going to buy you a mug in the White Hart this morning, but you vanished. Went back later, did you?'

'Well, I...' Kett tried to gather himself. 'See now, I didn't come here to wrangle. What I heard was, there's been another attack on a stranger.'

'You heard,' Cutler echoed. 'Where was this, then? And who was the victim?'

But he was watching Kett keenly, thinking he looked more than merely drunk; he appeared almost distraught.

Seemingly stuck for words, the little man blew out a breath.

'You sure it wasn't just tavern tittle-tattle?' Cutler persisted. 'The strangers have armed themselves and set a watch. I find it hard to believe there's been another attack.'

'Well, I can't be sure,' the other replied. 'There's so much gossip about... a man doesn't know what to believe.' On a sudden, he looked helpless, which led Cutler to a decision.

'Come into the house and eat something, Austen,' he said. 'Once you've sobered up a little, we may talk.'

It took an hour, but it was an hour well-spent. While Margery and the girls ate supper indoors, he took his fellow constable out the back, sat him on the bench and made him share a large bowl of broth along with hunks of rye bread. Mugs of plain well-water followed, until the man began to regain something of his usual self. Cutler then walked him round in circles and waited until he had made water profusely, before sitting him down again.

'There's been no attack, has there?' he said. 'It was but an excuse to come here.'

Kett hesitated, then sagged. 'I didn't know which way to turn, Matthew,' he mumbled. And when Cutler waited: 'It's all got muddled. I've been a fool... Got myself in over my head.' He looked up. 'Yet there's still a murderer to find. And since you didn't like my accusing the player – Wincott, I mean – we're no further on, are we?'

To which, Cutler stiffened. 'As it happens,' he said, 'I've learned more about Wincott today. Things I didn't like.'

On a sudden, Kett was alert. 'What have you learned?'

'Let's say that I've a bone to pick with him,' he answered, recalling his talk with Mary Martinhouse. 'If I thought it worth the trouble, I'd set out now and seek him at Ben Pimlico's. Except that...' He sighed. 'He won't be there. He'll be with his new lady, whoever she is.'

'Well... as it happens, he isn't,' Kett said. And when his host turned to him: 'I know where he is: carousing with some of the theatre folk in the White Hart. Or he was, when I left.'

'Is it so?' Cutler sat upright. 'Well then, would you like to take a stroll with me?'

Without hesitating, Kett nodded.

8

The inn was busy, it being Saturday night and no need for Bishopsgate folk to rise with the dawn. The two constables walked among the crowd, attracting glances here and there. Peering through the tobacco haze, they finally made out Nicholas Wincott seated by a window, evidently in his cups. But there was no raucous company of fellow players remaining now, merely one man who looked too unsteady to stand. Wincott appeared to be regaling him anyway, whether the other listened or not. Somewhat taut, Cutler moved forward to loom over them.

'May we join you?' he said, plonking himself down.

Bleary-eyed, Wincott looked round, then forced a smile. 'Constable Cutler! What an honour.' His gaze strayed to Kett, standing at eye level to him. 'And here's another of 'em! Two upstanding guardians of the law – or should I say one and a half? Here!' He shouted to one of the drawers, who looked round. 'Ale, for my friends!'

'Not for me,' Cutler said. Seeing there was no room, he eyed Wincott's drunken companion, who could barely lift his head.

'But I'd like to talk, if you'll allow. Mayhap your friend's had enough for one night. Constable Kett can have his stool.'

Wincott's grin faded; this was not a courtesy visit. Leaning forward, he tapped the drunken man on the arm. 'It seems I have business, Toby,' he said. 'Best get yourself home, eh?'

'Permit me,' Kett said abruptly. Whereupon with a strength that surprised all of them, he hoisted Toby to his feet, turned him about and gave him a shove. The man staggered, narrowly avoiding colliding with others. There was some indignant muttering, before a couple of helpful drinkers got up to ease the situation. Supported between their shoulders, the inebriate was marched off into the haze.

'How impressive,' Wincott said sourly. Kett sat down facing him, looking a good deal sharper than when he had appeared at Cutler's house.

'So, what's this about?' The player was frowning. 'Not more accusations?'

'I hope not,' Cutler said. The drawer having come over, he waved him away, then turned deliberately to Wincott. 'Yet I had a notion – nay, call it an urge – to ask you about a young girl who took her own life – drowned in the pond by Bunhill Fields. Her family said she died of the plague, but I've learned otherwise. What say you to that?'

But if it was a shock, the other managed to take it. He blinked, and looked quickly from Cutler to Kett. Having been told something of the sad tale on their way here, Kett wore no expression.

'What say I?' Wincott swallowed. 'In God's name, what do you want me to say?'

'A word of regret might help,' Cutler said. 'And some sympathy for her mother and father.'

'Sympathy?' The player frowned. 'Listen, I meant no harm – the maid was more than willing. I had no notion she was such a wilting flower.' He took up his mug quickly, tilted it, then realised it was empty and put it down with a thud. 'By heaven...' He took a breath, then eyed Cutler. 'You know me and my ways,' he said. 'What man would turn his nose up at such an offer? Now I think on it, there was a time when you'd have jumped at—'

'There's something more,' Cutler said, cutting him short. 'A matter of a gift you bestowed on Susanna Martinhouse. Far too grand a gift, I should add – and one she knew she could never wear, nor take home. Instead, she passed it to one of Alice Leake's trulls. Its scent was so powerful, it lingered for months.'

To that, Wincott lowered his gaze to stare down at the beer-stained table. 'What would you have me do?' he muttered. 'Flay myself, like some penitent? Nothing will bring the girl back.' On a sudden, he was indignant. 'God knows I'm no saint,' he added, looking up. 'But I've never set foot in Leake's den of harlots. I never pay for it – I do my wooing, and let nature take her course. So, if that's all you have to say to me—'

'It isn't,' Cutler said. 'There's the matter of the perfume – storax, that I believe came from Brisco's. A perfumed shift's a costly garment, though I'd wager a man like you would lay out the money if he thought it worth his while. Hence—'

'By the Christ!' Wincott showed his anger. 'Harping on that again? Having all but accused me of killing the man last time, you come here wagging the finger of piety about my foining some Shoreditch wench! Damn you, Matthew – and you too, master dwarf!' He eyed Kett with a look of contempt. 'You're no saint either, from what I've heard—'

'I think we should arrest him,' Kett said to Cutler, fixing Wincott with a glare. 'Skinner's eager for someone to blame. It might as well be him.'

Cutler decided to say nothing. Both constables eyed the player, who showed a measure of fear at last. 'No... you would not.' He swallowed again. 'Never try to bluff a seasoned gamester. You know there are men of substance I could call on, to aid me. Patrons, say, as well as—'

'Their wives?' Cutler broke in, in a casual tone. 'I wonder how many would drop a word in their husband's ear, on your behalf? Then again, perhaps that would be unwise—'

'Enough!' Wincott banged a hand on the table, causing a few heads to turn. 'In God's name, what can you gain from this?' he added, trying to calm himself. 'You know I didn't slay the perfumer – even if I did wrangle with him. As for that shift...' He paused, looking away. 'It was never meant for the Martinhouse girl – I swear it! It was bespoken for another, save that she refused it. Her husband would have wondered whence it came, she said. Though Hexham's such an old fool, I never thought it likely...'

He stopped abruptly. His tongue loosened by drink, he had betrayed himself – and it was past being remedied. At once, Kett's eyebrows shot up.

'Hexham? Do you mean Sir George Hexham, of the Queen's Privy Council?'

'I believe he does,' Cutler said, showing his own surprise. 'I know of no other with that name.' He eyed Wincott. 'I admire your nerve, Nick. Bedding the wife of a knight of the realm – a friend to the Queen, I hear – is bold indeed. Is that who you meant, when you told me of a *new and most pleasing acquaintance*?'

Lost for words, Wincott cursed under his breath.

'Well now,' Cutler went on. 'It's fortunate for you that neither of us is the sort to use duress. By such a slip of the tongue, you lay yourself open to demands for the price of silence. And yet...' He paused, his mind working. 'This could be your salvation. If, say, you had been with Lady Hexham on the night of Brisco's murder...?'

Leaving the sentence unfinished, he waited until Wincott looked up.

'I was with Albina Hexham all that Wednesday night, while her husband was at Greenwich attending the Queen,' he said heavily. 'I swear it on my life. Only...' He looked at each of them in turn. 'I beg that you tell no one. If you did...'

'You'd be well and truly in the shit, master player,' Kett finished. His tone was so bitter that Cutler looked round, to see his fellow constable wearing a look of disappointment. For some reason, he had wanted Wincott blamed for Brisco's murder, ever since he had first accused him... but now, the little man got to his feet. 'I've heard enough,' he said, with a glance at Cutler. 'I'm for home. I'm obliged for the bread and broth. I'll leave you to...' He shrugged. 'Whatever it is you want to do.'

And he was gone, head down, shoving his way through the drinkers. One or two men laughed – as they had always laughed at Kett, Cutler thought suddenly. Frowning, he watched his fellow constable disappear before turning back to Wincott.

'I never thought you and I would end up at loggerheads, Matthew,' the player said, with a shake of his head. 'After those times we had together.'

'Nor did I,' Cutler replied. 'Then, mayhap I misjudged you. I saw a likeable rogue, who cared not a fig for what folk thought. I never saw you as one who'd use a young maid so, and drive her to despair.' He sighed. 'In a way, that was a kind of murder, was it not?'

To that, Wincott merely lowered his eyes and, on a sudden, there was nothing more to be said. Cutler got up... whereupon a notion struck him. It had been at the back of his mind all along – ever since he had stood in Jean Meunier's shop and examined a blunted dagger.

'Do you know anything about a stage poniard, that might

have gone missing from the properties store?' he asked, looking down at Wincott.

Frowning, the other peered up. 'Jesu... have you eyes everywhere?' he asked harshly. 'There was a robbery, at the Curtain. Stuff of little value, apart from a dagger. I know not if it was reported. The watchman was remiss...'

He stopped, for Cutler had turned away. Through bleary eyes, Wincott watched him melt into the crowd, before slumping visibly.

* * *

Outside, the light was fading, but his day was not yet done. He knew exactly where to go, and would waste no time. Walking briskly, he headed northwards up Bishopsgate Street. On the way, he passed Brisco's shop, and slowed briefly to look through the window, but it was newly boarded. Turning away, he quickened his pace and did not stop until he was past Norton Folgate and walking down a narrow way lined by some of the meanest cottages in Shoreditch. At the last one, he stopped, saw a dim light within, and gave several loud knocks upon the door. At first, nothing happened, whereupon he knocked again. Finally, there came the squeal of a rusty latch, and the door opened a few inches to reveal a startled-looking Ned Broad, holding a lantern.

'Jesu, Master Matthew...' He drew back. 'You've frit me again... Have a care, will you? You'll wake the brats.'

'Then come outside, Ned,' Cutler ordered. 'I've questions for you.'

Broad complied, standing uneasily before his door. Putting the lantern down, he eyed the constable warily. 'What have I done now?' he asked. 'Naught, is the answer—'

'There were things went missing from the Curtain Theatre a

while back,' Cutler said sharply. 'They weren't worth much. But there was a dagger – blunted, though that could easily be put right. You know where to sell such – like the one I gave you this morning. So, will you confess here and now, or do I have to haul you off to Newgate first thing tomorrow?'

He waited, watching his man keenly – and was rewarded by his sudden look of fear. This time, Ned knew, there could be consequences. He put a hand to his ragged beard, and spoke up. 'I might have taken a pair of cups,' he said, avoiding the constable's gaze. 'They weren't much... not worth a fiddler's fart. As for—'

'The poniard,' Cutler broke in. 'What did you do with it?' His mind was racing – and yet, when the answer came, he was stunned.

'I... well, I gave it to Stephen Bland,' Ned said, speaking low.

'You what?'

'It was his garnish.' The miscreant looked up suddenly. 'By God, Master Matthew, what else could I do? He's had the measure of me for a long while – and I'm not the only one, I'd say. He's a sly bastard, is Bland... douses his lantern, comes out of nowhere and pounces like a hawk. So, what could I...'

But he trailed off, for Cutler was no longer listening. Thoughts flew up: firstly, the realisation that his suspicions about Bland taking bribes had been right all along. Yet now, there was something else: the blunted dagger that had been used to scare Jean Meunier.

He let out a breath, and realised how tired he was; it had been a very long day.

'So, what now?' Ned muttered, eying him nervously. 'I mean... could we not speak of the stocks, or even a flogging? God knows I deserve it, but...' He spoke faster. 'I won't offer you money, Master Matthew, for I know you wouldn't take it. Only, seeing as how I aided you this morning, I thought... well, mayhap...'

'Mayhap you've done more than you know, Ned,' Cutler said. And when the other gave a start: 'Forget about the stocks. But for pity's sake, don't let me catch you night-stepping again. As for Bland...' He paused, then: 'I doubt if you'll be dealing with him, after this.'

Open-mouthed, Ned Broad stared at him. For a while, he stood outside his door, long after Cutler had left him and walked off into the gathering dusk. Then with a lighter heart, he took up his lantern and went back indoors.

* * *

Cutler went home, intending only to sleep; reckoning was for the morning... Sunday, while Aunt Margery and the girls were at church. He would have much to do. Entering the house quietly, he closed the door, then saw a light at the rear: Katherine and Jane would be abed, but their aunt sometimes sat up late. Pausing only to pull off his boots, he padded into the kitchen and found her seated at the table with a candle, peering down at her sewing.

'Well now.' She looked up. 'You must be the busiest man in Bishopsgate, Matthew Cutler.'

He made no reply, only sat down heavily.

'Shall I fetch you a mug?' she asked, to which he merely shook his head. 'Katherine and I talked today,' Margery went on, laying aside her needle and thread. 'She will mend – I know it. As for you...' She put on a warm smile. 'You have brought comfort, to me at least. I know not how it was done, but I'm thankful.'

'It's I who should give thanks,' he said. 'You're my mainstay... a light that does not fail.'

She regarded him for a moment. 'I think you need something else just now – like someone to share your burden? It's been a while since you did that with me, is it not? Mayhap ever since you stood in for my too-busy brother, and became constable.'

'It may be so,' he admitted. 'But the tale isn't pretty. In truth, it should wait for another time.' And yet, he made no effort to rise. Margery was right, of course, as she usually was. He could hear Anne saying it – and more, he could guess what she would say now. On impulse, he straightened himself... and began to talk.

It took a little longer than he intended, but in the end, a weight was lifted. Aunt Margery had always been a shoulder for Katherine and Jane, a comfort to her brother, and a firm friend to Cutler himself. Piecing it out as he spoke, he told her everything: from what passed on the day of the perfumer's death, to what now looked like the bizarre events of today, leading up to his uncovering of Stephen Bland: as corrupt a watchman as could be imagined. This last revelation brought a gasp from Margery's lips.

'You know I never trusted Bland,' she said. 'Nor, I believe, did you.'

He said nothing, stifling a yawn. Now that he had told all, he was spent. Tomorrow...

'You'd best go upstairs,' she advised. 'Before you sleep where you sit.' And when he barely nodded: 'I know how weighed down you've been – and now, I see why. Yet it's better laid forth, is it not?'

'Likely it is,' he agreed, and got up stiffly to go to his bed.

* * *

Sunday morning brought rain again, and a gusty wind from the west. The family rose in good time, breakfasted and made ready to go to St Leonard's. Cutler was the last to appear, having slept more soundly than he expected. But he had formed a resolve, and felt better for it. He would accompany the others to the church, where Stephen Bland was sure to be. After the service... as yet he was uncertain. But whatever was needed, would be done.

They left the house in a group, following others up the street, Margery and the girls wearing their hoods. Little had been said, but Cutler was cheered by Katherine's manner; she was quiet, but appeared calm enough. Once inside, they took their usual seats. But as the service began, the constable found himself distracted. He scanned the congregation until he saw Stephen Bland sitting with his wife, a woman who was rarely seen. Bland saw him but gave no reaction, prompting Cutler to look away. By then he had seen others he knew, like Richard and Mary Martinhouse seated at the back. Margaret Fisher was there too in a front pew, accompanied by her servants; she did not look round. He saw no sign of Henry Deans, or of Austen Kett – but there was one, with whom he had no desire to speak: Roger Farrant.

Before he could avert his gaze, Farrant saw him and almost ducked out of sight. Cutler dismissed him and looked straight ahead. The parson, he realised, was talking of sin, and how a Christian must strain every sinew to overcome it.

Less than an hour later, having seen Aunt Margery and the girls off homewards, he stood some way from the church entrance in what had become a steady drizzle, and watched people file out. Margaret passed by, but gave no sign of having noticed him. So did Richard and Mary Martinhouse, in silence with their heads down. Finally, among the last of the stragglers, Stephen Bland appeared alone – to stop in displeasure as Cutler came forward.

'I thought you and I had naught to say to each other, after yesterday,' the watchman said.

'But we have, Stephen,' was the reply. 'I wish it were otherwise, yet I have a duty to fulfil.' He paused. 'Moreover, I think you know the what and the why.'

'Do you, now?' Bland frowned. 'Well, I say you're mistook. Now I've got things to attend to, so—'

'It won't do,' Cutler broke in. 'I spoke to Ned Broad last night, and got the truth out of him. You're in a mire, Stephen. Taking garnish from thieves, to look away while they're at work, is no better than thieving yourself. At the least, that's how a magistrate would see it.'

A moment passed, while Bland stared at him. He glanced round quickly, but to no avail. He seemed about to speak – until Cutler dealt a further blow.

'It's the poniard that troubles me most,' he said, watching the man carefully. 'Ned stole it from the Curtain Theatre, and you had it from Ned. It was blunted – it still is. I looked it over, along with Kett, when Meunier the button-maker was attacked in his shop. Do you know aught about that?' And when the watchman still stared, he went on. 'The matter is, I think someone hired a rogue to stage a little interlude at Meunier's,' Cutler said. 'Since Brisco's murder, the strangers fear a campaign to scare them, or even worse. Whether that's so or not, the poniard flung at the button-maker was supplied by you, so—'

'No more now… no more, I say!'

In dismay, Bland lowered his gaze, and a haggard look came over him. His shoulders fell, and for a moment, Cutler thought he would stagger. Glancing round, his eye fell upon the bench where he had sat the day before.

'Shall we rest there for a while?' he suggested. 'Mayhap there are matters you'd like to get off your chest before…' He trailed off. He had thought to say something like *before I arrest you*, but the words stuck in his throat.

After a moment, Bland gave a nod. Together, they walked over to the bench and sat down under the yew tree. Before Cutler could speak, however, the other stayed him.

'What has Kett told you?' he asked, his eyes on the ground.

'In regard to what?'

'You said he was with you at Meunier's... What else has he said?'

'About you, nothing. He's too eager to find someone to blame for Brisco's killer, though thus far, he's missed his aim by a mile.' Cutler found himself frowning; there were things to be uncovered here, his instinct told him. He found himself mulling over Kett's behaviour these past days – especially his troubled manner the previous night, when he had arrived drunk. On impulse, he raised another topic.

'It was you who told me Kett borrowed money from Brisco,' he said. 'And in truth, you've never had a good word to say about the man, have you? What was it you called him – a *twisty little runt*? Not to mention passing on idle gossip about him. Now, you fret about what he might have told me... I wonder why.'

He watched Bland again, and saw the look that passed across his face. Seemingly stuck for a reply, the watchman remained silent.

'Come now, Stephen.' Gathering himself, Cutler adopted a stern manner. 'I'm giving you a chance to spill your tale while you can. You know neither Deans nor Skinner would do that – once the alderman hears what's gone on, he'll want you imprisoned within the hour. I need to know about the poniard, and how it ended up being used to threaten Meunier – and more, I'd like to know what puts you and Kett at loggerheads. Call it curiosity, if you like.'

He stopped to let the words sink in. Bland was more than dismayed now; he was beginning to look desperate. And he was breathing somewhat quickly, wheezing as he did so. At last, with a great sigh, he seemed to come to a decision.

'It's all mummery... make-believe,' he muttered, almost to

himself. 'Austen Kett and I... we go back a long way. I fought off bullies who tormented him; he helped me to a trull now and again.' With a bleak look, he raised his head. 'It suited us to have folk think we're enemies. The truth is otherwise... as Alice Leake will tell you.'

'Leake?' Cutler frowned. 'What does she have to do with it?'

'Many is the time she's had need of a scrivener,' Bland admitted. 'One who can keep his mouth tight shut. A keeper of confidences... she knows enough to squeeze money out of those who'd rather pay than have their wives know where they go a-rutting.'

'You mean, Kett wrote letters for her, demanding a price for her silence?' Cutler was astounded. 'I'm surprised she's lived this long.'

'Important friends,' Bland muttered. 'Men who get to use the best harlots, free of charge.'

'And you?' Cutler's frown deepened. 'You're a married man, as contented as any I know. Now you speak of trulls—'

'By God, will you rack me?' the other broke in bitterly. 'Must I lay open my misery for you to pick over?' He paused, then: 'Contented in my marriage, you say... I wish to God it were so. But answer me this, master constable – for as one who lost his wife, you might understand. When a man has nowhere else to turn... when his own wife shrinks from his touch, as mine has these ten years past, what is he to do?'

Looking away, he fell silent. But Cutler's mind was busy, as a picture began to form. Bland and Kett, who on the face of it disliked each other, had a secret – as had Roger Farrant, before his and Cutler's embarrassing encounter. 'So, the gossip about Kett and his preference for men... that's what you meant by make-believe, is it?' he demanded. 'A mask, to conceal his true nature? And trulls cost money, mayhap more than he could afford... more, even, than Alice Leake allowed him for writing letters she couldn't pen herself. So, he borrowed – from Brisco. While you took things you could sell, from rogues like Ned Broad.'

To which, Bland's silence merely served for assent. Bedraggled and beaten, he was a forlorn sight. Cutler regarded him, and let out a sigh.

'By heaven, Stephen, it's a stony path you've trodden – and now you've stumbled. Did you think your luck would last forever?' And when the other gave no answer: 'Well then, tell me now of this damned poniard, and let's put an end to that riddle at least.'

'The poniard?' Bland met his eye. 'There's something I can reveal, though I doubt it'll bring much cheer. Send you down a different path, more likely... one that's a mite too thorny for a mere constable of the parish. But then again...' He nodded, as if reasoning while he spoke. 'Who knows, given the man you are, it might even win you plaudits.'

'What do you mean?' Cutler was impatient now. 'Speak, for I grow tired of this.'

'We were hired – Kett and I,' the watchman confessed. 'Paid to find some rogue who'd do as he was bid for a price, then disappear. He was to scare the living daylights out of the Frenchman, so as it would look like another attack on a stranger after Brisco was slain. And yes...' Seeing the look that came over Cutler's face, he gave a nod. 'I know it was foolish – wicked, even. Yet the price was more money than I see in a year – more even than Kett could make. But there was another aspect – a threat behind it. Do as we were bidden, and all would be well. Fail, and...' He drew a breath. 'There was no idle threat; I'd stake my life on it. I wasn't about to wrangle with a man like that.'

'What man?' Cutler's tone was sharp. 'Tell me!'

'I know not who he was,' Bland answered. 'But he found me

by night, and told me what to do. The same night, he'd been to Kett and demanded the same, so we would act as one and share the spoils. Kett found the varlet to threaten Meunier – and I gave him the blunted poniard, which wouldn't draw blood even if it struck home.' He paused, then: 'Whatever Austen Kett and I are, we're not murderers, Matthew – and despite all I've told you, I think you know that.'

Upon which, the man put his head in his hands, and bent almost to his knees.

Cutler watched him, then turned away. The rain had ceased at last, but he hadn't noticed.

9

Needing to think things over, he left Stephen Bland and walked to the churchyard gate – to stop short as he encountered the one man – perhaps the only man, just now – with whom he could share what he had learned.

'You're not going to arrest me for missing church, are you?' John Willard asked with a wry smile. 'I didn't know it was so late – I'm guilty as sin.'

'Guilty of working too hard, more like,' Cutler said. Whereupon, seeing his expression, his father-in-law's smile faded.

'You look as if you bear the troubles of the world,' he observed. 'Do you wish to share some of them?'

His son-in-law gave a nod, and relaxed somewhat. He turned about and the two of them began to walk, passing out of the rear gate of the churchyard into the orchards beyond. Soon they were in conversation, the substance of which stunned even Willard.

Cutler had not arrested Bland, of course... not yet. He believed the man had nowhere to go, nor had he shown any desire to flee. He was as miserable as anyone Cutler had seen: remorseful and afraid. As familiar a sight in Bishopsgate as the

Artillery Yard or the White Hart, he had served the Ward for decades, until plain appetite had driven him to recklessness. Beneath his bluff demeanour, the watchman was desperate, and it sobered Cutler to know it. Now, under the rain-dripping trees, he gave John Willard an account of what had happened since they last sat at supper.

'You astound me, Matthew,' the gunsmith murmured.

'No more than Bland has astounded me, I'd wager,' Cutler said.

'What then, will you do? The man could hang for what he's confessed.'

'I know it, and so does he. And yet...' He shook his head. 'I've no wish to see that. But as for Kett...' He took a breath. 'That slippery little rogue. He was part of the planned attack on Meunier, knowing what folk would think... the fears that would arise among the strangers. All along, he's been content to play the poor, downtrodden dwarf, pitied by some and laughed at by others – while taking money from a bawd to pen demands for money, and rutting like a stag at her house.'

'Some men are not what they seem,' was all Willard would say. 'It was always so.'

'More, he borrowed from Brisco,' Cutler went on. 'Which makes me wonder...' He stopped, as the idea struck him. 'And that would account for it. His eagerness to find a culprit for the murder – to accuse others. That's why he's been acting so oddly.'

'I don't follow you, Matthew,' his father-in-law said. 'If you mean—'

'I mean he's been scared witless, knowing that his owing money to Brisco would come out, sooner or later – and that some might even think he'd murdered the man.'

It was a grim notion. Cutler's mind raced, as he thought over his dealings with Kett: from finding him outside the perfumer's shop on the morning the body was discovered, to his rambling talk of a possible attack on another stranger. He had turned up at Cutler's door, speaking of things being *muddled* – of having *got in over his head*. Then there was his obvious disappointment of hearing Wincott's admission in the White Hart, which gave the player an alibi... followed by Cutler's last sight of Kett shoving his way out of the inn. He met John Willard's eye, as the other gave a nod.

'It may be so,' he allowed. 'Though there's something else, isn't there? Something a deal more troubling—'

'His being paid, along with Bland, to make the false attack on Meunier.'

They both considered the matter. Here was something, Cutler realised, that he had not imagined: that someone else – someone seemingly quite ruthless – could have a reason for contriving the affair at the button-maker's. But there, he realised, the trail went cold.

'I'm in a fog, John,' he said at last. 'Though I believe Bland when he says neither he nor Kett are murderers. That stretches fancy too far.'

'So...' Willard too was thoughtful. 'If the business at Meunier's was intended to throw the forces of law off the scent, the one who ordered it is likely your murderer. That, at least, is how it looks to me.'

'And to me,' Cutler said, after a moment.

'Moreover, whoever it was knew who to go to, to do his bidding: a wily constable who frequents the trugging-house – most likely after dark – and a watchman who's lost whatever scruples he had. Easy enough, when you've the means to persuade them.'

'That too, seems plain enough.'

'And yet, it is indeed a fog,' Willard said. 'I know not how I can

help, save to be at my house when you need to turn things about.'
Cutler nodded, whereupon the gunsmith changed the topic.
'Katherine's dandy of a suitor,' he murmured. 'Is she resigned to
the loss?'

'I hope so,' his son-in-law replied.

And soon after, they parted.

***

He walked briskly from the church and down Bishopsgate Street, where a few people were still returning from worship. He was thinking still of Kett – and felt betrayed, even foolish; his fellow constable seemed to have played him for a dupe – he a one-time player, who believed himself a fair judge of men's ways.

He was almost home, when he found find himself hailed. Looking round, he was surprised to see a figure dressed in black hurrying towards him: none other than the constable of St Leonard's parish, Roger Farrant.

'Cutler... if you please.' Somewhat breathlessly, the man came to a halt. He looked not only ill-at-ease, but flustered.

'Farrant.' Cutler eyed him. 'Is there something you wanted to say to me?'

'It's Bland, the watchman. You were talking with him a short while ago, in the churchyard.'

'I was, and what—'

'He's dead.'

They gazed at each other – and for Cutler, a troubling thought flew up, until his fellow constable's next words brought some relief.

'I found him slumped on a bench, lifeless as a doll. I'm no physician, but I'd guess his heart failed.' Attempting to assume something of his usual manner, Farrant grew brisk. 'As we know, he wasn't a young man. I've long feared the task of watchman was a burden—'

'Yes, I thought so too,' Cutler broke in, looking away. His mind whirling, he ran quickly over his conversation with Bland, realising it had almost certainly been the man's last. He turned back, to see Farrant standing stiffly.

'I... well, I thought you should know,' he said. 'The death has occurred in my parish, and I will do what is necessary – like breaking the news to his wife, and to the alderman. Likely, Master Skinner will wish to speak with you. For now, perhaps you would be good enough to inform our fellow, Austen Kett?'

'I will,' Cutler answered, somewhat absently. 'Is there aught else you wish me to do?'

'I think not.' Embarrassed, Farrant was eager to be gone; there was no forgetting their last sighting of each other. But before taking leave, he frowned. 'It may well be that you were the last person to speak with Bland,' he said. 'Is there aught you can tell, that may shed light on his demeanour in his last hour on earth? Anything that troubled him, say, or—'

'There was nothing,' Cutler said, his voice flat. 'He was a humble man, who tried to make do with what he had.'

He stood his ground eying Farrant, whereupon with a curt nod, his fellow constable hurried away. Cutler watched him go... and breathed a sigh. Stephen Bland may have spent his last moments unhappily, yet he had been spared arrest and imprisonment, perhaps even execution for his crimes. Nor had Cutler been forced to be the agent of such a tragic end, for a man he had once liked.

But for now, his duty lay elsewhere: to seek out Austen Kett.

* * *

He went at once to Kett's lodging: the lower half of a house on the corner of Bearward's Lane. Here the most diminutive constable in all of London lived alone, plying his trade as a scrivener. Cutler could not remember when he had last been inside; Kett was not one to entertain visitors. Then, knowing what he did now of the man, it seemed to fit. Arriving at the cottage with its first-floor jetty looming over his head, he glanced through the window, but all was gloomy within. He was about to knock on the door when a casement was thrown open, causing him to look up. A head poked out, framed in a linen cap.

'Master Cutler?' the woman called. 'I'm glad to see you, and no mistake. Pray wait, while I come down.'

He frowned, for the householder had appeared agitated. Unsure what to expect, he waited until there came the sound of a bolt from within, and the door flew open. A rotund little woman, still in her best Sunday frock, was before him.

'Come in, constable,' she said. 'I would have called someone soon, for all is not well – you'll see it is so.'

He followed her inside... and stopped. His first thought was that there had been a robbery: the room was in disarray, and with few possessions in sight. Then he saw the fireplace: papers had been burnt, perhaps hastily, leaving a pile of ashes. He glanced at Kett's work table, which had been cleared – and in an alcove, his bed had been stripped to its rope frame.

'He's gone, Master Cutler,' the dumpy woman said. 'I just know he has. He gave me his key – he's never done that before. Last night, it was... I was going to my bed when he came knocking. Not that it was his habit,' she added hastily. 'We were both lodgers, but never more – in truth, we weren't even friends. And yet...' She swept a hand to indicate the whole room. 'Look about you.'

He did look about, and soon decided that Kett's upstairs

neighbour was correct. For one thing, there were few clothes to be seen, only empty hooks on the wall. An oak chest was thrown open, showing only a few bits of old linen. More, the tools of Kett's trade were absent: no scrivener would part with those. There was nothing on the work table but a few broken quills and an empty inkpot. His mind busy, he faced the woman again.

'I forget your name, mistress?'

'Rose,' came the swift reply. 'My brother owns the house. More...' She hesitated, then: 'Kett owed him rent. He got behind at times, I don't know why since he had plenty of work and it's a skilled trade, is it not?' She spoke fast, nodding fiercely. 'If you ask me, that's why he's fled, the little—' She stopped herself, but Cutler's nod brought reassurance.

'Mayhap it is so,' he said.

'Well, I don't know what's to be done now,' Mistress Rose resumed. 'My brother will be mighty displeased... and yet, I never thought Kett would do this. He's a constable!'

'Is there aught else you can tell me?' Cutler asked, after taking another look round. 'Anything untoward?'

'I don't know that there is.' She made a show of thinking. 'He was out some nights; I'd hear him come in at dawn. I don't know where he was, since the city gates are shut... then, I don't pry. He's an odd sort... though you'll know him better than I.'

'I thought I did, mistress,' Cutler said, after a moment. 'But we all err at times, do we not?'

'We do, and that's God's truth,' Mistress Rose agreed. 'And for a woman who lives alone, I can tell you it was a comfort to me having a constable dwelling downstairs. Yet with all that's happened hereabouts of late, I don't know what's what.'

'I pray you, don't be afeared,' he replied. 'Tell your brother what's occurred, while I seek answers elsewhere. In the meantime, is there a friend who might stay with you?'

'There is,' she nodded. 'And I'm glad you were nearby... How odd is that? Did you have business with Kett yourself?'

'I did, and I do,' Cutler told her. 'And I will make haste to conduct it.'

* * *

He walked quickly, out of the Ward and up through Norton Folgate. Even before taking his leave of Mistress Rose, he had formed an idea as to where Kett might be. The man had left his lodgings in the night when, as his neighbour had said, the city gates were closed. Hence, if he had some notion of fleeing – and as yet, Cutler was uncertain why he would do that – there were few choices open. It seemed likely that his intention could simply be to hide while he formed a resolve – and the obvious place for that was Mistress Leake's.

It must be so; the more he thought on it, the more convinced he was. It had long been said that Alice Leake hid fugitives – for a fee, naturally. Her rambling old house with its many rooms, its dark passages and closets, had been searched in the past; Cutler recalled John Willard speaking of it, back when Martinhouse was constable. The searches had yielded nothing save angry and embarrassed customers, screams and insults from the trulls and a look of quiet satisfaction on the part of the bawd herself. But rumours continued – and with what Cutler had learned about Kett's connections with Alice Leake, he felt sure of his purpose. He strode up the road to Shoreditch... then found himself slowing down.

What did he intend? He stopped, standing in the rain-washed street. Even if Kett were at Leake's, and assuming he could be found, what was Cutler to do? Arresting a fellow constable was not unknown, and the man was as guilty as Bland had been –

perhaps more so. But now that Bland was dead, he might deny all knowledge of the scheme to frighten Meunier. As for his aiding Mistress Leake in her affairs – he was merely a scrivener, hired to write letters. And it seemed unlikely that copies of letters would ever be found; the pile of ashes in the fireplace could be proof of that. While, in the matter of neglecting his duties to frolic with harlots... Cutler found himself frowning. If such behaviour were to be punished, half the men in London would be flogged.

But he started walking again. He thought of Brisco, a bloodied corpse... and of Meunier, like his fellow strangers, a frightened man who had never done harm. He even thought of Wincott, a rogue and yet innocent of any crime... which brought him back to Kett, and the look on his face when he learned of the player's alibi. But most important of all was Bland's testimony of the man who had ordered the attack on the button-maker... This was the trail he must pursue, to find a murderer.

Thus resolved, he entered the trugging-house garden with the steps ahead of him, and the black-bearded giant regarding his approach once again without expression. This time, however, Cutler was not about to be hindered.

'I forgot that I owed you a penny, from last time,' he began, reaching for his purse. 'Pray take it now, and admit me. I've business with Mistress Leake that will not wait.'

The Cerberus hesitated, then seeing the coin held out, accepted it and stowed it away. But he remained where he stood, blocking the entrance.

'As it happens, I've been told not to admit you, Master Cutler,' he said calmly. 'Your pardon, but there it is.'

'No, it isn't,' was Cutler's stern reply. 'In truth, my business is not with your mistress but with another who's within – a fugitive. Prevent me, and I'll go to a magistrate and have a warrant sworn out. When I return, it shall be in the company of a sergeant-at-arms and his escort – not something Leake would welcome, I'm certain. So, do you persist?'

Upon which, though the giant made no move, there was disquiet in his gaze. He knew it was no bluff. Moreover, Cutler suspected, he was a man who had already seen the inside of a prison, with no desire to see it again.

After a moment, he spoke up. 'See now, will you tell Mistress Leake that?' he asked, speaking low. 'Will you tell her you threatened to make an arrest? Else, I might—'

'You might lose your place,' Cutler finished. 'Believe me, I wouldn't want that.'

So, it was done, the gate-keeper moving aside reluctantly. Cutler walked past him into the dimly lit lobby, seeking the proprietress, but the chair where she normally took her station was vacant. He stopped to look around, his gaze falling on the bench where he had sat with Petronella and learned the sad truth about the death of Susanna Martinhouse. The bench, too, was empty. He was on the verge of calling out when there came a sound from above that made him stiffen.

'You!' Mistress Leake cried, in a voice that could have stopped a regiment. 'Leave my house, before I have you thrown out!'

Taking a fortifying breath, Cutler stood his ground as she swept downstairs, while above her, faces peered over the banisters. The bawd wore a scarlet gown, cut low to display her enormous breasts, while her hair hung loose – which made Cutler blink. It had not occurred to him that Alice Leake still offered services to customers herself, but...

'You'll not have me thrown out,' he said firmly, as she gained the bottom step. 'I'll say to you what I said to your guard-dog: refuse to aid me, and I'll go to the magistrate for a warrant. When I come back, I'll bring armed men – who like as not, won't be too scrupulous as to how they deal with you.'

But she came forward, muttering an oath. Cutler glanced down; the woman was barefoot.

'And you know what I say to your threats?' she demanded, coming to a halt barely a yard away from him. 'I say you can put them up your fundament! By the time you've got your whoreson warrant, I'll have men at the gate who'll break the heads of anyone who comes. You know what some call this place? Leake's Leaguer – a fortress, when needs must. Now get you gone!'

'I've come for Kett,' Cutler told her, maintaining his calm. And when a frown appeared: 'I believe he's here, and he's in a deal of trouble. If you're concealing him, you could face arrest. I doubt even your best-connected customers could help you if that happened. Reputations might be at risk.'

She paused, her chest heaving, then: 'You canting varlet – do you truly think that would be the end of it?' she demanded. 'I could have your life snuffed out like a candle!'

'Not before I've seen you whipped at the cart's tail, from here all the way to Cheapside,' Cutler said, raising his voice. 'How you've escaped that punishment up to now is a miracle, to my mind. Alderman Skinner has his eye on you – and just now, he's not a contented man. I speak of the murder done in Bishopsgate Street, and the attack on another that followed hard upon it. Kett was a party to it. If he's here, as I think he is, you're harbouring a fugitive.'

He stopped to gauge the other's reaction. She was still angry – but she was uncertain. Whereupon, as the notion occurred, he played what he hoped was his winning card.

'So,' he resumed, 'will you give the rogue up, or must I mount a hue and cry for him? You know I have the power to do that, as you know what it would mean: an angry mob – likely half of Bishopsgate Ward – pouring in here, breaking everything in sight. A score of gate-keepers wouldn't be able to stop them.'

He held her gaze and waited – to be rewarded by a shudder that passed through her. For a moment, it appeared that she would speak, but no words came. She was thinking hard, weighing the risks... which prompted him to add a final word.

'Let me ask you this, mistress,' he said, raising his brows. 'Do you truly think your tame scrivener is worth the trouble? Let me have him, and I'll ask no more of you.'

'A curse on you, Cutler,' the bawd muttered. But she had lowered her gaze. 'You may have your way – but first answer me this: who told you he was here?'

'Does it matter?' he countered.

'It does to me.'

'Then I must disappoint you.'

She looked up, allowing a sigh to escape. But there was steel in her gaze; Cutler could imagine what might befall an informer, had there been one. The bawd had lost this battle, but remained a force not to be provoked. Her next words, however, took him by surprise.

'There are few men can resist Petronella when she works her charms,' she said, with an edge of scorn. 'If I didn't know better, I'd name you a sodomite – yet you are no such creature, Matthew Cutler. Is your petty office so important? Mayhap the law is your wife – and your harlot too.'

'If you wish to think so, then do,' Cutler replied. 'Now, will you bring me to my quarry?'

'Nay, but I'll bring him to you,' came the reply. 'And then I'll see you both out of my house – for the last time.'

She turned and walked away, her gown flapping about her bare ankles. Cutler watched her. She was an impressive woman, who could still entice men whenever she chose – yet a hard-nosed villainess, who wielded her own kind of power. He waited while she mounted the staircase and disappeared, listening for sounds overhead. For a while, there was nothing... then came voices, and the slam of a door, followed by more voices. Moving towards the stairs, he tensed... Was some deception being practised, or was Kett resisting? He was about to put a foot on the bottom step, when chaos erupted.

Cutler froze, gazing upwards – and the next moment, he might almost have laughed. What he saw was the struggling, protesting figure of Austen Kett, clad only in shirt and breeches, being manhandled to the stairhead by four of Mistress Leake's girls, one for each arm and leg. Stepping back, he could only watch as his fellow constable was carried down the staircase, red-faced and cursing, to be dumped in a heap on the floor. There he lay panting, with Cutler looking down at him, while the trulls wasted no time in going back whence they came. One threw down Kett's boots, his belt and cap before flouncing away.

Cutler reached down and offered a hand. 'Do you want to get up, Austen?' he enquired. 'Or shall I leave you there until you've caught your breath?'

10

It was past noon and the drizzle had ceased; it seemed there might even be a break in the clouds. Watched by Mistress Leake's giant, impassive atop the steps, Cutler marched his prisoner in silence through the trugging-house garden and out of the gate. He had no destination in mind at first, until he remembered it was Sunday and the theatres were closed. On impulse, he steered Kett to Holywell Lane and down as far as the Curtain, the space around it deserted save for a man passing with his dogs. There he stopped, shoved his fellow constable onto his rump on the grass, and stood over him.

'I know about the Meunier business, Austen,' he said. 'Bland's told me everything.'

Breathing hard, Kett gave no reply.

'I could almost praise you as a player,' Cutler added. 'For you've surely deceived me.'

'By the Christ.' The other eyed him balefully. 'What in heaven's name do you want of me?'

'I want all of it,' came the reply. 'From Brisco's death onwards.'

'What – surely you don't think I had aught to do with that?'

'The bribe, to find a rogue who'd scare Meunier,' Cutler snapped. 'The man who came to you with a fat purse – tell me about him.' Knowing that, as yet, Kett could know nothing of Stephen Bland's death, he was in no hurry to inform him. He waited.

'There's little I can tell – and that's the truth,' the other retorted. 'Save that he was mighty sure of himself, and his purpose. Bland and me...' He hesitated. 'If you know about the poniard, you'll know we wished no harm on the button-maker. It was only—'

'To make it look like some campaign against the strangers. A means of throwing light off the real reason Brisco was killed.'

'Well, mayhap it was!' Kett said, with some heat. 'I wasn't going to wrangle with a fellow who carried a pistol and gave me a simple choice: arrange the Meunier affair and get paid for it, or lose everything!'

'Everything... you mean your livelihood?'

'I mean my life! Did Bland not tell you the same?'

'Don't trouble yourself with what Bland told me. I know enough about you and he, posing as foes when you were up to all sorts of roguery together.' Cutler frowned at him. 'Bland taking bribes from thieves like Ned Broad, you borrowing money off Brisco, owing rent and all the while working for Leake. I wonder what else you've done—'

'To Hades with you!' Kett was sitting up, jabbing a finger up at Cutler. 'You think you're some kind of saint? We're not all so fortunate...' He broke off, turning aside. 'I know I've got into a tangle,' he mumbled. 'As I know what folk think of me – I'd be blind not to know. I've had to seize whatever came my way... so.' He let out a breath, and looked up. 'What do you propose to do?'

'In truth, I'm unsure,' Cutler admitted, as another notion arose. 'When I saw Skinner, he showed me a letter accusing

Henry Deans of Brisco's murder,' he went on. 'You wouldn't know about that, would you?'

He watched Kett carefully, but saw that the other's puzzlement was genuine. 'I would not,' he said. 'Yet...' He looked away. 'It smacks of the same purpose, I suppose, to—'

'To accuse others, and sow confusion,' Cutler finished. 'As you were hired to do.'

They were both silent until Kett spoke up again, looking sheepish. 'I'll speculate a little,' he said. 'I'd guess there are matters Skinner knows about, which he'd prefer to keep quiet. Like the rich folk he courts, against the day he becomes Lord Mayor. The sort of people Brisco did business with too, in the city.'

'That's no surprise,' Cutler said, though his thoughts were moving elsewhere. Once again, he had the vague notion that there was something dark behind the events in Bishopsgate that remained beyond his knowledge. He thought briefly of Wincott and his taste for women of wealth and substance, like Lady Hexham... the wife of a Privy Councillor.

'Men like the Italian, for one,' Kett said morosely. 'Scamozzi... Papist bastard.'

'You were content enough to borrow money from Brisco – another Papist,' Cutler replied. 'But what of Scamozzi? What else do you know?'

'Nothing more,' came the reply. 'Mayhap you should have asked Leake when you had the chance. There's little she doesn't know about the money that moves around Bishopsgate.'

'By God, Austen.' In exasperation, Cutler shook his head. 'Did you truly have to get yourself into such a pickle? And for what – favours from Leake's girls?'

The other lowered his gaze, then: 'I'll ask again: what will you do now?'

'You know where my duty lies,' came the reply.

'Aye... and you know what'll become of me.' Kett drew a breath. 'Is this how it ends, for you and me?'

'What else is there?' Cutler eyed him. 'Or did you think I'd let you escape?'

'Do you jest?' His fellow constable – for so he was still, for the present – wore a scornful look. 'I'd be caught within the hour. I stand out like a marigold in a midden!'

'Your tools, and your belongings,' Cutler said, after a moment. 'Are they yet at Leake's?' And when the other gave a nod: 'Mayhap you should go and retrieve them.'

He looked away, towards the great bulk of the Curtain Theatre. The times he had stood on the stage and performed before a crowd of two thousand souls now seemed a distant memory. He had learned then that most people are players, of one kind or another. Kett was one... but then, he had been dealt a poor hand from the start.

'Then, you do not jest?' Kett showed his surprise.

'In truth, I know not what I do,' Cutler told him. 'Though I'm certain you'd be a fool to linger in Bishopsgate. Likely there's a need elsewhere for scriveners. Now that the pestilence is over and we're free to travel, you might quit London and try some other part of England.'

Whereupon, hardly knowing why, he turned his back on Austen Kett and walked off towards Holywell Lane. Only when he had walked some distance did he recall that he had not told the man of Stephen Bland's death. Then, he would learn of it soon enough.

* * *

With a heavy heart, Cutler went home – to receive another surprise. He had barely entered the house, when a male voice was heard from the kitchen. He reached the doorway, then stopped as a figure rose from the table.

'Master Deans?' He nodded a greeting. 'This is unexpected.'

'Cutler.' The deputy alderman returned the nod. 'I knew not where you were, so I took it upon myself to wait here. Your daughters have made me welcome, as has your servant.' This with a glance at Aunt Margery, standing nearby, who bridled at the description. 'Now with your leave, I'll speak with you in private.'

'Very well...' Cutler met Margery's gaze; Henry Deans was another of those Bishopsgate men whom she would sometimes claim she had never trusted. Facing the deputy alderman again, he invited him to come out into the yard, but the man shook his head.

'We're called upon to attend Thomas Skinner. If you're ready?'

Without further word, they went out – and no sooner was the front door closed, than Deans turned quickly to Cutler; the man was in full righteous humour, and not to be gainsaid.

'What in heaven's name have you been doing, constable?' he demanded, with the familiar puffing out of his chest. 'Do you think you're the only guardian of law in the entire Ward?' And when Cutler gave no answer: 'From what I've heard, you've been running about Bishopsgate like a wet hen – and to what end, I ask? I've had no word from you, nor—'

'You said the alderman is expecting us,' Cutler broke in, curbing his impatience with the man as always. 'Can it wait until we're in his company?' Upon which he started walking, obliging the other to catch up.

'I've heard rumours,' Deans blustered, falling in beside him. 'You've been seen entering Leake's – that damned house of venery! Why did you so?'

'I'll give a full account when we're at Skinner's.'

He quickened his pace, heading down the street towards the gate. Deans muttered under his breath, but made no further remark. Thereafter, they walked in silence into the city, weaving through the Sunday throng to the alderman's house in St Helen's. Having been admitted by the servant, they greeted Skinner politely and waited. He was seated at his table, and there were stools nearby, but neither of them was invited to sit.

'Deans has told me of the inquest into Brisco, Cutler,' their host said, without preamble. 'Do you have anything further to tell?'

'I do,' Cutler nodded. 'But first, I have sad news.' And when the other two eyed him: 'The watchman, Stephen Bland – he's dead. He was taken ill after church this morning, and expired seated on a bench.'

'By heaven...' Deans was shocked. 'Why wasn't I told?'

'Roger Farrant told me, not long since,' Cutler continued, facing Skinner. 'He will inform Bland's wife and make all provisions.'

The alderman said nothing, merely glanced at Deans.

'He was ageing and tired,' Cutler went on. 'The task of walking the streets at night was becoming a burden. Farrant believed his heart gave out, and I've no reason to think otherwise.' He had realised that he had no desire to blacken Bland's name, but to let his crimes die with him.

'So... sad news indeed,' Skinner said, though with small sign of regret. 'A new watchman must be found.' He paused. 'What of Kett? Has he been told?'

To which Cutler hesitated, which allowed Deans to speak up. 'I've a notion the constable here has much to tell us before answering that, Master Alderman,' he said tartly. 'He would say naught to me on the way here.'

'Well, then...' Skinner let out a breath, and gestured to a stool. 'I suppose he'd better sit down – you too, Henry. I can but hope there's not more ill news.'

They sat, and the aldermen turned their eyes upon the constable. Deans maintained a disapproving look, while Skinner appeared somewhat distracted. But Cutler told his tale. He said nothing of Kett for the present, but summarised what John Willard would have called his *poking about*, for any hint that would lead him to solving the murder of Alessandro Brisco. By the end of it, however, there was no denying the lack of progress once again. He was drawing his account to a close, when:

'Wincott... the player?' Skinner frowned at Cutler. 'You questioned him again, you say?'

'I did. But he has an alibi for the night of Brisco's killing, and I've let him alone.'

'An alibi?' Deans gave a snort. 'How can you be sure he isn't lying?'

'Because I've known him for years,' Cutler replied. 'He's a hot-tempered fellow, it's true – it's well-known he fought a duel and slew a man, and paid heavily for it. He's no angel, but he's no murderer either. And...' He hesitated. 'The person he was with is a lady of substance, whom he was loth to name. Yet I got it from him, and that was enough for me.'

'Was it, now?' Skinner eyed him. 'Well, I should be the judge of that.'

'And rightly,' Deans put in, his manner setting Cutler's teeth on edge. 'Pray tell us, who is this woman you call a *lady of substance*?'

'She is Lady Albina, wife to Sir George Hexham.'

To this revelation, Deans merely reacted in the manner Cutler expected: with righteous dismay. Skinner, however, appeared stunned.

'Is that so,' he said, after a moment. 'Then, it shall go no further than this room. Do you understand me?'

Cutler said nothing, but his mind was working fast. Deans nodded, but the alderman's eye remained on his constable.

'And more... I'm minded to know why you've been at Leake's,' he murmured. 'Was that part of your enquiry?'

'I thought it might shed some light,' Cutler said, choosing his words carefully. 'I was mistaken.'

'As it seems you've been mistaken about other matters,' Deans scoffed. But Cutler ignored him, watching Skinner.

'This... this whole matter is a sore trial to us all,' the alderman said, looking aside suddenly. 'The inquest verdict on Brisco was clear, and I suspect we will never know why he was slain. Some personal grudge, or mayhap a robbery that went amiss...' He looked round. 'Does your mind move that way too, constable?'

He paused... and Cutler understood. Skinner wanted nothing more than to put the unpleasant business behind him. More, he seemed to be saying that his officials should do the same. Now, he saw the choice that lay before him: comply with the alderman's wishes, or...

But he could not. His innate stubbornness, his desire for doing what was right, had been with him since he had stood as a child in a Canterbury court and heard his father mete out justice. It would always be a part of him. He drew breath, then:

'In truth, Master Skinner,' he answered, eying the man squarely, 'I believe it's the duty of all of us to try and find whoever committed such a vile and bloody crime in our Ward. The folk of Bishopsgate are afraid – the strangers especially. If we fail to—'

'Oh indeed, we mustn't distress the strangers!'

It was Deans who broke in heatedly, regarding Cutler with almost a sneer. In some surprise, the other two looked at him, whereupon he gave a start – and began at once to bluster.

'I mean, of course they will fret,' he went on hastily. 'Why would they not, after the attack on the button-maker too? But as we know, they have mounted their own watch and must look to themselves... and I concur with you, alderman,' he added, facing Skinner. 'We should allow time to heal these wounds. The perfumer's body is in the care of his fellow countryman – let him be laid to rest. Haven't our people enough troubles, as they recover from the pestilence? Let alone the poor harvest we expect, after this sodden summer.'

Somewhat out of breath, he stopped himself. Skinner still looked surprised at the outburst – but Cutler was angry. He had always believed Deans was hostile to the incomers, despite his claims to be everyone's protector. And before he knew it, he was voicing it.

'Many of the strangers have done good service in Bishopsgate,' he said quietly. 'Even Alessandro Brisco, lending money to those in need. Kett was one of them, I've learned... mayhap you know of others?' He looked directly at Deans, who stiffened.

'What in heaven's name do you mean?' he demanded. 'Do you suggest that I'm—'

'Of course he does not,' Skinner broke in tersely. 'And I believe he will confirm that.'

He fixed his gaze on Cutler, and there was no mistaking his meaning: that the anonymous letter he had received was not to be mentioned. Cutler let out a sigh, and chose discretion.

'I make no suggestions, Master Deans,' he said. 'Though as you'll recall from the inquest, the perfumer appears to have had many debtors. It occurred to me that this might have some bearing on his murder.'

'Does it, indeed?' Deans retorted, with sarcasm. 'And what else has occurred to you, that might have a bearing on it? I pray you, enlighten us.'

'Henry, enough.' With a pained look, Skinner raised a hand. But Cutler sighed inwardly; nothing was to be gained by this meeting, and on a sudden, he wished to be gone. He was seeking some words by which to excuse himself, when the alderman turned to him again.

'I've heard you, constable,' he said, 'and I might commend your devotion to duty. Yet, I fear you've become so enamoured of this hunt for an unknown assailant that it clouds your judgement. I say again, I believe the culprit may never be found, and hence we should direct our efforts to restoring calm. To trust in God, if you will – and let matters rest.'

Trust in God... so, there it lay. Cutler lowered his gaze. This was not leadership from Skinner, who appeared instead to be warning him off pursuing Brisco's killer. Perhaps mention of Sir George Hexham had alarmed him, as one who had always sought the approval of important men. He looked up, to see the other watching him.

'I thank you for your advice, Alderman,' he said. 'Now I'd like to return to my parish.'

'Very well.' Skinner nodded. Deans remained seated, still nettled by their exchange, but Cutler rose at once and took his leave of them both.

Once outside, he recalled that not only was there need of a watchman in Spitalfields, there would soon be a need for a new constable at St Botolph's. On the matter of Austen Kett's imminent departure, however, he would plead ignorance.

* * *

He was back home within the quarter hour, taking a bite to eat before venturing out again. Margery and the girls were somewhat taut, exchanging looks; they had heard of Stephen Bland's death, already the topic of Bishopsgate gossip.

'They say you were speaking with him, just before he died,' Katherine said to her father. 'After we'd just seen him at church... so sudden. Did he seem ill?'

'I cannot say, Kate,' Cutler replied. 'But he was weary...'

'And troubled?' Aunt Margery broke in. 'Looking at him and his wife in the church, it struck me I've seldom seen such an unhappy pair.'

He made no answer; Bland's confession was still raw to him.

'You should rest today, Father,' said Jane, always the voice of concern. 'Could we not play at cards, as we used to?'

'When Mother was alive, she means,' Katherine put in.

A silence followed; his daughters seldom spoke of Anne nowadays, though their grief was ever-present, like a submerged stream. Cutler looked at each of them: different in many ways, yet so alike. He could hardly bear to recall the happiness they had all shared.

'Would that I could, my dears,' he sighed. 'But when this coil is over—'

'You will find something else to busy yourself with,' Katherine finished.

She met his eye, then lowered her gaze; clearly he was not yet forgiven him for the business with Edward Thorne. Somewhat heavily, he rose, and found Margery's eyes upon him.

'Have a care, Matthew,' she said kindly.

He managed a nod, and went out.

* * *

In the street, he began walking northwards, his mind in a turmoil; forcing himself to think of his reception at Skinner's, he realised that he did not know how to proceed. He had passed Holywell Lane and was in Shoreditch before realising that he was close to Margaret Fisher's house... whereupon he stopped. There was no point in deluding himself: this is where he had intended to go. And moments later, he was at the door.

She was at home, and he was admitted by her servant. As he entered her parlour, she arose from her chair with a look of surprise, which gave way to a smile. Soon they were seated together... and almost before Cutler knew it, he was telling her everything.

Later, he would wonder why he did so instead of going to John Willard, as was his habit. But talking to Margaret was different – and now, throwing niceties aside, he held nothing back. She was an attentive listener, and it was a relief to unburden himself. By the time he had spoken of the taut meeting at Thomas Skinner's house, she was gazing intently at him... until at last, as if coming to his senses, he shrugged and tried a smile.

'Your pardon... I've been like a stream in full flood.'

'Or like one making confession,' she said. 'Though to my mind, you've naught to reproach yourself for.' She paused, then: 'What you say about Skinner doesn't surprise me. He seeks patronage, even more than wealth. My husband did business with him in years past, as he did with men of far greater standing. Sir George Hexham was among them. I was presented to him once, at the Royal Exchange.'

Cutler raised his eyebrows. 'Was his wife present?'

'She was not, but I know of her,' Margaret answered. 'Nicholas Wincott isn't the first lover she's taken, from among men of a lower degree. Her husband's worn the cuckold's horns for years, though he seems not to know it. He may be the only one who doesn't.'

'Then he's to be pitied,' Cutler said. He was recalling his

encounter with Wincott in the White Hart, and the player's disparagement of the Privy Councillor as an *old fool*.

'Perhaps...' She looked away, frowning slightly. Feeling he had said enough about his troubles, Cutler was seeking some other topic of conversation when she startled him. 'I think you need to change horses,' she said, turning to him. 'If you truly wish to find the one who murdered the perfumer – as I know you do – then I fear that digging around in Bishopsgate will avail you nothing. You're no run-on-the-mill constable, when all's said and done. You were a player – and a good one. You should harness those skills you have, to greater effect.'

He was puzzled. 'In what manner? Just now, I see no way open to me.'

'Yet you must find one.' She hesitated, then: 'I'm mindful of the inquest, and the talk of Brisco's money-lending. He did good business, of course, but have you ever known a Catholic with money to spare, in these times?'

'He was a Church Papist,' Cutler said. 'Paid lip service to the liturgy to avoid paying recusancy fines, like others of his faith. Else he would have been ruined – and he was too clever to let that happen.'

'And that man Scamozzi?' Margaret sounded eager, which surprised him further; there was a light in her eyes that he had not seen before. 'Brisco's landlord, another Papist – and a rich man, despite having no ancestry here. Whence comes his wealth, do you think?'

'A merchant, like your late husband.' Cutler gave a shrug. 'Likely he imports wines or silks... the usual Italian trade.' But he was thinking hard upon what she had said. It looked now as if his desire to bring justice to a murdered man had been dulled by later events. He was wondering whether an enquiry into those

Brisco had done business with in the city might yield results, when Margaret spoke up again – and forestalled him.

'You spoke of the customer who found Brisco's body. What of other men of means, who spent lavishly on perfumed trifles? I don't mean the likes of Wincott,' she added, with a wry look. 'I mean those of true wealth. Had he offended someone, to the extent of making himself a target for revenge?' She smiled. 'I merely throw these burrs out, you understand, in the hope one might stick.'

'I see that,' Cutler sighed. 'But to question such men, I would be stepping far beyond my station. A parish headborough, to be kept dallying at their pleasure like a servant—'

'Oh cods, Matthew Cutler!' she exclaimed, to his surprise. 'Once more, you disparage yourself. Must I remind you again of those qualities you possess, that can take you beyond that station? In different apparel, you could pass for a lord – have you not played such parts often enough? Why should you not adopt some disguise, and venture into the city? Or...' She paused, eying him keenly. 'Have you not the courage?'

He stared at her – and something passed between them. It was not mere desire; Cutler had recognised that from the moment he had seen her again, after the intervening years. There was a challenge in her gaze.

'I believe I have,' he said quietly.

'As do I.' Almost fiercely, Margaret nodded. 'You could forge some strategy – like a campaign of war. Seek out those who did business with Brisco, and let them talk. It may not flush out a murderer – then again, it might. But come what may, it would be an adventure, would it not?'

Whereupon, before he could reply, she drew breath and spoke quickly.

'Now I think upon it, it strikes me that in the guise of a

gentleman of substance – if not a knight, or even an earl – you might take the role of a former customer of Brisco, who is distressed by his death and wishes to know more,' she went on. 'In which case, you'll need a wife for whom you bought perfumed knick-knacks.' And when Cutler gave a start: 'I always adored the stage – had I been a man, I would have gone upon it myself. So, shall I be that wife, and share your adventure?'

Whereupon, having delivered her proposal, she sat back and waited.

'By God,' Cutler murmured at last, 'I think I need a drink.'

11

It was dark when he came home, and the household were all abed. In the kitchen, he found a candle and lit it, then sat at the table to think. It seemed as if a new vista had opened before him – one that he had never imagined. If he rose to the challenge Margaret had set, no longer would he be hidebound by the feeble powers of a mere parish constable. Instead...

But by heaven, it was bold! He would be assuming a role that took him out of Bishopsgate and into the company of the rich – which meant using an assumed name, something he was uneasy about. Even wearing a sword was a risk, for a man of his station. And yet... he stared at the candle's flame, its brightness blurring his vision. Something stirred within him, that he had not felt in a long while... could it be excitement?

He ran over the conversation, in every detail. He and Margaret had talked long and late, fortified by fruits and Rhenish wine – though Cutler had drunk sparingly. He knew well enough how the evening might end, and was wary of it. Not that she had made overtures; she had made herself plain in their last conversation, and seemed willing to let the matter rest. Instead, they spoke of what had somehow gone from a wild idea to a plausible scheme: to pose as a well-to-do couple who had known Alessandro Brisco. They might visit other perfumers; they were few, and would surely have known the Italian. Among their customers would be some who had done business with him. It was, at least, a place to start.

'I have a name for you,' Margaret had said. 'How does Sir Amos Gallett sound?'

To which he had laughed, before observing that she was quite serious.

'I could be Lady Clarinda Gallett,' she had added. 'We hail from Kent – the county of your birth. You would be able to provide detail, if questioned. And,' she had added, before he could raise objection, 'there are still clothes in my husband's closet. I believe some of them would fit you. His sword, too, I have.'

And so, the matter had been settled, with an ease that took his breath away. Sitting in his darkened kitchen, he considered the plan they had made – and despite his early scepticism, realised that it might work. Provided he and Margaret could leave Bishopsgate unnoticed – which was possible if they passed through the fields behind Bedlam's graveyard, then crossed Moorfields to enter the city by Moorgate – they could then walk the teeming London streets to the Royal Exchange: a well-to-do couple, passing the time in leisurely fashion. There was at least one perfumer Margaret knew of, by the name of Segar. His shop, she had reasoned, was as good a place as any to begin their task.

And yet, he remained unconvinced. It seemed unlikely that, even if he were able to converse with people who had known Brisco, it would bring him any closer to finding his murderer. It tugged at him still: this feeling that there was something very murky behind it – perhaps something he was not destined to uncover. All that had happened since, like his entanglements with Wincott, Bland and Kett – even Edward Thorne – had amounted only to distractions. And once again, following today's conversation with Deans and Thomas Skinner, he felt very alone.

But he was not, not now. There was Margaret... the most unlikely *poker about* any constable could have imagined. With her picture in his mind's eye, he stood up, blew out the candle and went to his bed.

* * *

It was Monday morning, with the city gates open, and Cutler and his player-wife were already at work. In their new guises as Sir Amos and Lady Gallett, they left her house and set forth across the fields behind Bishopsgate Street in a light mist which the rising sun would soon burn away; mercifully, there would be no rain. Margaret – or Lady Clarinda, as he must call her henceforth – wore an elegant, saffron gown and a wide-brimmed straw hat tied beneath her chin. Cutler wore a cream-coloured doublet that had belonged to her husband, fawn breeches of Spanish cut and a short cloak of a mulberry hue. At his side was a light rapier in a tooled leather scabbard, along with his own poniard in its sheath. He also wore, a little self-consciously, a hat with a hanging jewel that had belonged to the late Master Fisher, instead of his own plain cap. Thus attired, they entered London by Moorgate and walked down Coleman Street through noise and bustle. Whereupon, somewhat to his surprise, Cutler began to feel more at ease. It was unlikely anyone would recognise him, if they even gave him a second glance. For Margaret, however, the case was different.

'It's possible I shall see someone I know, or who knows me,' she told him as they walked, arm in arm. 'If so, I shall rely on you to distract them.'

They passed by the Poulterer's Hall, turning left into Lothbury. Church bells clanged, drowning the street-sellers' cries. Another turn, to the right, and they were in Threadneedle Street with the Royal Exchange before them. Cutler slowed, readying himself.

'You should let me talk the most,' he said. 'I need to ease into the persona of Sir Amos. I may speak low to you, to confer over some purchase.' To which she nodded, as they approached the great portico of the Exchange – and soon, they were on.

It was a splendid building, its three stories towering over their heads. Coaches pulled up outside, disgorging people of fashion and their servants. In the vast, paved quadrangle within, surrounded by colonnades, merchants gathered to conduct business. Cutler and Margaret moved unhurriedly among them, towards the stairs that gave access to the upper floor – the Pawn – with its myriad stalls and shops. A citizen could buy almost anything in the Pawn: from a caged bird to a glass bowl, from a kirtle to a pistol. And soon, by making casual enquiries of other sellers, they found their way to the stall of the perfumer, Master Segar.

But Segar was a surprise to Cutler – and one look was enough to convince him that this middle-aged, balding man was something of a rogue. His glassy smile, his fawning manner, his eagerness to serve spoke of one who, in Cutler's eyes, was as slippery as an eel. Well dressed, wearing one of his own perfumed pomanders at his belt, the man bowed low to Margaret and asked her what she lacked. Would she care to sample one of his fragrances? He had every scent she could possibly desire...

'The small packets,' Margaret said, assuming a haughty air. 'May I see?'

'The *coussines* – by all means, my lady.' Segar hurried to select one. 'Newly arrived from France... here is ambergris. Others are steeped in rose oil, or marjoram...'

'Do you have storax?' Cutler enquired, more abruptly than he had intended. Margaret threw him a swift glance, before taking the scented sachet from the perfumer and inspecting it.

'Alas, sir...' Segar assumed a sad expression. 'I am at present without.' His accent was a further surprise: that of a northern man, though one who tried to temper it. 'Yet I have lavender, and so much more: tuberose, jasmine, fennel—'

'Yes, yes.' Cutler waved a hand airily. 'I'll let my wife choose. She is not to be hurried.'

'Of course.' The man bobbed and recovered his smile. 'In the meantime, might I know your name? I don't recall having had the pleasure of serving you before.'

'Sir Amos Gallett. I'm seldom in London...' He seized the opportunity. 'My custom in the past was to deal with an Italian named Brisco, out in Bishopsgate. Sadly, I learn that the poor man is dead.' He watched Segar carefully. 'No doubt you have heard?'

'Ah, yes.' The perfumer's sad face was back. 'Such a tragedy... a most knowledgeable man. A great loss to the art of perfumery.'

'Do you know how he died?'

'Alas, I do not,' came the reply, rather quickly. 'It was quite recent, wasn't it? Some ailment, perhaps...'

'In truth, I heard he was violently slain,' Cutler said.

'No... how terrible.' Segar looked aghast, before turning aside to attend to Margaret. His voice dropped to an intimate tone, as he asked her opinion of the *coussine*. It was a practised move, to exclude anyone else from the conversation. Cutler saw it, as he guessed that this man knew more than he liked to admit. It was followed by another notion: like the late Alessandro Brisco, Segar too was a Catholic.

He was unsure how he knew, but he did. Moreover, he was as certain as he could be that Segar knew how Brisco had died. So, why should he deny it? He was forming another question when Margaret turned to him and held up the perfumed packet.

'Do you care to make me a small gift, husband?' she enquired. 'It's a pretty trifle.'

'If you wish, madam.' He reached for his purse. 'Take it, and go where you please while I stay a little longer with this man.' He gave her a look which she understood at once: he would question Master Segar, alone.

'I will buy lace,' Margaret said. 'You may find me at the haberdasher further along the way.' With a languid gesture and a nod to the perfumer, she moved off.

Segar turned, but he was a fraction too late in assuming his sickly smile; behind it, he was uneasy. He raised a hand to draw attention to his stall, with its colourful array of small bottles and packets, but was interrupted.

'You know that Brisco was murdered,' Cutler said flatly. 'Why pretend otherwise?'

The man merely gulped.

'I regarded him as a friend,' he added, 'albeit one who had his secrets. His religion, however, was not one of them. He never denied his Papism, as some do.'

'I pray you, Sir Amos...' Segar caught his expression, and tried a puzzled look. 'Will you not say what you want of me? I'm a plain man of business. What else I am, can surely be of no interest to a highborn person like yourself.'

'Then, let's say this too is a matter of business,' Cutler said, thinking fast. 'I'm one who desires justice for a man I liked. Whatever you tell me, it shall be a private matter between us. And of course, I would not be ungrateful.'

But Segar was wary now. With a shake of his head, he was about to speak as Cutler produced a silver sixpence from his purse.

'Here's a token of my goodwill,' he said, holding it out. 'Next time I come, I may spend a good deal more. Now I think on it, I've a notion that Lady Gallett would like a pair of perfumed riding gloves. Brisco supplied such, I recall. Could you?'

'Well, I could...' The other hesitated. All about them, the hum of voices filled the Pawn, as the heady aroma of perfumes arose from his stock. Cutler raised his eyebrows, and waited until Segar took the coin and stowed it away.

'How can I aid you?' he asked.

'Did you see much of Brisco?' Cutler had lowered his voice. 'I know he was often in the city. Some of his customers were among the highest – Lady Hexham, I believe, was one.' And when the other did not reply: 'Did the two of you exchange news? For in truth, I know of no other perfumer hereabouts.'

'I saw him now and again,' Segar admitted, after a pause. 'As to his customers, I never asked.'

'I don't believe that,' Cutler countered. 'I think you would help him to business, as he would you. Or, did you consider him merely a rival?'

'Sir Amos, I beg...' The man was taut now. 'How can it matter to you whom Brisco or I served? Many people come here to buy my wares.'

'Call it curiosity,' Cutler said, affably enough. 'Or mere guile, if you will. I've said I'm not often in London, and need to widen my circle of acquaintances. Give me a name or two.'

'Names... is that all you require?' Segar looked sceptical.

'Well now, I spoke of Lady Hexham. They say Sir George is

always so busy attending the Queen or the Council, she often ventures out alone. Have you served her?'

'I have,' came the reply. 'I conduct business with many ladies of quality, whose husbands are so pressed – the Countess of Tanridge is one I could name. Lady Wheatley, the wife of Sir Titus Wheatley, is another. Whereas Brisco's habit, since you wish to know more, was often to visit them in their homes taking his goods with him, and so provide a private service.'

'Well, of course.' Cutler nodded impatiently, as if this was old news – but it was not. His mind busy, he was forming another question when, to his surprise, Segar leaned closer and spoke low.

'You're not seeking vengeance, are you, Sir Amos?' he asked warily. 'For I cannot be a party to such. I have my good name to preserve, and—'

'Vengeance?' Cutler frowned at him. 'What on earth do you mean, fellow?'

'Only that there have been... occasions, shall we say, when certain gentlemen believed their wives to be taken advantage of,' Segar said, speaking somewhat hurriedly. 'Having been alone with a tradesman who—'

'Ah – I see,' Cutler broke in. 'Is that what you meant by this *private service* provided by men like Brisco?'

He summoned a knowing look, but his mind had leaped. It had not occurred to him that the dead perfumer might have had relations with ladies of means that went beyond mere matters of business. He remembered John Willard's words, warning him not to listen to those who spoke too warmly of Brisco. He was eager to pursue the matter – but Segar was now reluctant.

'In truth, I know nothing more, Sir Amos,' he said, with a rapid shake of his head. 'One in my place must learn discretion.'

'Wise man.' Cutler nodded. 'Hence, I'll ask but one further

question of you: is that why Brisco was slain, do you think – for vengeance's sake?' And when the other gave a start: 'If so, would you be willing to speculate further as to—'

'Sir, I would not! And with your leave, I think we are done.' Segar was nervous now, clearly feeling he had already said too much. As Cutler watched, he turned and began busying himself at his stall, rearranging bottles to no apparent purpose. When a customer appeared, an elderly gentlewoman, he hurried to attend to her.

The brief interrogation was over – but for Cutler, a new door had opened. As he moved away from the perfumer's stall, he found himself recalling the bloody scene of Brisco's murder: a frenzied attack. And now, he might have stumbled upon the cause – but if so, what was he to do?

Scarcely looking where he walked, he eased through the throng of well-dressed men and women, their voices abuzz about him. He passed stalls without even noticing the goods displayed, while running over Segar's words – or rather, their implications. He had a different picture of Alessandro Brisco now: the elegant Italian, who had always dressed a little too grandly for a mere shopkeeper. A man who looked beyond Bishopsgate and served better-off customers – men like Master Whitney who had found the body, and who had considered him *a yeoman, yet in every other way a gentleman, almost the equal of myself.* And a man who, it now appeared, had done private – even intimate – business with the wives of overtaxed, and often absent, men like Sir George Hexham and Sir Titus Wheatley. It made him think of Wincott, and his taste for women far above his station. And so, was this the answer? Was Brisco's murder nothing more than the act of a husband driven mad with jealousy? Or even – which was far more likely – one who had hired some rogue to do the deed in his place?

He stopped, standing among the throng; on a sudden, his quest looked impossible. He would never know who had killed Brisco. All he could do – as it seemed clear Alderman Skinner wanted him to do – was let the matter lie. He was thinking on it when a familiar voice sounded close to his ear.

'Was the conversation fruitful?' Margaret asked, placing her arm in his. She was standing close to the haberdasher's stall, where people milled about. Cutler tried to smile, but failed.

'Oh... well-a-day.' She gave a sigh. 'Then I suggest, Sir Amos, that we remove ourselves to an inn with a private room, where you might unburden yourself. Does that suit?'

* * *

It was a small tavern in Walbrook, close by St Stephen's. In a tiny upstairs room with only two tables, the other occupied by several men arguing about the merits of their hawks, they sat and talked. Cutler took ale, Margaret a cup of Hippocras. Having told her what he had learned from Segar, he was silent.

'Well now...' She sipped from her goblet and considered. 'Here's a pretty tale: of bored and reckless wives, perhaps, whose husbands neglect them.' She raised her eyebrows. 'And who am I to judge, since I was one such? You'll recall it well enough.'

'I recall you attending the theatre,' he answered. 'Beyond that, I never speculated.'

'I confess I'm surprised that Segar gave Sir Titus Wheatley's name,' Margaret said, after a moment's thought. 'I know of his wife Joanna... a sombre and pious woman, seemingly devoted to her husband.'

'They're often the ones that need watching,' Cutler said, with a wry look. 'But what of the Countess of Tanridge? Is she too a sombre and pious woman?'

'I have no knowledge of her. Save that her husband is an old soldier, who fought with Leicester in the Low Countries.'

'Well, it's a revelation,' he resumed. 'Who could have guessed that the upright and respected Signor Brisco was seducing the wives of important customers behind their backs?'

'If he did so, he was risking a good deal,' Margaret said. 'Even—'

'His life,' Cutler finished. 'Snuffed out in a most bloody and terrible fashion.' He looked away. 'Which leaves me out on a limb, with nowhere to turn.'

They sat for a while, with the noise of the street coming in through the open window. Margaret watched him, then took a drink and set down her cup.

'The Matthew Cutler I knew was seldom downhearted,' she murmured. 'Mayhap Alderman Skinner was correct in saying that you have become too enamoured of this hunt for Brisco's murderer.' And when he looked sharply at her: 'You have taken on a burden, when you could easily set it down. Have you not enough to do as constable, without this?'

'More than enough,' he answered. 'And yet, I'm my father's son. He may be a stern man, even a cold man, but he has always believed in justice. I was raised to believe in it too.'

'Well, now I think upon it, so was I.' Margaret said, placing a hand on his arm. 'In which case, we must try and think how to procced, must we not?' She smiled and lifted her drink.

Raising his cannikin, Cutler clinked it against her cup... and felt his spirits lift a little.

And an hour later, they were back in Bishopsgate, stealing into Margaret's house by the back door like thieves. Here he changed into his everyday attire, ready to step out into the street again. He had decided to visit John Willard, to see if talking things over with his shrewd father-in-law would help once again.

But before leaving her house, he planted a hurried kiss on Margaret's cheek.

* * *

The gunsmith was glad enough to see him, if somewhat irritated. He had done poor business that morning, on account of a customer who quibbled about the cost of a new caliver. More than willing to close up for the hour, he took Cutler off to the White Hart for a dinner of pease and bacon. Seated at the same table by the window where he had confronted Wincott, he told Willard what had happened, ending with his encounter with Segar. His father-in-law was intrigued – and glad to talk of anything other than gunsmith's business.

'And yet, what you've learned about Brisco does not surprise me too greatly,' he said, wiping his platter with a hunk of bread. 'You'll recall what I thought of him. He's another of those my sister Margery would say she never quite trusted. Something of a dandy, she said once.' He shoved bread into his mouth and chewed.

'Well, it surprised me,' Cutler said. 'I thought him too clever to get himself into that sort of trouble. In truth, I wonder if we've leaped too readily to conclusions, despite what that fellow Segar said.'

'Mayhap it's wise to think on the names you've got,' Willard observed. 'A woman like Albina Hexham we know enough of, given your friend Wincott's tumbling of her. The Countess of Tanridge, now...' He frowned. 'If I remember aright, she was one of the Queen's favourite women, back in the time of the Armada. Pretty and flirtatious, while her husband's a good deal older than she is. Hence...' He gave a shrug. 'Such dalliances with men of a humbler station are not unknown, for women whose appetite is unsated.'

'What of Lady Wheatley?' Cutler wondered. 'Margaret called her sombre and pious, and a devoted wife, which—'

'Roused your suspicions at once,' his father-in-law broke in.

'Though I may well be doing her a disservice. This is mere speculation.'

'Sir Titus Wheatley.' Willard was thoughtful. 'There's another who played his part during the Armada summer. Close to Lord Howard, the Lord Admiral. A staunch fellow.'

'Well then...' Cutler took up his mug. 'It seems we have to give Brisco some respect. He plucked the choicest fruit, from the very top of the tree.'

'It would appear so. And yet...' The gunsmith was frowning again. 'It doesn't sit right with me.'

Cutler met his eye. 'How is that?'

'Men like Hexham the Privy Councillor, the Earl of Tanridge and Wheatley. They're upstanding noblemen, given to fair dealing. Even if... see now, let us speculate further. Even if one of them suspected his wife of being unfaithful, let alone had evidence, would he truly have ordered Brisco's murder? A heinous act, done at night... it's unworthy of any of them.'

'What if there are others, whom Segar did not name?' Cutler objected. 'There could be one husband who doesn't possess such scruples.'

'By heaven, Matthew.' Willard put on a sceptical look. 'The Italian wasn't a youth. How many such secret paramours could he have had? I doubt he was a rutting stag like Wincott – or Kett, come to think on it.'

'Yes...' Cutler frowned. 'I'm beginning to think myself a poor judge of character.'

'Or too trusting,' came the reply. 'Anne always said so.'

They were both thoughtful, until the gunsmith broke the silence. 'They say that old bull Josiah Madge will be made watchman in Stephen Bland's place. I don't like to think on what'll happen if he catches the likes of Ned Broad up to his tricks. Once a collector of scavage tolls, you'll recall, he lost his place during the pestilence. Too handy with a billet nowadays, is Madge.'

Cutler looked away, and shook his head. Dinner was over, and he would pass a quiet afternoon thinking on what had been said.

But when night came, matters took another turn.

* * *

'You're bowed down with care,' Aunt Margery said, as the two of them sat up late. 'Rest, and busy yourself tomorrow if you must. Find Madge and tell him his duties. Someone should.'

'I'll talk with him,' he allowed. 'But I need to walk now, clear my head. And no...' He lifted a hand to forestall her objection. 'I'm not about to play at watchman. You should get yourself to bed, and cease fretting about me.'

He left the house and stepped out into the darkened street. Bishopsgate was quiet, with a wind soughing in the trees beyond the Artillery Yard. For a moment, he thought of going to Margaret's house; yet, though they had grown closer, he was still hesitant. Gathering himself, he turned in the other direction and walked down towards the closed gate. He passed Brisco's boarded shop, then tensed on hearing the cries from Bedlam; some people never slept. He was about to quicken his pace, when a notion struck him.

Why could he not gain entry to the perfumer's, and look around? He had not been inside since the morning of the discovery of the man's body... Could he have missed something?

It was wrong, he told himself – unlawful. Yet he was no Ned Broad, but a constable seeking answers. Throwing caution aside, he slipped down the narrow ginnel beside the shop and gained a rear window. Thereafter, it was but the work of a moment to force the casement open with his poniard. Then he was climbing through, to find himself in darkness amid the reek of a dozen different scents.

Moving forward carefully across an unfurnished back room, he decided to risk a light; it would not be seen through the boarded front window. Fumbling with his tinderbox, he made a flame and peered about. There was a staircase close by, but he decided not to venture upstairs, to the man's private quarters. Instead, he made his way into the shop, where the proprietor's body had since been removed. The man's table had been set upright again, but was bare. And to his relief, the floor seemed to have been washed clean of bloodstains. Soon, he was moving stealthily about, finding to his surprise that most of the jars of perfume were still on their shelves. He thought then of the landlord Scamozzi, who would deal with his tenant's stock: as a well-connected merchant, likely he would have little trouble finding buyers. He was turning away, when his gaze strayed behind the table to fall upon the edge of what looked like a small basket, poking out from under the lowest shelf. Stooping, he pulled it free and found it contained a collection of ribbons. Taking one up, he examined it. Like the others, it was dyed a deep red – and heavily perfumed, with jasmine.

And at once, a thought flew up: that these items were not part of Brisco's stock, but were gifts, to be made privately. Why else would they be hidden from view? Standing with the heady odour of the ribbon in his nostrils, he imagined the perfumer tying it around the neck of one of his conquests, or fixing it in her hair...

Nodding to himself, he dropped it back into the basket. Then, after a final look around which revealed nothing of interest, he doused the flame and moved back to the rear of the shop. Soon he was outside, making his way out of the ginnel and into a silent Bishopsgate Street. He had barely started to walk when a sound from behind made him turn – too late.

'I'll have words with you, constable,' a male voice breathed, very close. 'And make no sound, or I'll be forced to use this.'

Upon which something sharp was pressed to his back, making him stiffen from head to foot.

12

They walked steadily up Bishopsgate Street before turning into a different dark ginnel – the same one that Cutler had hurried down two days earlier, before being seized by Edward Thorne's hired ruffian. This time, they stopped beside a wall where his captor made him turn and place his back to it. Thus far, since waylaying him in the street, he had said not a word. Now they faced each other, with nothing but dim candlelight from an upstairs window. Peering into the gloom, Cutler made out a pale, bony face under a cap pulled down low.

'Who are you?' He began – only to receive a jab in the ribs. The poniard pierced both jerkin and shirt, and would have drawn blood.

'I'll make it short,' the man said, in a tone that brooked no refusal. He was far from young, Cutler realised. 'You will listen and you will agree to my demands, or it'll go very badly for you. Do you understand me?'

But Cutler said nothing. Despite his predicament, he was in no humour to submit. The other paused, then made another jab with the dagger. 'I asked if you understood, Matthew Cutler,' he grunted.

'So, you know my name.' Cutler clenched his teeth at the pain; he could already feel warm blood at his side. 'What do you want?'

'It's plain enough,' came the answer. 'You are to cease this foolish delving into the death of the Italian perfumer. The inquest is over, the body is gone and there's no more to be done.'

For a moment, it shook him... until realisation followed, which shook him even more. Now at last, he knew with certainty that there was more to Brisco's demise than the slaying of a stranger by some fanatic – or even his being the victim of a jealous husband. Whoever this man was, he was sent by someone... Thinking fast, he tried to resist.

'Unlawfully slain by persons unknown, according to the coroner's jury,' he said. 'It was murder, and as constable, I—'

'As constable, you should look to your parish duties and no more,' the other broke in. 'Otherwise, when I say things would go badly for you, I make no empty threat. You have two pretty daughters. It would be a tragedy if anything ill should befall them.'

Something swept over Cutler then: a spasm of fear – followed by cold rage. His assailant, however, was ahead of him.

'That maddens you, doesn't it?' he said, almost mockingly. 'Then think on what I've said and act wisely. You're not a fool.'

'No...' Cutler tried to look the man in the eye, but his face was in shadow. 'I'm not a fool – nor do I forget.'

'Good.' The other stepped back, keeping his poniard levelled. 'Now do as I've ordered. And remember – you're an easy man to find.'

Whereupon with a rapid turn, he was gone. Cutler barely had time to watch his retreating back before he disappeared in darkness. Breathing hard, he moved away from the wall, then put a hand to his side and felt the stickiness of blood. For a moment, he had the urge to pursue this individual: to knock him to the ground, and take him by the throat. But it was fruitless; the man could be anywhere, and he was in no shape to run.

Moving slowly, he took off his jerkin and pulled up his shirt; even in the gloom, he could see the bloodstain. Pressing his palm to the wound – which mercifully, was not too deep – he walked out of the ginnel and into Bishopsgate Street, which was deserted. There he hesitated... before knowing exactly where he must go. Then he was walking again, up the road through Norton Folgate, to the house of Margaret Fisher.

* * *

He awoke with the dawn, having no idea where he was, save that he was comfortable and had slept deeply. He peered about, finding himself in a narrow bed in a small room, the window open and birdsong outside... whereupon the memories came back with a jolt.

He had been tired, almost drowsy when he arrived at Margaret's door, his arrival causing unease on the part of her servants. But he was recognised, and brought into the hallway while the lady of the house was summoned. Thereafter, Margaret had taken charge with efficiency. He sat in the kitchen, stripped to the waist, to have his wound bathed by her own hand, smeared with witch hazel and secured by a bandage about his body. Meanwhile, a servant made up a posset, which he drank quickly. Finally, he was led up the stairs to a spare chamber. Talking was for the morning, Margaret had said, before leaving him to rest.

And now it was morning – and the memory of the previous night's encounter struck him like a blow, prompting him to throw aside the coverlet. The girls... he must go to them at once. On his feet and finding himself clad only in his hose, he looked about and saw shoes, breeches and jerkin on the floor. His shirt was nowhere to be seen, but it scarcely mattered. Aware of pain in his side, he looked down but saw only a small stain on the bandage; the wound would heal soon enough. He dressed hurriedly, found belt and poniard and buckled himself. Then he was out on the landing, hurrying to the stairhead. No one else seemed to be up yet, which was for the best. Soon he was in the hallway, unbolting the main door and stepping outside.

As he walked home, with Bishopsgate barely astir, he tried to reason. The memory of the warning from the man who had waylaid him was stark. Jane and Katherine – and Aunt Margery too – must be sent away, out of danger. As yet he was uncertain where, but it had to be done. He had a few old friends, players from the theatres who might house his family, or Margery might know someone. He thought briefly of John Willard, but dismissed him; they should be far from Bishopsgate.

He was still turning over possibilities when he arrived home and stumbled inside, to find everything quiet. But he was not reassured until he had ascended the stairs and opened a door gently, to see both his daughters sound asleep in their beds. Relieved, he came down again and went to the kitchen to think. He was still sitting at the table when Margery came down, to halt in surprise.

'Where is your shirt?' she asked. 'You look like you've been a-wrestling.'

* * *

It was a taut gathering an hour later, after a hasty breakfast. Katherine and Jane sat in silence while he spelled it out. The two of them – and Margery too – must leave this morning for a place of safety. To their questions, his only answer was that he had been threatened because of his position as constable, and would take no risks.

'But what of you, Father?' Jane's face was filled with alarm. 'Are you not coming too?'

He hesitated, glancing from her to Katherine, who looked equally troubled, and then to Margery, standing with arms folded. And it was Margery who answered.

'Whatever's occurred, I think he means to stay and face it alone,' she answered quietly. 'If he was with us, we might all be in danger. Do I hit the mark?'

She was calm, and her unflinching gaze heartened him. He gave a nod.

'So...' Margery let out a sigh. 'We must decide where to go, for our holiday.'

'I know someone,' Cutler said, a notion having occurred. 'The old bookkeeper at the Curtain – he was a good friend. He lives quietly out in Surrey now... at Peckham Rye. If you will pack your clothing, I'll find a carter to take you and pen a letter for you to carry.'

'What, to someone we do not know?' Katherine demanded. 'Why do you not send us to Canterbury, to our grandfather's house?'

She was aghast now, as was her sister. But this was no time to consider his parents, whom the girls had not seen since they were small. He would not speak of his father, who had grown crabbed with age, or of his mother, who was now so taciturn, she barely spoke. There would be a poor welcome at the home of Edmund Cutler the magistrate – only disapproval for his son's having put his children in danger.

'It's too far, Kate.' Aunt Margery was regarding her niece

sternly. 'Your father hasn't the time to seek a wagoner for such a journey.'

To Cutler's relief, Katherine hesitated, then appeared to submit.

'Yet, for how long shall we be gone?' Jane asked. 'We shall fret every hour, not knowing what happens to you.' She was close to tears, prompting Katherine to put an arm about her. But now, their aunt was brisk.

'We've not the leisure to think on that,' she said. 'Your father knows what he must do, and he can fadge for himself. Pray, go to your room now and find what you need to take.'

Mercifully, it was enough. The two girls rose, but as they were about to leave, he stayed them. 'I'm filled with shame for what I've brought upon you,' he said, getting to his feet. 'I'll do what I can to make amends, yet I cannot know how long it will be.'

And so, all was set in motion. Properly clad in a clean shirt, he went out and soon secured the services of a carter he knew, who would arrive before noon and take his family through the city and down into Surrey. Having given Margery a purse of money and a hastily scrawled letter to his friend, he took farewell of his daughters at the door. His heart was heavy as he kissed both of them, before turning away. From the street, he glanced back once to see Katherine raise her hand before going back inside. Then he was walking, setting his face grimly to the tasks ahead.

For, since rising that morning, he had found a strength he barely knew he possessed. No one, he told himself, would be allowed to threaten his family as that hard-nosed messenger had done, and get away with it. And a messenger the man clearly was – which raised the question of who had sent him, and why they were so keen that he drop his investigations into Brisco's death. A plan of how to proceed was needed now, and he was impatient to speak of it with Margaret. But first, perhaps an apology for his rapid departure would be in order.

She was up when he arrived back at the house, and relieved to see him. After finding him gone, she told him, she had not known what to think. They were soon seated in her parlour while he told her about the previous night's encounter, of which she knew little. Now, after hearing his account, she showed alarm.

'Who could have sent this warning, to be delivered in such a threatening manner?' she wondered. 'It makes little sense to me.'

'Nor to me,' Cutler said. 'Or not yet – but it's helped me form a resolve.' He paused, then met her eye. 'Call me stubborn, or reckless, or what you will. But I mean to pursue this to the end, with every breath in my body. I owe it to the man who was murdered in my parish, I owe it to the strangers who are afeared, and to my family. Moreover—'

'You owe it to yourself,' she finished.

They were silent. On the way here, another thought had occurred to Cutler: that he could be putting Margaret in danger too – something he was loth to do. But first, he would express gratitude. 'I owe you a good deal,' he said. 'Not just for your aid yesterday, but for last night. Mayhap it's best that I stay clear of you now. I need to pummel my brains, seek a path through this fog.'

'Do you?' Margaret frowned slightly. 'Well, I like that not a jot. I thought we had formed a most promising partnership... poking about in the fog, as you term it. I enjoyed playing Lady Gallett at the Exchange – and it's cruel of you to deny me the chance of another performance.'

That jolted him. 'Are you serious?' he asked. 'After what's happened, I thought—'

'I know,' she broke in. 'But let us think on it together. Now that your family is gone away to safety, you're free to act as boldly as you dare. As Sir Amos, you can move in the highest circles if need be – even question those ladies of quality we know of, who knew Brisco. I cannot be certain, but I've a notion you may learn something of value... that *we* may learn something. Or does your mind not move that way?'

'Well, it might.' He was taken aback by her words. But that eagerness was there again – a desire for excitement she had shown before. He was about to speak further, but again she forestalled him.

'And in the meantime, you should stay here at my house. You may use the spare chamber where you slept last night. That's wise, isn't it?'

'Is it?' He raised his eyebrows. 'I'm grateful, yet...' But he broke off, feeling suddenly foolish. What was he afraid of? He had duties to discharge, which had nothing to do with where he spent his nights. And it drove him – this desire to find Brisco's murderer, and restore some calm to the people of Bishopsgate. Seeing Margaret waiting for an answer, he nodded.

'Well then, I'm doubly in your debt,' he said. 'And it will make attiring myself as Sir Amos a lot easier. I only hope I'll avoid being recognised for a while longer.'

'But you're a player,' Margaret said, with a smile. 'The clothes and the hat, together with the sword and the way you carry yourself, are your disguise. As for myself, folk around here had almost forgotten me. We will jet upon our stage with aplomb.'

To which, despite everything, he laughed. And with remarkable ease, the two of them fell into making plans for their afternoon's excursion: to intrude upon one of Alessandro Brisco's former customers, who might even have been his lover.

* * *

Sir Titus Wheatley's London dwelling – one of several he owned, scattered about the southern counties of England – was a large house in Hart Street, within sight of the Tower. That afternoon, Sir Amos and Lady Gallett arrived at the gate and announced themselves to a servant as having business with Lady Wheatley. As Cutler had hoped, Sir Titus was away, but Her Ladyship was at home. In view of the obvious status of this distinguished-looking couple, the servant asked no questions, but led them through the house to a well-kept garden at the rear. Here they were presented to the lady herself, who was seated on a bench under the shade of a tree. While stools were brought hurriedly by servants, Cutler made his bow. He and his wife were in London for but a short time, he announced, and had been desirous to visit before leaving for their country residence.

'Most kind,' the lady said. Setting aside her book, she regarded them both with a faint smile. 'Though I confess, sir, I have not heard your name before.'

Cutler inclined his head, and took a moment to observe this *sombre and pious woman*, as Margaret had called her. His first thought, as he regarded a brown-haired, plainly dressed gentle-woman with a modest demeanour, was that the description seemed apt enough. His second thought was that it was a persona – as false as was his role of Sir Amos. The notion came from her eyes: large and green, which moved about rapidly before settling on his.

'I rarely come to town, madam,' he told her as he sat down. 'My estate keeps me well occupied, and the hunting is good. Does Sir Titus hunt much, these days?'

'Rarely,' came the reply. 'As you may know, he's much occupied with state business. Ships and seamen... or ropes and sails, if you will.' She regarded Margaret, who was taking her seat at his side. 'Does country life suit you too, Lady Gallett?'

'In truth, madam, it bores me utterly,' Margaret said, making Cutler blink. She was adopting the languid tone she had used at the perfumer's stall. 'I relish my all-too-infrequent visits to London – the theatres in particular.'

'Indeed?' Lady Joanna assumed a look of disapproval. 'I do not attend them. They are places of disorder and frivolity.'

A pause followed, which Cutler was about to fill – but Margaret was quicker. 'Though I'm always eager to visit the Exchange too,' she said. 'I was there yesterday, buying perfumeries. There is, of course, no opportunity for that in the country.'

'Indeed,' their host said again, somewhat frostily. 'I seldom go there. My needs are few, and my servants make the purchases.'

'Of course... and may we talk of other things?' Cutler asked, regretting that their encounter had got off to a bad start. 'For in truth, there is a reason for our visit which I'm hesitant to broach. It's a delicate topic.' He paused, throwing a swift glance at Margaret in the hope that she would know how to respond... and to his satisfaction, she did not fail.

'Husband, I pray you.' She put on a pained expression. 'I'm certain Lady Wheatley has no desire to discuss that – assuming it's what I think it is?'

Cutler put on a faint smile. 'As you please, yet I had in mind—'

'You had in mind what, sir?' Lady Joanna interrupted. 'For in truth, I begin to find this conversation wearisome. Perhaps you should say why you are here, while the day lasts.'

'Very well, madam – but it's a tragic matter,' he replied, in a grave voice. 'It concerns the death of a man I did business with, out in the suburb of Bishopsgate. An Italian perfumer named Brisco. I believe you were acquainted with him.'

He was watching her carefully, to judge her response – but when it came, it was unexpected.

'I knew no such person,' Lady Joanna said, sitting up sharply. 'And I regard perfume as a tawdry affectation, for women of the meanest sort.'

For a moment, neither of her listeners reacted – until Margaret got quickly to her feet.

'You disappoint me, madam,' she said brusquely. 'I had heard well of you – yet you choose to insult me. Would you truly besmirch me as a woman of the meanest sort? If so, I'll trouble you no longer. Husband?' She turned to Cutler, who had maintained his composure. 'Will you accompany me, or will you linger?'

But she threw him a look which was plain enough: she was giving him the opportunity to question Lady Joanna alone, as he had done with Segar in the Exchange. Seizing the moment, he lifted a hand.

'Peace, Lady Gallett,' he said, in a tone of reproach. 'I suggest you go and summon our coach, and I will join you anon. In the meantime, I shall try to make amends for your hasty words.' Turning to their hostess, he inclined his head. 'With your leave, madam?'

'There is no need,' Lady Joanna said, matching Margaret for haughtiness. 'The matter is forgotten, and I'll not delay you longer.' But Margaret had turned, and was already walking off to summon the non-existent coach. A moment followed, as Cutler gathered himself; once again, he was on... and in no mood to waste words.

'Forgive my abruptness, Lady Wheatley, but I'm certain you were acquainted with Master Brisco,' he said, facing her without expression. 'As I suspect you have heard of the circumstances of his untimely death.'

The lady caught her breath, but made no reply.

'Moreover, I should say that my relations with the man extended to more than mere business dealings,' he added. 'He was a friend, whose loss weighs heavily upon me – particularly in view of his being cruelly murdered.'

Again, she remained silent – but he was aware now of a sharp mind at work, forming a response. After a glance towards the house to see that no servants were near, he pressed on.

'I seek justice for Brisco. Whoever took his life should be made to pay for it with his own. I also wish to speak with those he had dealings with – whether they deny it or not. Hence, I—'

'Who are you, sir?' she demanded, finding her voice at last. 'And how dare you come to my house in this manner? Do you forget who I am?'

'I do not,' Cutler replied. 'Nor do I forget who your husband is – a man of honour and high standing in England. I wonder also, how much he knew of your relations with the perfumer.'

'What?' Drawing a breath, she rose to her feet. 'Do you threaten me?'

'In truth, I'm uncertain,' he said, remaining seated. 'Should I have grounds?'

'By the Lord – you are a scoundrel!' But she was not only angry: she was alarmed too. He saw it, and guessed at once that the rumours had foundation: she had indeed had close relations with Brisco.

'No, madam.' Somewhat sadly, he shook his head. 'I'm merely a man seeking answers. If you won't provide them, I'll go elsewhere.'

But he met her gaze, thinking that this was a passionate woman beneath a prim exterior: one of those Margaret had described as *bored wives, whose husbands neglect them...* and on a sudden, he felt ashamed. Who indeed, was he to judge? And in the end, would it bring him any closer to finding Brisco's murderer?

'I believed I might learn something from you,' he resumed. 'Believe me, I bear you no ill will. And had you viewed my friend's body, as I and others did, I don't believe you would censure me. The inquest provided no comfort, and those who knew him are undone...'

He paused, as a notion flew up unbidden. He was uncertain, but he seemed to hear Anne's voice urging him on: *cast a pebble in the pond, and see how the ripples spread...*

'I speak of men like his landlord, Niccolo Scamozzi,' he said, pronouncing the name carefully. 'He took charge of Brisco's body, to arrange the kind of burial he would wish.'

But to that, there was no sign of recognition on Lady Joanna's part; the name, it seemed, meant nothing. Somewhat heavily, she sat down again.

'You saw the body,' she said, after a moment. And when he nodded: 'Was it...'

'Despite what he had suffered, he was at peace,' Cutler said. 'An upright and respected man, gone to his maker.'

He watched her lower her gaze, surprised at the change in her manner. He even wondered if she had tried to avoid facing the fact of Brisco's murder. Yet here was a stranger who claimed to have been his friend – who had seen his corpse, and wanted justice. Perhaps her secret relations with the perfumer had been more than merely lustful; had they been lovers, in the truest sense?

'I ask your pardon, with all my heart,' he said, on impulse. 'You feel his loss, as do many who knew him. I should not have raised it in such a callous manner.'

'No, you should not. And yet...' She raised her eyes, letting out a sigh. 'I was remiss in my rebuke of your wife. I've even been known to buy perfume, at times.' She thought for a moment, then: 'You say Master Brisco has been given the burial he would have wished?'

'By his fellow countryman – another Italian.' Cutler nodded.

He rose from his seat, realising that the encounter was over; Lady Joanna may have been Brisco's lover, but it hardly seemed to matter now. He made his bow, remembering on a sudden that he was supposed to be Sir Amos Gallett. But the lady, it appeared, had almost forgotten his presence. When he murmured some words of farewell, she made no response.

Outside the gate, he found Margaret waiting.

'How was I this time?' she asked. 'Did I give a worthy performance?'

His mind busy, Cutler did not answer.

13

It was afternoon, and after a hurried return to Margaret's house, Cutler stepped forth into Bishopsgate Street, clad once again in his usual attire. He was constable of Spitalfields, and needed to remind himself of it. And he had barely walked a hundred yards before he was accosted by Henry Deans, who brought him down to earth with a bump.

'At last, I find you,' the deputy alderman snorted. 'You seem to be everywhere but in your parish. Have you not heard the news?'

'News?' Cutler echoed. 'I'm uncertain what—'

'Austen Kett's up and gone!' Deans broke in, in a voice of outrage. 'Left his lodgings owing rent, took his belongings and fled like a felon!'

'Is it so?' Cutler raised his eyebrows. 'How unfortunate.'

'Unfortunate? It's a gross neglect of duty,' Deans huffed. 'He's told none of us – unless you know something?'

'Alas...' He shook his head. 'How did you learn of it?'

'The landlord – his sister lodges above Kett's. Now he's disappeared, there will be no constable in St Botolph's. Until one is appointed, you and Farrant will have to shoulder the added burden.'

'I suppose we will. And in the meantime, should someone not inform Master Skinner?'

'I've already done so,' came the brisk reply. 'Moreover...' A frown appeared. 'Following our talk at his house, can I take it you've heeded his words? His advice to put the Italian's death behind you, and look to your duties?'

'I always listen to advice,' Cutler said. But his mind went at once to the previous night, and the bleak warning from the man who had spiked him; the wound in his side was still tender. It seemed as if there were some hidden party, bent on making him abandon his pursuit of Brisco's murderer – something he had resolved not to do.

'Did you hear me?' Deans asked, rousing him from his reverie.

'Your pardon...' Cutler met his gaze. 'You were speaking of Skinner?'

'I spoke of duty,' Deans retorted. 'The maintaining of order in our Ward. What with Bland's demise, and Kett's flight to heaven knows where, we are sorely depleted.'

'I heard Josiah Madge will be watchman. Is that true?'

'I've asked him to serve for the present. Skinner will make the appointment.'

'So... it seems all is in hand,' Cutler breathed. 'And with your leave, I'll be on my way.'

'All is not in hand,' Deans said. 'As deputy alderman, I'm troubled by what I've heard about the strangers. Hoarding weapons in their houses, and so forth. It's almost as if they consider themselves a militia... a trained band, yet without authority.' He paused, then: 'Since you appear to consider yourself their friend, you might remind them of the law in that regard.'

'The law?' Cutler stiffened. 'There's no law that I know of

against keeping a poniard or a cudgel to protect yourself or your family. Or mayhap you regard a baker's knife or a joiner's chisel as a weapon?'

'That's frivolous talk, constable,' came the other's retort. 'You know what I speak of.'

Cutler bit back a retort of his own. There was no use arguing with Deans... He despised him, and realised he always had. Now he thought on it, the deputy alderman reminded him of his older brother Giles: a haughty man who had often railed against the Huguenot refugees who had settled in their home city. Was that why Cutler had always found sympathy for the underdog? he wondered.

With a curt nod, he moved off down the street.

He would go to Willard's – and now, it struck him that he had not told his father-in-law of Katherine, Jane and Margery being sent away. In the haste of that morning, Margery had left Cutler to tell her brother of their departure – instead, he had been preoccupied with his quest. Quickening his pace, he hurried to the shop and pushed at the door – only to find it locked.

He put an ear to it, but could hear nothing. It was unusual... Frowning, he knocked loudly. Receiving no answer, he knocked harder – until to his relief, came the sound of a bolt being drawn. The door opened to reveal Willard, holding a large hammer.

'By heaven, Matthew,' he muttered. 'I thought...' He broke off. 'Nay, never mind what I thought. Get yourself in here, and bolt the door.'

'What's the coil, John?' Cutler asked.

But Willard merely shook his head, and moved to his customary station at the workbench. When his son-in-law had secured the door and joined him, he produced a scrap of paper and held it up.

'This was put under my door last night,' he said. 'You'd better read it for yourself.'

Cutler took it, and read.

Master Willard: your kinsman who serves as constable in your place toys with matters that he should not. He has been warned. Tell him to cease, or he will bring mayhem upon all of your family.

There was no signature. Lowering the paper, he let out a sigh.

'Can you shed any light on that?' The gunsmith was eying him grimly. It occurred to Cutler that never before had he seen his father-in-law shaken.

'I can,' he answered. 'But first, be assured that Margery and the girls are safe, and gone from Bishopsgate. I sent them away this morning, to a trusted friend in Surrey. I should have told you sooner.'

'Well, that's balm to my ears.' Willard too gave a sigh. 'But what of this warning?'

'I'll tell you – the whole sorry tale,' Cutler answered, before dropping the paper on the bench. 'I've been remiss. Things have moved apace since I saw you last, and in truth...' He shook his head. 'In truth, it might be best for everyone if I did as I've been ordered, and forgot the whole, sorry business of Brisco's death.'

His father-in-law observed him for a moment, then drew up a stool for each of them. Soon they were both seated... but as the saga unfolded, ending with Cutler's and Margaret's visit to Lady Wheatley, Willard grew agitated.

'It looks as if you've kicked open a hornet's nest,' he said finally. 'Have you formed an opinion as to what lies at back of it all?'

'Only that the whole world, it seems, wants me to cease

hunting for a murderer, and look to my duties as a humble constable.'

'That is indeed how it looks.' Willard eyed him. 'And yet, you won't comply.'

'They – whoever *they* be – have threatened my family,' Cutler replied. 'What would you do, John?'

His father-in-law hesitated, then got to his feet and took up the scrap of paper with its anonymous message. As Cutler watched, he took it over to his small furnace, opened the door with tongs and placed the offending note inside.

'I'm having a drink,' he said. 'Will you have one too?'

* * *

They talked for almost an hour, sifting the events of the past days. Willard was alert, asking questions which Cutler answered quickly. But by the end of it, the mystery remained: who was it who was so determined to stop his search for the murderer of Alessandro Brisco?

'The man with the poniard,' the gunsmith murmured. 'How did he appear to you?'

'No common villain,' Cutler said, and touched his side. 'And he knew how far to press his point, to achieve the desired effect.'

'Press his point... very apt,' Willard said with a wry look. 'But what troubles me is his reminding you that you're an easy man to find. Apart from those occasions,' he added, 'when you jet forth as Sir Amos Gallett.'

At that, Cutler looked embarrassed. 'It seemed worth the attempt. And Margaret can be most persuasive.'

'I remember. I also remember that she's a clever woman. Your visits to the perfumer in the Exchange, and to Lady Wheatley... mayhap they were not entirely in vain.' His father-in-law was thoughtful, staring at the floor. 'Do you not think so?'

'I've learned that Brisco was a man with secrets... how many more remain to be uncovered, I cannot know. But I feel certain he and Joanna Wheatley were lovers. They had occasion to be private together, when he brought her perfumes... which she at first denied.'

'Brisco was a close fellow,' Willard said. 'Had the air of one who thought his trade was somehow beneath him, I always thought.' He frowned. 'Now you say that the Countess of Tanridge was another of his customers? If so, he ventured on to dangerous ground. The Earl's not a man to be trifled with – though, as I told you, I cannot see him stooping low enough to have Brisco murdered.'

Cutler too was thoughtful now. 'The Countess sounds like a headstrong woman. Young and flighty – and bored, Margaret would say. If Brisco was as bold as he now appears, he might have seen these women of quality as a kind of prize... a triumph.'

But at that, Willard shook his head. 'I never thought him as vain as that. A Papist, who would have made confession when he got the chance. As with his money-lending, he could merely have seen it as good business, dealing with these rich women. Though, from what you've said, it could have led to something more.'

'If so, it strikes me that there is one avenue left to explore,' Cutler said then, deciding as he spoke. 'As a friend of the late perfumer, I should visit the Countess of Tanridge.'

'You're not serious?' Willard frowned. 'What would that avail you?'

'I'm uncertain... Call it a whim, if you will.'

'By God, you are serious. Haven't you upset enough people already?'

'It would seem so,' Cutler admitted. 'But I'm in a fog still, and mighty eager to see it lift.' He gave a sigh, touched his father-in-law on the arm and got to his feet. 'Or mayhap I'm just tired, and want to see my family home and safe.'

'I wish to see you safe too, Matthew.' Willard levelled a gaze at him. 'I pray you tread carefully, whatever you do.'

'I'll try,' Cutler nodded, and left him.

* * *

But that evening, when he was at supper with Margaret, the two of them fell into a dispute that threatened to become tempestuous.

'You mean to go alone to Tanridge House, without me to add credence to your disguise?' She faced him across the table, her colour rising. 'That's cruel of you.'

'I'm afraid to draw you further into this mire,' Cutler said. He had eaten well, and found it difficult to argue on a full stomach – especially with the woman in whose house he now appeared to be lodging. 'You know the danger is real... You cannot doubt it since my father-in-law too received a warning.'

'I do not doubt it... and yet, I've not asked you to appoint yourself my guardian.' And when he made no reply: 'I gave you the chance to speak with Lady Wheatley. You've not asked what I was able to discover after I left you.'

He frowned. 'I thought you went outside at once, to await me.'

'Not at once.' Margaret wore a somewhat mischievous look, which he had come to recognise. 'I practised a little deception on her servant. Asked to use the closed stool, and when he left me alone, I ventured up the stair and found her chamber. There was a distinct reek of perfume – civet and musk.'

'That was bold of you,' Cutler said. 'But it's no surprise. She admitted in the end that she'd done business with Brisco – and that it was remiss of her to rebuke you.'

'Did she, indeed?' Margaret said frostily. 'A pity she did not say so to my face.'

'Well, it's over and done,' he sighed. 'But I mean to stick to my resolve, and see if I can learn anything from the Countess of Tanridge.'

'Without me to hinder you, it seems.'

'It isn't that. I cannot go as Sir Amos. Assuming she even receives me, she could be suspicious. She might want to know of my family, ancestry...' He shook his head. 'It's best I claim to be a friend of Brisco, who wishes to continue his business.'

'What, pose as a perfumer?' Margaret was sceptical. 'You have neither the skills nor the knowledge.'

'Nevertheless, I mean to try,' Cutler said stubbornly. 'After all that's happened, I need to—'

'Pick up the scent,' Margaret finished. 'And more...' A frown appeared. 'I almost wonder, given the countess's reputation, if you mean to fill Brisco's shoes. You're handsomer than he was... if you played your hand well, who knows what might happen?'

'By God.' He raised his eyebrows. 'Are you jealous?'

'Am I what?' With a sudden movement, she seized her napkin and threw it down. 'You forget yourself, master constable.'

'Mayhap I do,' he said. 'But I'm certain it would be unwise for us to go as Sir Amos and Lady Gallett this time. Though,' he added, 'it's possible we may do so again.'

'I will think on that,' she allowed, after a pause. 'And now, I propose to read before going to my chamber. I'm somewhat fatigued.'

Upon which she rose, calling for the servants. Cutler watched her go, before getting to his feet. He would retire to his own chamber, and ponder the role he must adopt on the morrow when he ventured down to the river, to the London residence of the Earl of Tanridge.

He had decided to go by boat.

* * *

To call it merely a house would be doing the Earl a disservice: it was a mansion, occupying an impressive river frontage beside Durham House, the residence of Sir Walter Raleigh. Visitors might arrive on horseback or by coach via the entrance on the Strand, or by wherry at the Thameside jetty. Cutler, clad in a green doublet and breeches belonging to the late Master Fisher, but without a sword, had walked down through the city that morning to the Old Swan Stairs by London Bridge and hailed a waterman. Once settled in the boat, he ignored the man's gruff attempts at conversation. He was thinking about his new persona as Edward Watkins, a man of business who had known Alessandro Brisco.

He knew this was a risky venture; perhaps it was also a waste of time. Yet his visit to Lady Wheatley had not been in vain, he told himself. He believed he knew a good deal more about Brisco now – moreover, the attempts to make him give up his quest had angered him. Though a visit to Lady Dorothy Hibbert, Countess of Tanridge, was of a different order entirely; her husband was one of England's Great Men, and a friend to the Queen. As yet, Cutler was uncertain how to present himself; he could only hope that his old talent for impromptu would not forsake him. He was still musing on it when the boat struck the jetty post with a thud, jolting him into action. Having paid the fare, he stepped on to the landing and arrived at the garden gate, to be greeted by a liveried servant.

'Watkins of Bishopsgate, come to attend the countess,' he said breezily. 'I carry perfumes.'

He tapped the leather bag which hung from his shoulder, hoping the man who stood before him would not wish to inspect it. If he did so, he would find only a small jar of rose oil loaned by Margaret, along with the *coussine* they had bought from Segar in the Exchange. These, she had told him that morning, would have to serve for his samples. Those were almost the only words the two of them had exchanged since breakfast.

'You're a perfumer?' The servant looked him up and down. 'What's happened to the Italian fellow?'

'Alas, he died,' Cutler said, with a look of regret. 'Has the news not reached you here?'

'It has not.' The other frowned. 'What was the cause?'

'It was most sudden... In truth, I know little of the ailment, whatever it was.'

'Yet, you are quick to arrive in his place,' came the sharp response.

'He was a good friend... He would wish me to act,' Cutler said, thinking fast. 'He was devoted to your mistress, and loth to disappoint her.'

But the man was wary. 'What mean you by that?' he demanded.

'Why, nothing more than a desire to do business. Master Brisco considered her his most gracious and noble customer... He was proud to attend her.'

'By the Lord...' To that, the other shook his head. 'Here's another damned flatterer.' With a look of disapproval, he opened the gate and stood aside. 'The countess may yet be abed,' he muttered. 'In which case, you should wait in the kitchens.'

With a nod, Cutler left him and passed through a garden with fruit trees and flower beds. Gardeners eyed him as he gained the entrance, where a maid in a hurry directed him to a side wing of the house. He entered the kitchen, clouded with steam and stifling hot from the fire. Having stated his business, he was told to step out to the passage, where one of the countess's body servants would find him. Only then did he realise that he was to be admitted to Lady Dorothy's bedchamber.

It was something of a shock... but then again, perhaps not. It was unlikely the countess would be alone; perhaps she ate breakfast in her rooms, before the elaborate business of dressing took place at the hands of her women. It could be midday before she arrived downstairs. He pondered the matter for almost half an hour, pacing the passage, until at last, a maidservant arrived to escort him. He was led through the house to a grand staircase, then up to a landing with several doors. Assuming a casual air, Cutler enquired whether His Lordship was up.

'The Earl is not here, master,' the young woman said. 'He stays in his house in Surrey, with his dogs.'

They stopped outside a painted door, where he waited while she went inside. A moment later, the door was opened by a different woman, considerably older... then at last, he was ushered into the presence of the Countess of Tanridge. Ready to make his bow, he saw that the huge four-poster bed was unoccupied, as was the padded couch before it. He was about to look round, when a rather shrill voice broke the silence.

'I'm over here, Master Wilkins. There's no need to look like a startled rabbit. Pray, approach so that I may inspect you.'

He put on a smile, turned... and froze.

She was sitting on a cushioned seat by an open window, with a small table to one side, on which stood only a jug and a chased-silver goblet. And, she was quite evidently drunk.

'My Lady.' Cutler took a few steps and bowed low. 'It's most gracious of you to receive me.' He kept his smile, while darting a glance at the other two occupants. The younger maidservant was leaving, but the older one remained, regarding him somewhat severely.

'I suppose it is.' The countess eyed him with vague curiosity. She was indeed young and attractive, wearing an elaborate morning gown of primrose yellow, and loose slippers of velvet. Her dark hair hung loose, and there was no jewellery. Surprised to be admitted in such seemingly intimate circumstances, Cutler was subdued. But he knew a drunken woman when he saw one, and realised he must adapt – quickly.

'I regret I must begin by bringing sad tidings,' he ventured. 'I'm told that the news has not yet reached you, of the death of my good friend Alessandro Brisco. I pray you will accept my condolences, for I know that he served you often.'

'He's dead?' The countess gave a start. 'Good God.' She turned to her companion, who to Cutler's eyes appeared tense. 'Why has no one told me?'

'I knew nothing of it, my lady,' the woman replied. 'He had not been here for some time, as I recall.'

'No...' Lady Dorothy considered for a moment – then startled Cutler by facing him abruptly and breaking into a laugh. 'Well, no matter. We all have to leave this earth sometime... Is that the sole reason you come here, Wilkins? To bear the sad tidings?'

'It's Watkins, my lady,' Cutler said. 'And I confess I have other motives. I follow the same trade as Master Brisco – fine scents, of which I know you are a connoisseur.'

She gazed at him, as if failing to comprehend.

'Perfumes?' He raised his eyebrows, beginning to wonder whether coming here was wise. 'He would visit you with his wares, to let you select at your pleasure.'

'He did, on occasions.'

It was the woman-in-waiting who had spoken, rather curtly. 'Yet he was always careful to choose a propitious time,' she added. 'This early in the day is inapt, if not discourteous.'

A moment followed, in which he sought for a reply... but he was forestalled.

'Leave us,' the countess said, in a bored voice. For a moment, Cutler thought she was addressing him, until her woman looked round sharply.

'My lady?' She was ill-at-ease. 'I must dress your hair, while Bridget fetches the silks...'

'I will call you both,' her mistress broke in. 'Surely you can find something else to do, while I confer with the perfumer?'

And she turned away until, after a moment's hesitation, the woman moved off without a word. At the door, she threw a swift look at Cutler before going out, which might have conveyed a warning – or could it have been one of sympathy?

'Well, we're alone,' the countess said with a smile. 'Would you care to drink with me?'

He managed a look of regret. 'I fear it's somewhat early in the day for me,' he began – but he was too late. She was pouring something from the jug into her goblet, which she held up.

'I said, would you care to drink with me?' she repeated.

He hesitated, then moved closer and took the cup from her outstretched hand. He sipped, tasted Malmsey of the finest quality, and handed it back.

'Delightful,' he said, but his spirits were sinking; the situation looked impossible. Whatever the countess might have in mind, he now wished to be gone.

'So, what have you brought me?' She took a drink from the cup herself, while regarding him over the rim. 'Civet, storax? Alessandro always gave me first choice of his latest stock.'

'Alas, I have only rose oil and a little *coussine* today,' he answered, before falling silent. With a brazen motion, the Countess of Tanridge had opened her gown to display an embroidered shift beneath.

'It's somewhat humid, isn't it?' she murmured. 'This summer is unbearable.'

Cutler blinked, but stood his ground. 'True enough, my lady' – which prompted a peal of laughter.

'What on earth are you frightened of?' She patted the window seat. 'Come now, sit and talk. Talk of Brisco, if you like. How much did he tell you of me?'

She waited while Cutler sat down beside her. Keeping his eyes on the floor, which was covered in a fine Turkey carpet, he tried to remain true to the role of Watkins the perfumer, a tradesman from Bishopsgate.

'That you were his most valued customer, my lady,' he answered. 'Attending you was a joy.'

But at that, her face clouded. 'I don't believe you,' she pouted. 'I hear flattery, of the basest sort.' And seeing Cutler had no answer: 'I demand conversation,' she went on, somewhat languidly. 'Alessandro was a man of fine words... that charming Venetian accent. We exchanged many confidences.'

In spite of everything, Cutler was intrigued. 'Confidences... yes, he told me so. Hence, may I take it you were aware of his religion?'

'Oh, that.' The countess plonked her cup down on the side table, before stifling a yawn. 'I cared not a fig for his popery.' To add to his unease, she chuckled like a girl. 'It's well that my husband isn't present to hear that. Is it your religion, too?'

'It is not, my lady,' he replied, but she did not appear to be listening. A moment passed, then:

'Alessandro would apply perfumed oils to my body, with his own hands,' she said, turning to face him. 'Would you like to do the same?'

Cutler blinked again, seized the goblet and took a drink.

14

A short silence had followed, before Cutler managed a contrite smile and raised his hands in a gesture of apology.

'Your pardon, my lady,' he began. 'I have only a *coussine* with me, which I intended as a gift by way of introduction. Perfumes fit for your skin would have to wait for another occasion.' Without waiting for her to reply, he opened his bag. But when the small packet appeared, the countess was unimpressed.

'Is that all?' she murmured. 'Have you brought no bottled scents?'

'Alas... in truth, I thought it would be forward of me to do so. I wished to learn first what you will have from me.'

'What I will have from you?' A sly look appeared. 'Now there's a question.' And when he said nothing: 'Although, now I ponder the matter, it would be somewhat forward of me, too, since we do not yet know one another.' She paused, looking him over... and it struck him that she was growing drowsy. How much had she drunk? He caught a whiff of her breath, and barely avoided frowning.

'You are handsome,' she said. 'I would not have said that about Alessandro. His art was in his ways.'

'My lady...' Cutler drew breath. If he was to learn anything at all, he should strike before the occasion was lost. 'Did your husband know Brisco? Was he aware of his visits to you?'

'The Earl?' She gave a slight shrug. 'I never asked him. Always occupied with matters of what he calls *state*... in truth, he pays more mind to his hounds than he does to me.'

There was a scornful edge to her voice now. When her gaze drifted towards the goblet, Cutler lifted it and handed it to her.

'Not a jealous man, then,' he said, as she drank.

'The war hero...' She lowered the cup and stared into it. 'He was with Sir Philip Sidney when he fell at Zutphen, you know – as everyone knows, for he reminds them often enough. Fifteen eighty... whatever it was.'

'Fifteen eighty-six, if I recall rightly,' Cutler murmured.

'We used to laugh about it,' she went on, as if she hadn't heard. '*Tell me his secrets*, Alessandro would ask while he dripped oil on my shoulders. And I would do so – just to spite the old fool. Tanridge deserves it.'

'His secrets?' Cutler echoed. 'Do you mean matters of intimacy between you and the Earl?'

'What intimacy?' She turned suddenly, and would have dropped the goblet if he hadn't caught it. 'Do you see that bed?' She gestured clumsily. 'The great Earl of Tanridge hasn't visited it in months – not since the pestilence! Husband? He might as well be a eunuch. Is that a way to treat a wife who's...' She waved a hand. 'Who is a woman, yet one who enjoys less pleasure than her servants? Can you answer that, my pretty fellow?'

Placing the goblet gently down on the table, Cutler shook his head. 'I cannot, my lady. Nor can I do more than...'

He stopped himself.

He had been about to say something like, *Nor can I do more than offer you my sympathies*, before realising how trite it sounded. But since the countess was no longer listening, it hardly seemed to matter.

'A pox on him,' she muttered, almost to herself. 'I know his duties, his assignments, better than he knows them himself. Have I not talked long and late with Privy Councillors – some of the best in England – of everything from arms to armadas? Some men of worth are content to visit me, to be at ease and trade their troubles with mine. I could serve the Queen as well as any of them – if she ever listened to the counsel of women.'

She stopped talking and shook her head; she had grown maudlin, for which Cutler knew there was no remedy save sleep. But his mind was busy as he ran over what she had said: here was a revelation, that as yet he barely grasped.

'You talked of state matters?' he prompted. 'With Brisco?'

'Why should I not?' came the slurred reply. 'We told each other everything: his wife back in Italy whom he loathed – and his landlord, whom he adored. I used to mock him, ask if he and that Italian landlord of his were more than mere friends... He grew angry at that. I liked to make him angry – his passion was of a Roman kind: hot and heady.' Upon which, to Cutler's alarm, she looked up suddenly and grasped his arm.

'And you...' With half-lidded eyes, she peered into his. 'What is your passion? Did you truly come here to sell scents, or...' She paused, then let out a gasp. 'By the Christ, I don't believe you're a perfumer at all! I should have known from the start... There's no smell upon you! Where's your smell, master intruder?' And before he could react, she lurched to her feet. 'Get out!' she cried. 'You weak-kneed varlet... you worm... I can call men who'd slit your gizzard!' She staggered, putting a hand out. 'Get out,' she repeated feebly. 'Go off and tug your yard, you...'

But that was all she said. As Cutler too got to his feet, the Countess of Tanridge slumped to her knees, then fell sideways. Muttering to herself, she stretched out on the Turkey carpet, eyes closing while saliva dripped from her mouth.

Cutler watched her lapse into a stupor, then picked up his bag. The scented *coussine*, which she had all but ignored, had fallen to the floor. Let it serve as a gift, he thought, to one of the unhappiest women he had ever seen.

He turned from her and walked to the door. Outside, the woman-in-waiting was seated on a stool by the wall. As Cutler appeared, she got up at once.

'Your mistress is unwell,' he said. 'With all my heart, I hope she recovers.'

* * *

He did not leave Tanridge House by the water gate, but via the main entrance on The Strand. From there and along Fleet Street he walked back into London, with a longer walk to follow, through the city and out to Bishopsgate. He needed to think, and walking had always helped. But one notion rose above all others, that almost took his breath away.

The Countess of Tanridge had talked with abandon to Alessandro Brisco, in moments of intimacy. And their private talk had included matters of state, known to her husband and others she had spoken of – those *men of worth* in whom she confided – which put a new light on everything.

He tried to reason, sifting the events of the past week – for it was almost a week, since the morning Stephen Bland had come with the news of Brisco's death. Now, in the space of less than an hour, he had learned more about the perfumer than he had known in all the years he had lived in his parish. And an unexpected picture had emerged: of a clever, even manipulative man who appeared to have played his distinguished customer the Countess of Tanridge with ease. Aside from receiving money for his wares, he had presumably enjoyed her body too. And what else had he gained, from the gossip concerning her husband?

The more he thought about it, the more it troubled Cutler. *Tell me his secrets*, Brisco had urged Lady Dorothy as he fondled her – and she had obliged, with abandon if not with glee. She was shameless and embittered... a dissatisfied woman, fated to languish at home while the Earl was elsewhere. She had spoken of important men who visited and confided in her, which suggested she had other lovers. She had even claimed, if drunkenly, that she could *serve the Queen as well as any of them* – was that merely a boast?

He frowned as he trudged the streets, almost oblivious to the din of the city. From Ludgate to Paul's, then through West Cheap to the Poultry. People jostled him, beggars whined, horsemen and carts clattered by, but he barely looked up. In Threadneedle Street, he glanced at the entrance to the Royal Exchange and thought of Segar the perfumer who had – unwittingly, it seemed – set him on a trail that had led to discoveries he had never imagined. He thought then of Lady Wheatley, another distinguished customer of Brisco's – and likely another of his lovers.

He stopped suddenly, narrowly avoiding colliding with a passer-by. The Alessandro Brisco whom Cutler now saw was a figure of menace: the courteous shopkeeper of Bishopsgate was but a persona – no different from his Sir Amos or Watkins the perfumer. How long the man had been the confidant and lover of these women of distinction, he could not know – and what his dalliance with them might amount to, was also hidden. He should seek advice, he decided... or at least, tell someone he trusted, who might help him piece things out. John Willard, of course, sprang to mind – and Margaret too. He would speak to them soon.

But first, there was something else: since rising that morning, he had felt a desire to go home to his house, empty as it was. To sit at his own table, and pour a mug of his own beer, and try to step back from this puzzle – this thankless quest that so far had brought him only trouble. The notion calmed him as he set off again, passing by St Anthony's and at last into Bishopsgate Street. He had barely cleared the city gate when it started to rain hard, sending people scurrying for cover.

But it suited him. Without hurrying, he walked past Bedlam, past Brisco's still-boarded shop where he had ventured in secret, relieved that no one was likely to accost him just then on parish business. Dripping wet, he arrived at his house, drew the key which he always carried and entered. It was a relief to close the door behind him and stand in his hallway, with only the sound of rainwater falling outside. A short while later, he was seated in his kitchen, cool and lifeless with no fire in the chimney... and no bustle of women to fill the place. How Katherine, Jane and Aunt Margery had fared since leaving, was just another thing he did not know; he could only hope they were safe.

He reached for the jug and poured. The beer was flat and sour, but he drank anyway. Thereafter, he leaned back against the wall, closed his eyes and let out a sigh. Only then did he remember that he still wore a doublet and breeches belonging to the late Master Fisher... but that could wait. He yawned and stretched, as an image rose unbidden of the Countess of Tanridge in her primrose-yellow morning gown, slumping to the floor.

Within minutes, he was asleep, and when he awoke, it was dusk.

He came awake with a start, looking round in the gathering gloom. His neck was stiff... He sat upright and moved his shoulders, wincing at the stab of pain. The house was quiet... He listened, realising that the rain had ceased. The reek of stale beer assailed him, prompting him to push his mug aside. Then he was on his feet, hunting for a candle... only to remember that Margaret would have expected him hours ago. How long had he slept?

He stumbled about the kitchen, found a candle and tinderbox and made a flame. His clothes, he realised, were still wet... With an oath, he took up the candle-holder and moved out to the hallway. He needed fresh attire – and to wash too, though there was no fire to heat water. Holding the light aloft, he ascended the stairs and went to his chamber. In his oak chest, he found a clean shirt and breeches, and threw them on the bed. He was starting to remove his damp clothing when he heard a sound from below, and gave a start; someone had opened the door.

His first instinct was to call out, but he did not. In his hose, he stole softly across the room and through the open door to the landing. He listened, but heard nothing... then came the sound of the latch, as the house door closed. It was followed by a footfall; the intruder, whoever it was, was in the hallway.

He had no weapon; his belt and poniard were on the kitchen table where he had left them. Again, he had an urge to challenge the incomer, but again, he resisted. Instead, he moved silently to the stairhead and peered over the rail, but could see nothing. He was on the point of going down, relying on his bare hands for whatever action was needed, when he caught a scent that made his heart jump: the smell of whale oil. And in seconds, he was running down the stairs, two at a time... to confront a figure that loomed up.

'Fall to your knees!' Cutler snapped. 'I'm armed – and whatever you do, I'm ready!'

A brief moment followed... then as his eyes adjusted to the

gloom, Cutler saw the man duck aside. 'I hold a poniard,' he bluffed. 'And I'm constable – I can spike you in self-defence.'

'The devil you will.' A voice rose, low and menacing in the dark. 'Back off, or—'

But he was cut short, as Cutler struck out with his clenched fist. The crack itself would have startled anyone, let alone the force of the punch. The man reeled backwards – and as he did so, something fell from his grasp to land with a thud. Again, Cutler smelled whale oil – but by now, he had understood. With rising anger, he lashed out again using both fists, heedless of where the blows would fall. To his relief, the intruder staggered and fell.

'So – you would have set fire to my house,' he breathed. Peering down in the darkened hallway, he made out the man's pale, gaunt features. When he took a step forward, his foot struck something. He reached down and found a narrow-necked jar on its side, the reek of the oil inside it strong in his nostrils.

'Arson's a capital crime,' he murmured, as he picked up the jug. 'The penalty is hanging.'

There was no response.

'Stay down there, damn you,' Cutler ordered. He needed light – but first, he needed his poniard; the bluff would not hold. Stepping aside quickly, he darted into the kitchen, set the jug on the floor and caught up his belt. But he had barely time to pull the weapon from its sheath when the sound of movement came from the passage. Spinning round, he darted to the doorway – in time to see his captive lurching away from him. The house door flew open and the man was through... whereupon a surprise followed.

'Caught you, you varlet!'

A bulky figure appeared from nowhere, blocking the intruder's escape – and even as Cutler hurried forward, he knew the voice.

'Madge?'

'I have him, master constable!' The scavenger – who was now acting watchman, which Cutler had forgotten – sounded jubilant. 'Take his arms, before I down him!'

It was over in seconds. The would-be arsonist, grunting and struggling, was manhandled roughly by Josiah Madge, who shoved him back into the hallway. Cutler gripped the man's arms, pulling him backwards. Between the two of them they forced him into the kitchen and over to the chimney corner, where Madge put a foot behind his victim's leg and sent him, arms flailing, to the floor. With a gasp, the man lay still.

'Hold this while I make some light,' Cutler said, thrusting his poniard unto the watchman's hand. 'And in the meantime, you have my thanks.'

'I knew something was amiss,' Madge muttered. 'I saw no light and thought you were all abed – and I saw this bastard. Likely, he thought the house was empty – easy pickings.'

Taking the dagger, he stood menacingly over the one who was now their prisoner. Meanwhile, Cutler went upstairs to fetch the candle, brought it down and lit it. In the kitchen, he found another, and lit that too. At last, he and the watchman could gaze down upon the scowling man... and Cutler stiffened, as recognition dawned.

He should have known the voice... In the turmoil, it had barely registered. But he knew now, with cold certainty, that the person slumped in his kitchen was the same one who had accosted him two nights before, warned him off enquiring into Brisco's death and spiked him in the side for good measure. More – he had threatened Katherine and Jane. He drew a sharp breath, then saw Madge looking him up and down.

'You were abed?' He gestured, prompting Cutler to recall that he was clad only in his hose.

'Not quite,' he said.

'Shall I bind him?' the watchman asked, in a conversational tone. 'The matter is, he's the first rogue I've caught. I could lock him up somewhere till morning, then take him to the magistrate. Or...' His face fell somewhat. 'I suppose you'll want to do that?'

'There's no need, Madge – but you've done mighty well, and I'll not forget.' Cutler threw him a look of approval. 'Though you can tie him if you will, while I find some clothes.'

It was done swiftly. Cutler brought leather laces and stood guard with the poniard while Madge trussed their victim's wrists before him, drawing the bonds so tightly that the man winced. Then he stood back while Cutler went off to put on shirt and breeches. He came down to find the watchman sampling the beer from his mug, before plonking it down on the table in disgust.

'Jesu, that's sour,' he complained, wrinkling his nose. 'And what's that smell?'

'Nothing to be concerned about,' Cutler said somewhat quickly. On a whim, he had decided not to tell Madge about the prisoner's intentions. The risk of fire, among the thatched and timber-framed cottages, was always a cause of great fear. And he saw an opportunity now to turn the tables on the man who had bested him – and perhaps to get some answers at last, to the mystery that dogged him still.

'Your family,' Madge said, as if he had just remembered. 'Are they above?'

'They're away, visiting.' Cutler faced him. 'I'm alone, and will hold this one here until morning. There's no need for me to keep you from your watch.'

Madge frowned. 'Well, if that's what you wish.' He wiped his mouth and sniffed. 'I left my lantern and staff outside, so I'd best retrieve them.' Having rotated his stout body and started for the doorway, he paused to look down at the silent figure in the corner. The man had lost his cap in the struggle, revealing a head of close-cut, white hair.

'Good thing you were home and I was near, is it not? Else who knows what he'd have took.'

'That's true, Madge.' Cutler nodded. 'And I'm in your debt. Till the morrow, then?'

'Till the morrow, master constable,' the watchman answered. And he was gone, stamping along the hallway and out to the street, closing the door behind him.

Cutler waited for the latch to fall, before turning to his prisoner.

'Unlike you,' he said quietly, 'I don't intend to make it short.'

* * *

It began calmly enough. Cutler brought a stool and sat down before the bound figure, making it clear this was to be an interrogation. While the other eyed him balefully, he repeated the fact of arson being a crime that merited only one punishment.

'And I'll make sure you hang,' he said flatly. 'No one will take your word against a constable and the watchman who caught you. I'll show the whale oil, and swear on my oath that I saw you spill it. Doubtless you've a tinderbox about you somewhere – even if you didn't, I'd provide one. The magistrate hates fire-setters, and will show no mercy.'

The tied man said nothing.

'Although...' Cutler made a show of considering. 'You might want to make a clean breast of everything – like who sent you to warn me, two nights ago, to cease his *foolish delving*, as you termed it. It might make things a little easier for you... A comfortable bed and a meal in your last hours, say.'

'You can go hang yourself, constable,' came the snapped

reply. They were the first words he had spoken since his capture. 'You're a fool, who has no inkling of what he does.' A grimace appeared. 'And whether I hang or not, things will go badly for you.'

But if he intended to alarm his captor, he failed. Remaining calm, Cutler raised an eyebrow.

'Will they? Do you care to say more?'

'I could, but I'll pass. In the meantime, you'd best think harder about what I said the last time we met. I'm not one to bluff.'

'You mean, about my daughters?' Cutler's anger was rising. 'That was a mistake, for which I mean to make you pay.'

'For pity's sake...' The other let out a breath, glanced down at his hands and uttered a muffled oath; clearly, the bonds Madge had tied were beginning to trouble him. 'Don't be a simpleton,' he added. 'Free me, and do as I told you. You can still walk away from this, and be at peace.'

'At peace?' Cutler echoed. 'No... not while I'm still in the dark about what drove you to make such threats, and to warn me off hunting for Brisco's killer – what drives you still, to do what you came here for. I've not been idle – I've talked with people who knew the perfumer better than anyone here did. And I've learned—'

'Whatever you've learned, it will avail you nothing, Cutler!' the man threw back, with sudden vehemence. 'It's a fool's errand you're on – it'll bring only mayhem upon you.'

'Who sent you?' Cutler demanded, his mouth set tight. 'I'll sit here all night until you tell me – tomorrow too, if need be. By then, I wager you'll be feeling somewhat uncomfortable.'

'God's heart...' A sigh came, followed by a shake of the head. 'I heard you were stubborn, but I never took you for a dolt. Believe me, if I told you that—' But he broke off, lowering his gaze. Cutler watched him, thinking hard... until a notion flew up that shook him.

'Was it you who bribed Kett and Bland?' he demanded. 'That assault on the button-maker, to make us think Brisco's death was all of a piece... an attack on the strangers... you?'

There was no reply.

'By heaven...' Cutler leaned forward suddenly, making the other start. 'You're no more than a lackey – both messenger and servant. Carrying out orders and taking risks, while whoever sent you stays out of sight. Would you truly hang, rather than give them away? If so, you're the dolt and not me.'

'A pox on you,' the other retorted through his teeth. 'I'll say it once more: for your own sake, untie me and let me go. And forget about Brisco. I swear, it's the best course.'

'Best for whom?' Cutler held the man's gaze. 'Answer me, and mayhap we can trade.'

'Trade – what chaff!' He snorted. 'You've said I'm for the noose. Take your weasel words, and shove them down your gullet!'

But a look of uncertainty appeared on his features, as he eyed his captor. A notion had just occurred to Cutler which might break the man's refusal to talk... He paused, then sat back.

'There might be a way open to you, after all,' he said. And when the prisoner frowned: 'I could bring you to the magistrate on a charge of attempt to rob. No one else knows of your real aim. You'd get a flogging and a branding – yet you would live.'

The other drew a breath, but remained silent.

'You should consider it, at least,' Cutler resumed, thinking swiftly as he spoke. 'For what have you achieved? I'm closer to finding Brisco's murderer... I've learned much about him.' He paused, then: 'The aldermen here are ready to set his death aside, put it down to a robbery. But you and I know better than that – do we not?'

A moment passed – whereupon to Cutler's surprise, the man sagged visibly. 'You don't understand,' he sighed, lowering his eyes. 'If I fail, someone else will come.'

'Who will?' Cutler demanded, leaning forward again. 'For God's sake, why don't you tell me and be done with it?'

'I cannot!' the other retorted, with a shake of his head. 'Leave this... I'm imploring you now. Forget what you think you've learned about Brisco. Believe me, he wasn't worth the trouble you've gone to. His death was a blessing... There.' He looked up suddenly. 'Is that not enough for you?'

'It is not,' Cutler replied.

'Then, there's nothing more I can say.' And with that, the tied man closed his eyes and leaned back weakly against the wall. Bruises showed on his face, where he had been pummelled in the struggle. He looked so forlorn that Cutler could almost have pitied him.

Without further word, he rose and made his way to the table, where he sat down heavily. He snuffed out a candle, leaving the other lit. He would wait until morning, then decide what to do...

On a sudden, he felt very tired. Within minutes, he had fallen asleep.

When he awoke with a start, it was dawn. Coming to his senses, he stood up so quickly that his stool fell to the floor behind him. His gaze flew at once to the corner, where his prisoner still sat with eyes closed, exactly as he had left him...

And he almost called out, though it would have done no good. The would-be fire-setter – the one who had spared no pains in his attempts to silence him – was dead.

15

'His heart failed him, I'd wager,' Josiah Madge said, in a phlegmatic voice. 'I've seen it often enough... like poor Stephen Bland's did. This one was too old for night-stepping.'

He and Cutler stood in the kitchen, looking down at the corpse. Cutler had checked the great artery in the man's neck, and found no pulse. His flesh was as cold as glass.

'Went sometime in the night, I'd say,' the watchman added. 'Did you hear anything?' And when his only reply was a shake of the head: 'Well, master constable, here's a pickle. What are we to do with him?'

It was indeed a dilemma. Cutler had gone out soon after discovering the body, and found Madge as he finished his night watch. Now, in the chill light of early morning, decisions had to be made. 'I don't even know his name,' he said, after a pause. 'As for his crime...' He shrugged. 'It's too late for punishment now.'

'Or for magistrates,' Madge muttered. 'And it's but a week since we had the inquest on the Italian. I doubt if anyone's eager for another one – not Alderman Skinner, for sure.'

Death of a Stranger

With spirits sinking, Cutler barely nodded. He had all but forgotten the alderman of late... Now an event had occurred that could bring only more trouble. He thought briefly of his fellow guardians of the laws. Farrant, he decided, would be of no help, while Deans...

'I could lose him,' the watchman said, breaking his thoughts. 'Others do it – cart a body out of their parish, leave it for someone else to find. Take his clothes, things that would identify him, roll him into a ditch and make it look like he drowned. Christ knows, there's been rain enough this summer to fill every gulley in London.'

'By God, Madge...' Cutler stared at him. 'That's hard.'

'What else shall we do?' Madge spread his hands and let them drop. 'Neither you nor I killed him – nobody did. Knocked him about a little, but he looked tough enough to take the blows... unless you did worse, after I left you?'

'I didn't touch him,' Cutler said. 'Just told him what would happen to him.' He looked away. 'Whether that scared him enough to bring on some sort of seizure, I can't say.'

'Mayhap it did,' Madge allowed.

Despite the nature of the deceased and the things he had done, Cutler was troubled. He had never killed anyone – except on a stage with a blunted rapier, after careful rehearsal. And yet, though he may have been partly to blame for this death, the intruder had surely been the cause of his own misfortune. What Cutler regretted more was that he had failed to get anything from the man, other than renewed attempts to make him give up his quest for Brisco's murderer. On a sudden, the matter looked even murkier than before.

'I'll do it, and we'll keep it between us,' Madge said then. 'I can fetch a barrow, cover him up and wheel him out beyond Finsbury Fields. I'll drop him in the ditch by the corner of Moorfields and Postern Lane. That's in Cripplegate Ward – makes it their business.'

'By God,' Cutler said again, meeting the watchman's gaze. 'I'm almost persuaded to let you.'

'You should, master constable,' was the firm reply. 'After they stopped me collecting scavage on account of the pestilence, I carried bodies day and night. One more won't make a deal of difference – especially a varlet like this one.'

It was the best, if not the only solution; Cutler saw it, and managed a nod. It was a relief – until he recalled the dead man's chilling words, that if he failed, someone else might come. What, then, was he to do? He thought briefly of yesterday's walk back from the city, and his resolve to talk to Willard. As for Margaret Fisher...

'I said last night I was in your debt, Madge,' he said at last, facing the watchman. 'After this...' He sighed. 'It's a secret you and I will share until we die. In the meantime, let me give you a payment for your trouble.'

But Madge shook his head. 'I don't want your money. I can sell that one's belt, shoes and dagger to a fripperer... They'll fetch a goodly sum. Buy me a mug in the White Hart now and again, and we'll forget it happened.'

And without further ado, he started for the door, saying he would return with a barrow and a blanket to cover the body. Cutler let him go, and set himself to wait. Only then did he remind himself how fortuitous it was that his family had been absent – whereupon a shock followed: it struck him that that the dead man would not have known that. Had he really intended to put the lives of everyone in the house at risk of severe hurt – even of being burned to death?

On reflection, the notion of allowing his corpse to be dumped uncermoniously in a ditch sat somewhat easier upon Cutler's conscience.

* * *

It was almost midday when he arrived at Margaret's house. He had expected her to be uneasy, or even angry with him, but he was wrong. She was sitting calmly in her parlour taking a light dinner, and merely acknowledged his arrival with a nod before ordering her servant to set another place. Conversation, it seemed, should wait until after the meal. For his part, Cutler was so hungry that he fell to with alacrity, hardly lifting his head until he had cleared his plate. A pudding of apricots with cream then appeared, but he demurred.

'I think my guest is sated,' Margaret said to her servant. The man, discreet as always, left them alone, whereupon she poured ale from the jug with her own hand and passed a cup to him. 'Was your visit to the Countess of Tanridge profitable?' she enquired.

'I didn't spend the night there, if that's how your mind moves,' Cutler said. 'Matters turned out somewhat unexpectedly.' He paused, wiped his mouth with a napkin and met her gaze. 'Are you in the humour to hear my tale, or...?'

'You know full well that I am.' She looked him over, now with some concern. 'But you alarm me, Matthew. What's happened?'

He told her, leaving nothing out. She listened in silence... but when he spoke of the events of the morning, she grew uneasy. Josiah Madge, true to his word, had taken the body of the unknown man away. Cutler had done no more than put the house to rights and dispose of the jar of oil before leaving.

'I have your late husband's clothes, tied in a bundle,' he

finished. 'They're somewhat damp, but none the worse for wear. I don't expect to take the role of perfumer again.'

'By heaven...' Margaret let out a sigh. 'This business troubles me now, more than ever.'

'As it does me,' Cutler said. 'I need to talk to John Willard, try to puzzle it out.'

'Without me, you mean?'

He shook his head. 'I thought, after all that's occurred, that the three of us might put our heads together – if you're willing, that is?'

'And if I were not?' She arched her eyebrows. 'Given the fact that I seem to have become an accomplice to deception of various kinds, what would you have me do?'

'Heaven only knows,' he replied – then caught the look in her eye, and relaxed. 'In truth, I feared I'd outstayed my welcome here, even that—'

'If you're about to speak of putting me in further danger, and all that follows, you may save your breath,' Margaret said. 'I'm angered by what's been done.' She lowered her gaze. 'Had that fellow succeeded in what he intended last night, I would have...'

She broke off, took up her cup and drank. After a moment, Cutler did the same.

'Nonetheless, I abhor what I've brought upon you, and upon my family,' he said.

'I know it,' Margaret murmured. 'I'd think less of you if you did not.'

Upon which she rose and, since the rain was holding off, suggested a walk in the fields to settle their dinner.

* * *

In the evening, as John Willard was shutting up his shop, the two of them surprised him by arriving together. Bishopsgate Street was quiet, apart from the occasional roar of cannon-fire from the artillery yard, it being Thursday. The gunsmith, whose house was too close to the yard for comfort, had stuffed his ears with scraps of cloth. At sight of Cutler and Margaret, not quite arm in arm but looking suspiciously like a couple, he pulled out the wadding and looked them over.

'I'm honoured, Mistress Fisher.' He inclined his head. 'And master constable... will you come indoors? Something tells me you've tidings to impart.'

After brief greetings, the two of them followed him inside. Willard closed the door while Cutler found stools and saw Margaret seated. For himself, he was restless and remained on his feet. Their host brought his jug of watered wine and cups, which Margaret accepted. She and Willard had long known each other, but had not spoken since her return to Bishopsgate. Some small talk followed, before the gunsmith's gaze drifted towards his son-in-law.

'I've thought a little, since our last talk,' he said. 'Done some fitting together, you might say... like fashioning a snaphaunce pistol. Only, you never know how well it'll fire until you take it outside and try it. Mayhap you'd like to speak first?'

It was done swiftly: Cutler recounted his tale again, as he had for Margaret. He was impatient, and could not hide it. When, once again, he came to the end of his encounter with the now-deceased fire-setter, Willard was as uneasy as she had been. In his case, however, the potential threat to his sister and grandchildren was hard to bear.

'Jesu...' he breathed in, shaking his head. 'I'd like to have been there, when you had that devil at your mercy. It seems to me he got what he deserved, after all he's done.'

'Yet, I like it not,' Cutler admitted. 'I think he could have been made to talk, sooner or later.'

'And what do you think he could have told you?' Willard asked.

'The name of whoever it was who sent him, at the least.'

The gunsmith was thoughtful. 'Well, I doubt that. But even if he had, I fear it would bring you no comfort.' And when his son-in-law frowned: 'Have you no suspicions yet, as to who gave the fellow his orders?'

'Let's say that I haven't, John,' Cutler replied, somewhat wearily. 'And I've pummelled my head for long enough. Some say you've the best mind in Bishopsgate...' He glanced at Margaret. 'Though Mistress Fisher here would run you close. Give us your thoughts.'

'Well, I will...' Willard hesitated. 'But first, think again on all that's happened over the past week, will you? Since Brisco's death, the assault on Meunier after Kett and Bland were bribed... the hard warning to you, and now the attempt to burn your house. You could say that someone's grown desperate, could you not?'

'You said the fire-setter claimed he was not one to bluff.' Margaret spoke up, facing Cutler. 'It seems that last night's action was proof of it... In short, you were supposed to die.'

'It would seem so,' he agreed.

'And upon which, all would be over,' the gunsmith said, with a nod. 'Since the only one who's been concerned enough to find out who murdered the perfumer would be gone, no difficulty would remain for those who wished the matter closed.' He paused, then: 'Hence, we should wonder who stands to gain by that.'

It was indeed the nub of the matter, and Cutler knew it well enough. 'Aside from our alderman, who would prefer to forget the whole distasteful business – and whoever killed Brisco, of course – that remains dark to me,' he said. 'And no,' he added, 'I don't believe the man who threatened me was the one. A hired lackey, and hard enough, but I can't see him stabbing the perfumer to death in the way it was done. In truth, I see now that he was somewhat clumsy in his attempts – and he failed.'

'Well then.' Willard nodded again. 'Let's consider Brisco afresh, shall we? What could he have done – or who could he have angered enough, to end up as he did?'

'When you speak of him, I can't help but think of his paramours,' Margaret put in. 'Those bored wives... In truth, I still struggle to see that man as a rutting scapegrace, who used his moments of intimacy so shamelessly.'

Cutler said nothing, thinking of his encounters with both Lady Wheatley and the Countess of Tanridge – but Willard, it seemed, was ahead of him.

'It's what passed between those women and him that sits badly with me,' he said. 'I've pondered it ever since you spoke of it. Those private matters of state, that the countess babbled to Brisco about. Whether she was drunk, or merely consumed with bitterness, it was most reckless. To my mind, it amounts to treason.'

'But surely Brisco must have known that?' Margaret was frowning.

'By God...' Cutler looked up sharply. 'Do you mean that gathering such material was his intention?'

'Bullseye, Matthew!' his father-in-law exclaimed, startling them both. 'That is indeed the way my mind moves. Those men we know of, whose wives Willard served – Wheatley, and the Earl of Tanridge. Privy Councillors both, and concerned with the defence of the realm. Have we forgotten that we're at war with Spain – a Papist power, that would overrun us and return

England to the old religion? And here among us, live men who privately wish the armada had succeeded!'

He was nodding fiercely; his words hung in the air, causing Margaret to start. 'Do you mean to suggest that our perfumer, a respected citizen of Bishopsgate, was a spy?' She gazed at Willard. 'Can it be possible?'

'Well, in truth, I'm uncertain. What think you, master constable?'

They looked to Cutler, whose mind had leaped. He had already formed another picture of Alessandro Brisco: a courteous man who minded his business, yet was intimate with the wives of important men – at least one of whom had been willing enough to tell him things known only to those in government. What if the sober and seemingly pious Lady Wheatley had done the same, wittingly or not?

'What do I think?' He met Willard's eye. 'I think – nay, I fear you may be right.'

They were quiet, each taking in the notion. Margaret, who was stunned, took a drink from her cup. Willard had calmed – and it was Cutler's turn to become animated.

'If one of the husbands – Wheatley or Tanridge, say – had learned of his wife's dealings with the perfumer, there would be little question of their wanting him dead,' he said. 'Yet' – this with his eyes on his father-in-law – 'you doubted they would stoop to such. And surely Brisco would have been arrested, to be hauled before interrogators? The Queen's servants would be eager to know what he had discovered, let alone—'

'Let alone what he had done with such knowledge,' Willard broke in. 'Is that not the sticking point? Who would he have told?'

'By heaven – this feels almost like a council of war,' Margaret murmured, almost in disbelief. 'Yet, who are we fighting?'

'We fight Spain, Mistress Fisher,' the gunsmith answered. 'As we've done for almost a decade... yet wars are not only fought on land and at sea, or even in rooms of state. They're fought in the shadows, between unseen enemies... men like Brisco, perhaps.'

But Cutler wasn't listening. Still on his feet, he had taken a few paces away, before turning abruptly. 'You asked whom he could have told.' He eyed Willard. 'Well, here's a notion: his old landlord, Scamozzi, whom the countess said he adored, is another Papist – if one of a different stamp. Rich and haughty... one who cares little for the country he resides in, I might even say. What if—'

'Hoxton!' his father-in-law broke in sharply. 'You've said he dwells in Hoxton – where he's not alone among Catholics. The ambassador of Portugal had a house there... So does Sir Thomas Tresham, as notorious a Papist as any in England. By the Christ – there is your link!'

They stared at each other, astounded by the conclusion. Here, it seemed, was a truth exposed, as stark as it was alarming.

Brisco had wheedled state secrets out of the wives of Privy Councillors, by charm by and guile... secrets he could then have passed to Scamozzi, who could have passed them on to someone who knew how to use them.

'I'm supposed to be a constable here,' Cutler said at last, with a shake of his head. 'Not an intelligencer. All I tried to do was find a murderer, and bring justice to my Ward. Now what have I done?'

Neither of the others had an answer. Willard drank and lowered his gaze; even he was subdued, as the implications of their discovery sank in – if, indeed, it was correct. Proving it, Cutler realised, would be a far harder proposition. The weight of it fell upon him, almost visibly as he pondered it.

'It's too grave a matter for me,' he said. 'I've no choice but to take it to a greater authority... which means Thomas Skinner, I suppose.' He grimaced. 'He'll be angry that I've ploughed this furrow against his wishes. Likely, he'll dismiss me as constable... and do you know?' He looked at the others. 'I care not a jot if he does. Let someone else shoulder the burden.'

'I confess, in your place, I'd feel the same, Matthew.' His father-in-law shook his head. 'Even if these are but suspicions on our part, the Queen's council must hear of them. Let them act as they will – although...' His face darkened. 'I fear it's you they'll haul in for questioning. They'd want to know how much the flighty Countess told you, while she was soused.'

'She told me nothing of value,' Cutler said. 'Even if they racked me, they'd learn no more.'

'I pray you, don't speak of such!' Margaret exclaimed. 'You've done no wrong, save to exceed your powers, perhaps. Let Skinner do his worst.'

'Well, it's settled,' he told her. 'I'll go to him in the morning. It will be a relief to get it off my chest...' He faced Willard. 'In the meantime, I'll ask you—'

'Save your breath,' the gunsmith broke in. 'I'm saying nothing to anyone. Yet...' He shook his head. 'I don't envy you, Matthew. And I'll not be at ease until I see my grandchildren home safe with you, and this whole affair behind us.'

Cutler barely nodded; there was no more to be said. Having made his resolve, he was already thinking of the morrow, and what would surely be a fraught meeting with the alderman.

Having bade John Willard goodnight, he and Margaret took their leave, stepping out into Bishopsgate Street. A wind had got up, bringing a threat of more rain.

'You're not going home again, are you,' she said as they began walking. It was more of an instruction than a question.

Cutler shook his head.

* * *

Friday dawned, as rainy as he had expected. Had it not been for the hooded cape borrowed from Margaret, he would have arrived at the alderman's house soaking wet. Walking determinedly, he passed through the city gate and into St Helen's parish. To his surprise, his heart was light. He had escaped being burned to death... Just now, whatever Thomas Skinner might say or do would seem somewhat trivial. Gathering himself, he arrived at the door, knocked and was admitted.

This particular morning, however, would soon pass out of his control.

To begin with, Cutler's visit being unexpected, the alderman kept him waiting in the hallway while he conducted business with a gentleman in his parlour. By the time the guest had departed, he was on edge, having turned his position about until he was weary of it. The notion of making a clean breast of everything now looked less like affording him relief, and more like provoking the irascible Skinner to anger. When he was finally shown into the man's presence, he was as tight-wound as a bowstring. He found the alderman seated at his table and made a perfunctory greeting, whereupon:

'I know what you've come about, constable,' Skinner snapped. And when Cutler blinked: 'Deans was here yesterday, bewailing his lot again – how Bishopsgate Without is almost bereft of officers. I speak not only of the loss of Kett and Bland, but the fact that, according to Deans, you're seldom seen about the Ward. Moreover, even Farrant seems elusive these days. It must be remedied – and soon. Do you not agree?'

'I do, alderman.' Cutler suppressed a sigh. 'Yet in truth, that's not why I've come. I'm here on a matter of some gravity.'

The other frowned. 'In God's name, don't tell me you're still harping on the Brisco business?'

'I fear I must. For it's grown far beyond my compass. Will you hear me?'

'By heaven...' Skinner gave a start. 'There's not been another murder, has there?'

'No, but there could have been – and I mean mine,' Cutler rejoined, before he could stop himself. 'You might say I'm fortunate to be standing here...' He broke off. 'It's not a pretty tale,' he added. 'Yet it must be laid out. You will see why.'

'Will I?' It was the alderman who gave a sigh. 'Well then, you'd better tell it.'

He did, for perhaps the third time – or had he lost count? It was become a litany. Starting from the events of the previous Sunday, following his last meeting with Skinner, he told of the warning he had received at dagger-point that same night. After that, while his listener grew more incredulous by the minute, he gave a day-by-day account of all that had happened, leading up to yesterday's talk with Willard. He was obliged to include Margaret Fisher too, given her part in their outings as Sir Amos and Lady Gallett. The only thing he omitted was the death of the would-be fire-setter – Skinner would have taken a dim view of Madge's disposal of the body. Instead, he was obliged to concoct a tale of the man running away on being discovered. Having told all, he felt both unburdened – and somehow, guilty.

'I know you'll dislike what you've heard, Master Skinner,' he finished. 'As I know I've disregarded your advice. I believed I was acting for the best, but doubtless you'll form your own opinion.' Seeing the look on the other's face, he awaited the explosion.

'Great God, constable...' For once, the alderman was almost speechless. 'Brisco a spy for the Papists – for Spain?'

'It looks that way to me,' Cutler replied, after a pause. 'I can only tell you what I've – what we've – learned.'

'But it's... fantastical!'

'Speculation, I'll admit. Either way, it's too great a matter for me.'

'Too great?' Skinner was staring down at his table, as if the quill and inkpot might concur in his disbelief. 'Not just for you – for all of us.'

Cutler remained silent.

'As for accusing Privy Councillors' wives of such perfidy... such recklessness...' He looked up helplessly. 'Can you not see what you've done?'

'I suppose I can,' Cutler answered, somewhat wearily. 'And in truth, alderman, I'm at the end of my tether. Dismiss me if you will, or do what—'

'Enough!' At last, Skinner seemed to be recovering. 'I'll hear no more of your notions.' With another sigh, he leaned back in his chair. 'Just now, I could curse you to Hades and back, and yet...' He shook his head, then eyed his constable grimly.

'And yet, what if it's true?' Cutler suggested.

It was the alderman's turn to say nothing. The silence grew, until finally, he slapped a hand down on his table. It came almost as a relief.

'You can't go back to Bishopsgate,' Skinner announced. 'You'll stay here, while I get word to others... though as yet I'm uncertain who to tell.' He glared at Cutler. 'God knows what they'll do with you, after your preposterous adventures.'

'If I'm to be interrogated,' Cutler said, 'I can tell nothing more than I've told you.'

'But by heaven, will you think on it?' The alderman leaned forward. 'If there's a shred of truth to your accusations, the Privy Council will be dismayed. Whatever news or tidings the Countess of Tanridge might have passed to Brisco – and I'm yet to be convinced that she did any such thing – the result could be terrible. We speak of the safety of England!'

'I realise that, alderman. It's why I'm here.'

'Well, you'd better make yourself comfortable,' Skinner retorted, growing brisk. 'You can wait in the pantry down the hall, and take dinner in the kitchen. I'll issue orders to my cook – in the meantime I've messages to send to men of rank... I hope to God they don't think I've lost my sanity!'

Upon which, Cutler found himself dismissed.

16

Outside the pantry, matters may have been moving at pace – but for Cutler, it was a long and tiresome wait.

Two or three hours had passed, and he was beyond feeling restless. He had paced the cramped little room with its shelves of dried herbs and jars of preserves, venturing at times out into the hallway. He had heard the front door open, and footfalls, but no one came for him. Around midday, the mousy-haired maid brought him into the kitchen for a dinner of mutton pie and small beer. Apart from the cook, there were no other servants present. Afterwards, having no desire to kick his heels any longer, he was on the point of going to Skinner to protest when footsteps sounded from the hall. On leaving the kitchen, he saw the alderman himself approaching.

'With me, Cutler,' he said brusquely. 'There's someone wishes to speak with you.'

He followed Skinner into his parlour, to find a man he did not know seated at the alderman's table. He was well-dressed, young and alert, with an air of authority which Cutler found reassuring. Having been invited to take a vacant stool, he sat while Skinner removed himself to a chair near the wall. Whereupon, the one who was clearly in charge spoke up.

'I'll spare you having to recount the whole tale again, Cutler. Master Skinner has furnished me with the gist of it.' Seeing that his words came as something of a relief, he added, 'I confess I'm surprised that a constable has done so much in pursuit of justice in his parish. To my mind, you're an odd man for such an office... then, I understand you used to be a player. At the Rose, was it?'

'At the Curtain, and the Old Theatre now and then,' Cutler answered, wondering where this was leading. 'I'm content to leave those days behind me now...'

'Save when you impersonated a knight, and bluffed your way into the homes of two of the Queen's Privy Councillors,' the young man finished, somewhat curtly. 'That was rash.'

'If it please you,' Cutler said quickly, 'I do not wish that my friend – the lady who posed as my wife – be censured for her part. It was entirely my ploy, which she undertook merely to please me.'

'You're clearly a persuasive man, then,' the other said. 'So – will you tell me more of your encounter with Lady Wheatley?'

'There's little more to tell. She clearly had feelings of affection for the perfumer, and was saddened by his death. I... Forgive me, sir, but might I know who I'm addressing?'

'I serve the Queen's council,' came the terse reply, 'and my name is unimportant. Pray continue.'

'Very well.' Cutler drew a breath, and gave a brief summary of his and Margaret's short sojourn with Lady Joanna in the garden of her house in Hart Street. As he finished, he heard Skinner give a snort of disapproval from his place by the wall, but ignored it.

'And your visit to the lady was prompted by a chance remark of a perfumer in the Exchange?' the Queen's man enquired, regarding him keenly.

'Nothing more – a whim, if you like.'

'Yet for all of that, you've no evidence that Lady Wheatley spoke to Brisco of matters touching on her husband's duties.'

'I have not,' Cutler answered. 'Only suspicions, sharpened by what I learned when I attended the Countess of Tanridge.'

'Suspicions?' the young man echoed. 'That's what drove you, and nothing more?'

Cutler nodded, finding himself eager to speak of his far more momentous visit to the countess, but for some reason, the questioner seemed reluctant to move on.

'How much do you know of Sir Titus Wheatley, Cutler?' he demanded.

'Only that he was active in our defence during the armada summer. His wife spoke briefly of his preoccupation with ships and sailors, as she put it. The topic seemed to bore her.'

By the wall, Skinner stirred impatiently, but the Queen's man seemed not to notice. 'Do you believe she cuckolded her husband with the perfumer?' he asked abruptly.

'In truth, I cannot answer that.'

'Yet you suspect it.' And when Cutler hesitated: 'Come now, constable. A wise man – let me call you that – knows the world he lives in. Do you think Lady Wheatley shared moments of intimacy with Brisco, during which she may have – inadvertently or not – spoken to him of Sir Titus' duties as aide to the Lord Admiral?'

'I think it possible,' he answered. 'Though I'm more certain of my ground with regard to what the countess told me—'

'I will come to that,' the other broke in.

A moment followed, in which Cutler grew aware of a quick mind at work, sifting facts from fancy. But when the young man spoke up again, he had shifted ground.

'This attempt to set your house alight, and your timely

prevention of it,' he said. And when Cutler stiffened: 'You insist that you have no idea who the intruder was?'

'Only that he was the same man who threatened me some days before, when he ordered me to cease looking into Brisco's death.' With a frown, he added, 'I also believe he was the one who bribed Constable Kett and the watchman Bland, to stage the attack on a button-maker in our Ward, and hence divert attention from—'

'By heaven, not that again!' It was Skinner, half-rising from his chair. 'We've been all over this tedious ground – sir,' he added, looking at the Queen's man. 'Do you not wish to delve into Brisco's alleged treachery, and what stems from it? It strikes me—'

'Will you kindly leave the room, alderman?' the other asked, turning to him.

'Your pardon?' Skinner stared. 'This is my house, sir...'

'I wish to question the constable further.' The man's tone was adamant. 'And I don't have all day at my disposal.'

A moment passed, but there could be no refusal. Cutler watched, and despite everything, suppressed a smile of satisfaction as the alderman stood up angrily. He looked briefly at both men, but said nothing as he made his way to the door.

As soon as it closed, the inquisitor relaxed visibly.

'Now, constable,' he said, affably enough. 'Tell me what you really did with the fire-setter, rather than spin me this cock-and-bull tale about letting him escape.'

* * *

It was, he would think later, one of the strangest conversations he had ever had. His instinct was to be evasive, being loth to involve Josiah Madge in the business of concealing a death and preventing a lawful burial – let alone a possible charge of causing the man's demise. He considered, before deciding what he would say.

'I fought with the fellow, and overpowered him,' he said. 'But he made a run while I got my poniard – it was mere luck that the watchman, Madge, stopped him at the door. Thereafter, we dragged him inside and bound him, and Madge returned to his duties. I told him nothing of the man's attempt at arson, which would have troubled him. He thought him merely a thief, and left it to me to bring him to the magistrate in the morning. I tried to question the prisoner, but he would tell me nothing. I decided to let him stew, and fell asleep. On my waking, I found him dead. I believe his heart failed... He was not a young man, and likely unsuited to his task.'

'So, you had a corpse on your hands?' the Queen's man prompted. 'That must have been inconvenient.'

Cutler blinked; the man's tone was almost conversational. 'It was,' he admitted. 'Hence, I borrowed a wheelbarrow, covered the body up and took it out through Finsbury Fields, to Moorfields. There's a ditch by Postern Lane...'

He stopped himself, for the inquisitor had raised a hand quickly. 'There is, save that it's hardly deep enough to drown a man,' he said, with a wry look. 'Unless he were so drunk, he couldn't even lift his head to breathe. And I've never known a drunken man strip himself down to his hose, before falling into a ditch which is a long way from the nearest alehouse. In short, when a body was found there yesterday morning, the constables of Cripplegate Ward thought it suspicious and reported it to the Lord Mayor's office, whence by roundabout means, I learned of it.'

Stunned, Cutler remained silent.

'I learned of it,' the other went on briskly, 'because the fellow who was unlucky enough to fall foul of you and your watchman is no stranger to some of us. Though he had clearly lost his skills of late, since he's proved to be such a consummate bungler.'

'You knew him?' Cutler stared in disbelief. 'Then, who in—'

'His name is of no consequence.' The Queen's man waved a hand dismissively. 'Call him Burrell. He's used so many over the years, I doubt he remembers his true name anyway. It's what he did that's of consequence: to whit, hiring himself out to those who will pay handsomely to make their troubles go away. As he tried to do – most clumsily – with regard to the killing of the perfumer Brisco. Bribing your fellow constable to stage that feeble attack on the Frenchman, warning you off, and—'

'And sending letters, accusing other people of committing the murder?' Cutler broke in. 'One was sent here, to the alderman.'

'That doesn't surprise me.' The other gave a shrug. 'As I said, all done clumsily... and to no avail, since it appears merely to have spurred you to greater efforts.'

'By heaven.' Cutler sagged. 'I thought I was in a fog. Now it's lifted a little, and yet...' He frowned. 'The question still remains: who hired him to do what he did, to try and put everyone off the scent?'

'That is, indeed, the proper question,' came the reply.

A silence fell – but to Cutler, the Queen's man's words brought relief. He had been right about most things: that none of those at first suspected, like Martinhouse or Wincott – let alone accused, like Henry Deans – had killed Brisco. Moreover, the man whose death he still felt responsible for had been a rogue of the first order, working for the true culprit – yet he was not the murderer either. He nodded to himself, and found the other man eying him.

'Now tell me more about the Countess of Tanridge,' he invited. 'Did she try to seduce you, or was she too drunk?'

* * *

It took only a short time for Cutler to tell of his visit to Tanridge House on the river. Feeling a deal calmer, he spoke freely of all that had occurred, ending with his last sight of the unhappy woman stretched out on her Turkey carpet. The Queen's man, whose name he did not know and suspected he never would, listened intently. Then:

'What a tawdry business,' he said, after Cutler had ended his account. 'And what a deal of trouble the countess has caused – more than she could imagine, I'm certain. As for her husband...' He shook his head. 'That is not for your ears. In truth, you've already learned far more than is good for you.'

'I suspected as much,' Cutler admitted. 'I know I've gone beyond my duties – I even broke the law by removing a body. But I came to the alderman to own what I did.' He gave a sigh. 'It was a burr that stuck, which I couldn't dislodge.'

'A strong desire for justice is not to be made light of, constable.'

He frowned, as the other man regarded him keenly.

'You've been forward – even reckless,' he added. 'Yet, inadvertently or not, you've done the state good service. You may be as loyal an Englishman as any I know.'

'Well, I may be a magistrate's son, but I never dreamed of revealing a Papist spy,' Cutler said, feeling helpless. 'If that's what Brisco was.' And when the inquisitor said nothing: 'What will happen now? Am I to sign a paper swearing secrecy, or am I—'

'To be arrested?' The other raised his eyebrows. 'Do you think you deserve it?'

Cutler had no reply.

'Well now, let us speculate,' came the rejoinder. 'And I want your word that nothing I say will go any further than this room. Is that understood?'

This was unexpected. Cutler blinked, then nodded.

'Very well. Let's say that Brisco was all that you – and I too, for argument's sake – suspect he was: a stranger in our country who, despite appearances, remained fiercely loyal to his religion and to the Papacy. He was in contact with others of his faith, who secretly favour Spain. Brisco had charm and wit, and under the harmless cover of a perfumer attending the wives of important men, was able to draw intelligence from them. Who, then, would he pass such tidings to? An agent of Spain, of course. A Portuguese exile, for example, or—'

'Another Italian?' Cutler broke in. It had hit him once again: the man the Countess of Tanridge had spoken of as one Brisco adored – his landlord. He drew a breath and named him: Niccolo Scamozzi.

'Scamozzi.' the Queen's man repeated it. 'You reason well, constable.'

A moment followed, in which Cutler's thoughts flew wildly. He pictured the imposing figure who had spoken at Brisco's inquest... and who had been at pains to settle matters quickly, taking charge of the body. But then, doubts soon arose. The man was successful in business, seemingly content to dwell in England... Would he really be a party to aiding in its overthrow?

'In truth, I'm uncertain now,' he said at last. 'It's a leap to judgement.'

'It is,' the other agreed. 'And without proof, most hard to justify. The man is well known to city merchants, even to noblemen.'

'Through money-lending?' Cutler put in. 'Brisco had many debtors, I've learned. I wondered where he first obtained the funds for such...' He stopped, for his inquisitor was nodding.

'One sure way to gain men's confidence is to aid them when they're in need,' he said.

It was beginning to make sense. Using money supplied by Scamozzi, Brisco had made loans and gained access to various people – even aiding lesser folk like Austen Kett, perhaps merely to demonstrate good will. Cutler considered, while the other man regarded him shrewdly.

'And while we're speculating,' he murmured, 'tell me this: what would you do, to expose a powerful man like Scamozzi as an agent for a foreign power – one with which we're at war?'

'I?' Cutler frowned. 'Do you toy with me, sir? You said I've already learned more than is good for me, hence—'

'Pray, indulge me,' the other broke in. 'You were a player. You're blessed with a skill for invention... I might say extempore. Sir Amos Gallett – wasn't that the role you chose, in your investigation? I almost wish I'd been there to see it.'

But Cutler was uneasy now; this was more than unexpected. On a sudden, he wondered whether this was why the quick-witted young servant of the Queen's Council had told Skinner to leave the two of them alone. He hesitated, then:

'If you truly wish me to speculate, I might suggest that someone go to Scamozzi on some pretext... asking to borrow money, say. Then try to get him to incriminate himself, and—'

'Crack this nut,' the other finished. 'I applaud you.'

'Your pardon, sir...' Cutler showed his unease. 'This is beyond me. I've told you all I can. I wish nothing more now than to return to my parish – if I'm allowed to, that is.'

'No doubt – and yet, you underestimate yourself.' Having adopted a conversational tone, the Queen's man grew brisk again. 'I said you were an odd fit for a constable,' he resumed. 'Educated, yet seemingly content with a humble post in an outlying ward like Bishopsgate... a backwater, some might say. Is that truly enough for one like you, Cutler? Or – answer me plainly now: did you not secretly enjoy playing Sir Amos and Lady Gallett with your obliging friend, and mingling with noblewomen?'

'And if I did?' Cutler drew a breath – and in an instant, he understood. 'By God... you cannot mean that the someone who goes to Scamozzi should be me?'

There was no answer.

'You are serious?'

'Tell me, which university did you attend?' the inquisitor asked. But when Cutler replied that he had done no more than waste a year at Cambridge, he nodded. 'I thought as much. I was at St Benet's – and you?'

'St John's – though somewhat before your time, I think.'

'Yes... but let's return to the notion of visiting Scamozzi. It would be brave, would it not?' To Cutler's unease, the young man appeared excited. 'And most profitable for England, should it succeed in its aim. There might even be rewards, for those who undertook such a venture.'

'Forgive me, sir, but this grows fanciful,' Cutler objected. 'If you truly imagine me going to Scamozzi alone, and trying to get some kind of intelligence from him, then—'

'Oh, you would not be alone. I would be there too, posing as your servant.'

They eyed each other. The man did indeed appear to be making a serious suggestion, which was alarming enough... whereupon another notion occurred to Cutler. And since things had gone this far already, he felt bold enough to voice it.

'This... deception you describe,' he began cautiously. 'Should it succeed, if that's not too wild a notion – I suppose it would win great approval from the Council, that one of their younger servants had accomplished such a feat? You spoke of rewards...?'

'I did,' came the swift reply. 'And your part in the venture would not be overlooked, constable. You have my word on it.'

So, there it stood: this ambitious young man had his own agenda – to unmask a servant of Spain, and win plaudits for his efforts. Moreover, he was prepared to use Cutler in the process. It almost took his breath away.

'Think on it,' the other said. 'For it's not so fanciful as you imagine. Scamozzi, so I hear, entertains people of note on Saturdays at his house in Hoxton: merchants, speculators and so forth. It's a popular gathering – and there's no reason why, say, Sir Amos Gallett should not attend along with his servant, seeking a private word with the host. As you suggested, it could be that Sir Amos wants a loan, to aid him in a forthcoming venture. They repair to a private room – given the importance of the matter, Sir Amos has insisted on it – where Scamozzi finds himself confronted and given a stark choice: leave quietly with us now, or—'

'Or what – sir?' In exasperation, Cutler shook his head. 'Do you truly think it would be so easy? A man like that would be wary of anyone he doesn't know – he would have people nearby, and—'

'Of course he would.' As before, the inquisitor waved a hand airily. 'But I believe it can be done. With your powers of persuasion – and mine too, if I might be so boastful – we can get something from him. Enough, at least, for me to take to my masters.' He paused, then: 'I know I ask a great deal from you. But the gains could be great – you have a family to think of, do you not?' And when Cutler stiffened: 'I pray you, consider well. After this, you might not have to remain a mere constable. And I, for one, would gladly see you rewarded.'

'I came here expecting censure,' Cutler said, after some moments had passed. 'Now...' He frowned. 'Did you have this scheme in mind from the start? Is that why you asked the alderman to leave us?' And when the other gave no answer: 'Is there nothing more you will tell me? Your name, perhaps?'

'I will be Barnabas – your devoted servant,' came the reply. 'That is, if you're prepared to step forth as Sir Amos once again.'

'Well, do I have a choice?'

'You do. Although, given your neglect of your duties, along with your casual regard for the law...' The other met his gaze squarely. 'Who knows what might follow?'

At which, Cutler lowered his gaze. A part of him wanted to tell this manipulative young man to go hang himself, and damn the consequences. Fortunately, he had enough self-possession to dismiss such an action... He looked up.

'Tomorrow afternoon, you say?'

The inquisitor – or Barnabas, as it seemed he should be called – nodded. 'I will meet you, clad as Sir Amos, on the road out of Shoreditch, two hours after midday.' With that, he smiled, which startled Cutler. The change in the man's demeanour was striking: a handsome charmer, not unlike Nicholas Wincott – and used to getting his own way.

Though how the two of them would fare together, he could not imagine.

***

A short while later, he was walking back to Bishopsgate in the rain, heedless of all about him. All he could think of was that he had been cajoled into taking part in the attempted entrapment of a suspected agent for Spain, alongside a man he had just met who would pose as his servant. It was as absurd as it was dangerous – and to his mind, almost certain to fail. He was through the city gate and back in his home parish before he realised that he had forgotten all about the hooded cape he had borrowed, and was now soaked to the skin.

But the matter paled to insignificance after he arrived back at Margaret's house, and told her what had occurred. For without a moment's hesitation, she announced that once again, she would be taking the role of Lady Clarinda Gallett, and accompanying her husband Sir Amos to the house of Signor Scamozzi on the morrow.

And she would remain deaf to his protests.

17

'You cannot go,' Cutler told her, for perhaps the third time. 'The venture is dangerous, and the outcome uncertain. Nor did this man suggest you should be involved. I—'

'You forbid it?' Margaret wore a severe look, even though her eyes sparkled with excitement. 'On what authority, pray?'

They were sitting at supper, though Cutler had barely touched his. The enormity of what he had somehow agreed to do lay heavily upon him. Having changed out of his sodden clothing and dried himself, he had taken a welcome drink before telling her of the plan, expecting her to be abashed. Later, he would realise that he should have known better.

'You could ruin the scheme,' he tried. 'Aside from the risks, will you not consider that?'

'So could you,' she retorted. 'I'm sure Scamozzi's no fool... He might suspect from the start that you're no more a knight of the realm than his stableboy. You need a well-bred wife with you to add credence, as I did with Lady Wheatley.'

'And displeased her,' he replied. 'Would you use such haughtiness again?'

'So, you can see me in the role after all?'

She had a look that he recognised: more mischievous than anything. To Margaret, it was an adventure, while to Cutler... He sighed, and surrendered.

'Well, it seems you're determined,' he said. 'I can hardly prevent you... and in truth, you may be right that it would help in the deception. But I'm not the one you must convince. If this man... this courtier, or whatever he is, refuses to have you along, there's the end of it.'

'I see that,' she replied. 'Clearly, I must use my powers of persuasion. But it's all to the good, is it not?'

Upon which she lifted her cup and urged him to drink to the success of their venture. With a resigned air, he took up his own cup, his thoughts already drifting to the morrow. In her excitement, Margaret may have relished the thought of helping to entrap a Spanish agent. For his part, Cutler could not help thinking of all the things that could go wrong – starting with the disapproval he expected from his new servant Barnabas, when they met with him on the road to Hoxton.

As it turned out, in that matter at least, he was mistaken.

* * *

Saturday dawned, warm and breezy but mercifully dry. Having spent the morning choosing their clothing and making ready, Cutler and Margaret, now suitably clad as Sir Amos and Lady Gallett, left her house at the appointed time and walked for half a mile along the highway out of Shoreditch. There were people on the road, but with Margaret keeping her face shaded by her straw hat, and Cutler with his jewelled headpiece pulled low, they were not recognised. Having passed the last cottage, they were nearing a thicket by the roadside when someone stepped out in front of them... causing Cutler to stop in surprise.

The confident young Queen's servant he had encountered the previous day was gone, and in his place was a fawning lackey, plainly dressed, who touched his cap and bowed low. The transformation, he had to admit, was striking.

'Well met, Sir Amos,' the man said, smiling broadly. 'Are you well today?' Whereupon his gaze fell on Margaret, causing him to lose the smile at once.

'I thought you would come alone,' he said.

'My wife, Lady Clarinda,' Cutler said, feeling utterly foolish. 'She insisted, but if you—'

'Barnabas, is it?' Margaret lifted her head and regarded the newcomer with a supercilious air. 'I trust you know your duties. I'll be your mistress henceforth – and I will brook no slackness.'

A short silence followed. Cutler looked aside, expecting a riposte. But the other, having gazed at his companion for a while, suddenly brightened.

'What a splendid idea,' he said. 'I mean... your servant, my lady.' He bowed low again.

'Well, that's settled then.' Margaret turned to her player-husband. 'Are you content now, Sir Amos?'

But before he could respond, the one to be known as Barnabas laid a hand on her arm.

'I'll quit my role just once and say this, madam,' he murmured, leaning closer. 'Lest you forget yourself, I have charge of the projection. It's not a game. Whatever I instruct you to do, you must comply. Your friend here understands that.'

Whereupon, without waiting for a reply, he stepped back and assumed his servant's role again. In spite of himself, Cutler was impressed; the man was a natural player, who could work upon the stage if he chose. Not to be outdone, he cleared his throat.

'I think we've wasted enough time, Barnabas,' he sniffed. 'Signor Scamozzi awaits us. Though it would have been more fitting had you brought a coach, or at the least, horses.'

'Indeed, it was remiss of me, sir,' came the swift response. 'Yet, I feel certain your host will be unaware of how you arrive. Might I suggest you get familiar with the house as well as the company, before you approach him?'

Upon which, the three of them exchanged looks... and despite his unease at what might lie ahead, Cutler breathed more easily. The first hurdle was over; henceforth, he could only play his part to the utmost, and be guided by the man who went as his servant.

It was an odd reversal of roles. And yet it was real – and once again, he and Margaret were on the stage.

* * *

Scamozzi's house, both of them would admit, was more luxurious than expected. Set well back from the road, it sat apart from the dwellings of other prominent citizens who chose to live here in the quiet hamlet of Hoxton, well removed from the summer stink of London. Sir Amos and Lady Gallett, along with their servant, were admitted at the gate by a close-mouthed attendant, and approached the broad, two-storied building. Horses stood riderless on the forecourt, their reins held by boys. A flight of stone steps, flanked by statues of nymphs, led up to an imposing entrance where another servant bowed the guests inside. They were in a wide hallway hung with tapestries, above chests displaying silver plate. Even Margaret was subdued; the trappings of wealth were everywhere.

But there was no time to admire. While their servant Barnabas moved off, murmuring that he would return later, Sir Amos and his spouse adopted courtly airs and walked towards the strains of music, passing through an archway into a large room beyond, where they stopped. A consort of viols and horns played in one corner, though the musicians could barely be seen for the company – which seemed to be made up entirely of men. Cutler stared about, and realised that by including Margaret in their scheme, he and his superior in the enterprise had made an error.

'Welcome, sir... Might I know your name? I don't believe we've seen you here before.'

He turned to find a soberly dressed, middle-aged man at his elbow, eying him curiously: a steward by the look of him. Cutler nodded briskly and announced himself. He was thinking how to account for Margaret's presence, but the other anticipated him.

'And do I have the pleasure of greeting Lady Gallett?' He made a brief bow. 'It's rare for my master's guests to bring their wives.' He eyed Cutler. 'Nonetheless, I pray you will enjoy his hospitality. There are sweetmeats and candied fruits in the cerise room.'

'In truth, I'm come here on a matter of trade with Signor Scamozzi,' Cutler said, thinking fast. 'My wife was merely curious to see the gardens, of which we've heard so much... I'm sure she would like to stroll outside. With your master's approval, of course?'

'That would be most apt,' the steward said. 'I will have a gardener show you the roses—'

'I pray you, do not bother,' Margaret broke in haughtily. 'I've no wish to impose myself further. Will you have a cup of cordial sent out, while I walk?'

'Of course, my lady.' The man inclined his head. 'A boy will attend you.'

It was settled quickly. With a glance at Cutler, his player-wife swept imperiously out into the entrance hall, the steward following. For his part, he allowed his gaze to wander across the assembled guests, talking in groups. Attentive servants moved among them with jugs and trays of cups, while three or four small dogs frisked about their feet. After accepting a drink of sweet wine, he was looking for Scamozzi when someone tugged at his sleeve.

'I forgot to tell you – you should speak to him of the Levant Company,' Barnabas whispered, bending low. 'There's the cause of your speculation: a voyage to Aleppo, say, for which you're seeking funds. And by the way – we're Papists.'

'We're what?' Cutler snapped. But seeing that other men had noticed him and Barnabas, he managed an air of irritation and waved his servant away. Struggling to digest the revelation, he moved slowly among the guests, before finding himself accosted by a florid-faced gentleman who was already somewhat the worse for drink.

'Is it you, Buckley?' he muttered, drawing close and almost spilling his cup.

'It is not, sir.' Cutler looked him up and down. 'I'm Sir Amos Gallett—'

'By God, you're the very image of him,' the other exclaimed. 'I ask your pardon... Here for the gaming, are you?' Without waiting for an answer, he added, 'Pinero's my choice – and my bane. Lost twenty crowns to Scamozzi last time, the devil.'

'Do you know where he is, just now?' Cutler asked casually.

'I may have seen him under the colonnade,' came the vague reply. 'Had it built to remind him of home, I believe... tawdry Italian affectation.'

The worthy raised his cup and drank, giving Cutler the opportunity to escape. Moving away with alacrity, he caught sight of a pair of open doors and headed towards them. It was a relief to step outside and find himself under an arched colonnade overlooking the extensive gardens. There was no sign of Margaret – but here was Scamozzi, seated at a small table with two other gentlemen. A jug and goblets of Italian glass sat before them, and all were taking tobacco, blowing out streams of blue smoke. Girding himself, Cutler made his entrance.

'Signor Scamozzi.' Approaching the table, he inclined his head. 'I pray you'll permit the intrusion... Sir Amos Gallett.'

All three men looked up – whereupon Cutler tensed inwardly. He had almost forgotten that Scamozzi could have seen him when he attended Brisco's inquest, in his capacity as constable. He recalled the man's imposing presence, and the stir he had caused. Today, however, he looked relaxed and wore neither sword nor poniard. One of the dogs sat at his feet, seemingly asleep. And he gave no sign of recognising Cutler, presumably because of the difference in his attire. After a moment, he too inclined his head.

'You are welcome, sir... Have you come here with friends?'

'I have,' Cutler answered. 'But in truth, I came to seek you out on a matter of business. A speculation, which I'm assured might be of interest to you.'

'Ah...' Scamozzi assumed a smile of regret. 'I never discuss such topics on days like this. You might visit me at my premises on the river... next week, perhaps?'

'Alas, I cannot do so.' Cutler matched his regretful look. 'I'm in London only briefly. I must return to my estate in Kent tomorrow.'

'Another time, then.' Scamozzi was about to turn away, bringing an end to the conversation.

'And yet, I was told you would be the ideal man for this venture, sir... *il uomo perfetto*,' Cutler pressed on, with a smile. 'I'm readying a fleet for the Levant... since the Venice Company is no more, one must adapt. As you, of course, will understand.'

A moment followed, but his hopes rose; the host appeared

interested. The other men, nettled by this newcomer's intrusion, regarded him coolly.

'A fleet, you say?' Scamozzi narrowed his eyes. 'How many ships?'

'At present, only four,' Cutler answered, improvising rapidly. 'Yet with your involvement, that could be doubled. I need hardly add that the returns would be great.' And when another moment passed, he added, 'I would be most glad if you could make an exception to your habits today. I swear it would be greatly to your... our mutual advantage, if we might discuss the matter – in private, of course.'

He fell silent, judging it best to say no more. Another moment passed, then:

'Sirs.' Scamozzi turned to his companions. 'Will you indulge me, while I hear Sir Amos?' Leaning down, he fondled the little dog's ears. 'There are times when matters of business must take precedence.' Upon which, with that air of authority Cutler recalled from the day of the inquest, he laid aside his tobacco pipe and waited.

It was enough, of course. Whoever the other two gentlemen were, they had no intention of disappointing their host. Both murmured their assent and rose, taking their pipes with them. Cutler stood aside politely while they ignored him and strolled towards the house. He tried a smile of approval... but before he could direct it at Scamozzi, his attention was caught by a figure standing – or lurking, he might have said – close to the colonnade: Barnabas was watching them intently.

'I pray you, sir, take your ease.' Scamozzi indicated a vacant stool. 'Do you need your cup refilled?'

'No, no...' Cutler sat down, wondering how to play this scene. He needed Barnabas to come to his aid – but likely, as a servant, he would be dismissed. His mind busy, he distracted himself by throwing a glance at the dog.

'Does your friend here have a name, Signor Scamozzi?' he ventured.

'She does...' The other eyed him. 'You spoke of the Levant, Sir Amos. I don't recall your face from the last meeting of that company.'

'I was formerly of the Venice Company,' Cutler told him.

'Before they joined with the Turkey group, then?'

'That is correct.'

'So... you have four ships at your disposal already, you say. Which ones?'

He was regarding his guest keenly. It had not occurred to Cutler that Scamozzi would know the names of ships. To buy time, he put on a smile and glanced towards the spot where he had seen Barnabas, but there was no sign of him.

'As yet, I do not have such particulars,' he said. 'But my associates assure me that all is in hand. As I said, your investment would greatly increase the returns...'

'I will need more than this, sir.' Scamozzi was growing brisk. 'It occurs to me that you are new to the Levant trade. Perhaps when you have the particulars, as you call them, we could talk again. I suggest at my warehouse by Queenhithe.'

At that, Cutler was stuck for a reply; the projection appeared at risk already. With a casual air, he took a drink from his cup... whereupon a figure loomed up from nowhere.

'Master Scamozzi.' Barnabas was at his side, leaning over the table. 'Your pardon for the interruption, but this man has not come to talk trade, and nor have I. We wish to discuss the late Alessandro Brisco, and your relations with him.' Whereupon he pulled a stool out from the table, and sat.

A long and tense pause followed, in which a number of things might have happened. Taut as a post, Cutler braced himself for the arrival of servants with orders to throw him and Barnabas out... but the outcome was quite different.

'So, you have come,' Scamozzi said, very quietly. 'I thought someone would, perhaps even sooner.' He glanced at each of them. 'What do you want?'

Not knowing how to proceed, Cutler kept silent. But Barnabas, it seemed, was prepared.

'It must have been difficult for you, this past week or so,' he said smoothly, looking intently at their host. 'Losing your source of intelligence, I mean. Those snippets, wrought by Brisco from his dainty customers...'

'I asked what you wanted.' Scamozzi's shoulders had tensed, as he met his questioner's eye. 'You must know that I can summon men to overpower you, and—'

'Yes, I know.' Airily, Barnabas dismissed the threat. Cutler was struck by the speed with which he had abandoned his fawning-servant act; he was the interrogator again, who had faced him across Skinner's table the day before. He had discarded his plain coat to reveal an expensive-looking shirt of fine linen. 'But I think that would be unwise, don't you?' He went on. 'We speak of matters of importance, gathered in the interests of Spain and passed from Brisco to you. Now he's dead... which is most unfortunate.'

With that, he waited to allow the words to sink in. But Scamozzi, it seemed, was recovering quickly. With a glance towards the house, he leaned back from the table – but Cutler had begun to recover too. On impulse, he leaned forward.

'Brisco was murdered, most bloodily,' he breathed. 'And since that day, someone has ordered rumours and accusations spread as to the identity of his killer. The result has—'

'Sir Amos.' Barnabas cut him short. 'We're not here to speak of that, are we?' He threw Cutler a warning look. 'No doubt our host here has done what he needed to, in order to settle matters. It's his present predicament that concerns us, is it not?'

But Cutler's anger was rising, as he recalled the injustices of the past week. He was about to speak, when:

'Who are you?' Scamozzi demanded harshly, looking at each of them in turn. 'Or shall I ask, who has sent you?'

'Why, have you not guessed?' Unflustered, Barnabas raised his eyebrows. 'Come, sir. We're men of the same faith as you.' Upon which, he reached inside his shirt and pulled out a small crucifix on a chain, before stowing it away again.

'No... you will not beard me this way,' Scamozzi said angrily. He was the master here; he was a quick thinker and he was gathering his resources. 'Whoever you are, I can have you bound and thrown in a pond, and that will be an end to this. As for your little cross of silver—'

'You forget yourself, master stranger.' In a tone that brooked no argument, Barnabas silenced him. 'Do you think we came here unprepared? Others are aware of our visit, and will act if we do not return. Think now, on your own position – for you should. Your actions are treasonous, as were Brisco's.' And when the other flinched: 'The Queen of England and her Council have no mercy for those who treat with the enemy – I speak of a traitor's death. You'll know what that means.'

A silence fell. Impressed by Barnabas's words, not to say his style, Cutler put on a hard look and eyed their man grimly. A moment followed, then:

'So, what is it you demand?' Scamozzi glanced about swiftly, but no one was nearby. 'That I should buy your silence, or...?'

'Oh, no... nothing so tawdry.' Summoning a wry smile, Barnabas took up one of the glasses left by Scamozzi's departed guests.

'May I? Now, I spoke of your predicament. Here you are, without your friend – your collector of intelligence. Who was also your tenant, I believe. Did he live rent-free, for his services? He seems to have had plenty of money to spread around. Or was serving his religion enough, against the day it might be restored to this country? Either way...' He paused, took a drink and set the glass down. 'My friend and I may be men of similar opinions, but we are not saints. We came here with an offer, and thought it best to do so in full view of your company. Call me reckless, if you like – but I'm no water rat, to come skulking about your wharves.'

He stopped and allowed another silence to fall. Cutler kept expression from his face, but his mind was racing. What did Barnabas have in mind? Silently, he cursed the young man for telling him nothing of what was supposed to happen. But he kept quiet and waited.

'Where did you learn this... these things?' Scamozzi asked, in a different tone.

'In Bishopsgate, among other places,' Barnabas replied. 'Although my friend here went further afield, diligent fellow that he is. Visits to Lady Wheatley and the Countess of Tanridge, who was most obliging, I understand – was she not?'

He eyed Cutler, who gave a brief nod; at last, he was on somewhat safer ground. 'The countess is the most indiscreet woman I've ever met,' he said, turning to Scamozzi. 'She told me a good deal about what she and Brisco did together... and about you too.'

Brisco's former landlord – and receiver of intelligence, it was becoming evident – bristled.

'So... master stranger.' Barnabas eyed him. 'We've made our case, I think. It merely remains for us to trade, does it not?'

'Trade?' Scamozzi frowned. 'But I thought...'

'You thought us a couple of rogues, here to back you into a

corner and then disappear in exchange for a fat purse.' Barnabas summed another wry smile. 'I trust you've now modified your opinion.' He paused – then delivered what Cutler realised was his killing blow. 'As I said at the outset, you've lost your source of intelligence. I'm merely proposing that we fill the void – pick up where your unfortunate perfumer friend left off. In return for our expenses, of course. I expect you can be a generous man when pressed.'

'What?' Scamozzi sat bolt upright. 'Do you jest with me?'

His dark eyes flashed in sudden anger – but for Cutler, a revelation was about to follow. For a second, his gaze strayed to the man's dog... and around its neck, he now saw, was a red ribbon. At the same moment, a faint whiff of jasmine rose, taking him back to Brisco's shop and a little basket of such trifles... and in an instant, everything fell into place. Later, he would be astonished at how he had guessed – but he had.

'By heaven,' he blurted, 'you killed Brisco! You!'

Whereupon, matters unfolded at speed. Without warning, Scamozzi stood up abruptly, dashed jug and glasses aside with a sweep of his hand, and turned towards the house. He was about to shout, causing the others to jump up too – at which point, the little dog, which had thus far remained still, leaped to its feet and barked. Distracted, its owner leaned down as if to brush it away – whereupon Barnabas darted forward.

'Be silent,' he muttered, clapping a hand over the man's mouth. Upon which, Cutler grasped Scamozzi's arm.

'Seize him,' he ordered. 'We must get him away – now!'

Barnabas looked startled, but recovered immediately. Together, they grabbed hold of the man and marched him between them, out from under the colonnade into the garden. He began to struggle, but they were stronger. Quickly, without looking behind, they were able to get him round a corner of the house, towards the rose beds... only to stop at the sight of Margaret, straw hat in hand, regarding them in astonishment.

'Why, Sir Amos. And...?' She gazed at their prisoner. 'What in heaven's name are you men doing?'

18

The situation was hopeless, if not absurd. With Margaret following behind in bewilderment, Cutler and Barnabas hurried their prisoner across the garden, trampling flowers in the process. Meanwhile, Scamozzi's little dog yapped and barked, scurrying about their heels. Where they were headed, they had no idea. There were people in the courtyard at the front, and probably elsewhere... They could have been followed. Looking about, they found themselves beside some outbuildings: stables, and one that could have been a brewhouse.

'In there, quickly,' Cutler breathed.

'And then what?' Barnabas retorted.

'I don't know, but we need to get him out of sight.'

There was no time for argument. Together, they walked their struggling prisoner to the door of the low building and wrenched it open. Then, as Barnabas was pushing Scamozzi inside, there came voices from some distance away. Cutler glanced round quickly, then stepped back.

'I'll try to bluff,' he said. 'You rack him – for he's the man I've been hunting, I'd stake my life on it.' Then, as Barnabas disappeared, he closed the door on him and turned to Margaret, who was still following. 'The dog,' he said, somewhat out of breath. 'Pick it up.'

After a moment's hesitation, she dropped her straw hat, stooped and gathered the squirming creature in her arms, murmuring some soothing words. To Cutler's relief, it quietened, whereupon she frowned at him. 'For pity's sake, Matthew...'

But he had moved to her side, and was taking her arm. 'We were about to return it to its owner,' he said. He managed a smile as two men approached. One was the steward, the other looked like a gardener, stout and muscular.

'Master steward.' Cutler beckoned him close. 'We were at pains to rescue Signor Scamozzi's excitable pet, before she tore herself frisking among the roses. Perhaps you would care to return her?'

'Sir Amos?' The man was frowning. 'I saw someone with you...'

'That was my servant. I've allowed him to go and relieve himself.' He sniffed. 'I shall chastise him later for his incontinence.'

But both men were regarding him, seemingly unconvinced – whereupon Margaret spoke up.

'Will you take her?' she asked. 'She's a charming little maid, but I fear she will stain my frock.'

There was a pause, before the steward gestured impatiently to the gardener, who came forward to take the dog. Having let go of her charge, Margaret threw the man a smile.

'Take good care of her now,' she ordered.

'My master...' the steward began.

'I left him under the colonnade,' Cutler said.

'Well... in that case...' To his relief, the man relaxed somewhat.

Cutler stooped to pick up Margaret's hat and handed it to her, saying, 'We won't detain you longer. Signor Scamozzi being unwilling to discuss matters of trade with me today, I'm taking my leave.'

He assumed a bland smile and waited – until mercifully, the danger passed. With a brief bow, the steward backed away, ushering the gardener to follow. Cutler and Margaret watched until they had disappeared round the corner of the house, whereupon he faced her.

'If you'll walk to the forecourt, I'll meet you there.' And before she could react, he added, 'You did well.' He turned away, opened the door to the brewhouse and stepped inside, blinking in the dim interior. He had barely closed the door before Barnabas' voice startled him from close by.

'You took your time,' he muttered.

* * *

There was small possibility of questioning Scamozzi, though this was what Cutler wished to do. Barnabas had fashioned a makeshift gag from a kerchief, and forced the man to sit on sacks of malt piled against the back wall. The little room with its single window, cluttered with pails, casks and brewery trappings, reeked to its rafters. Standing together, the two looked down at their prisoner. Barnabas had drawn his poniard, which he held menacingly.

'How in God's name are we going to play this?' he demanded, under his breath. 'Do you not see what you've done?'

'I've caught a murderer, that's what I've done,' Cutler answered.

'And I've caught a spy,' Barnabas threw back. But he stepped aside, drawing Cutler with him. 'And yet, I'll allow it's a golden chance,' he said urgently. 'I need one thing from him: the name of the person he passed his intelligence to, once he had it from Brisco. After that, my masters can take the matter in hand.'

'And you think he'll tell you?'

'If we put the fear of God into him...'

But he trailed off. To Cutler's eye he looked agitated; matters had spiralled out of his control, and he was somewhat at a loss. Meanwhile, their prisoner eyed them both; he was angry – and yet, he was afraid too.

'Well, it's enough,' Cutler decided. 'We're both right – this man's as guilty as sin. You can inform your masters.'

'Yes...' Barnabas looked away briefly. 'Provided they'll listen.' He hesitated. 'In truth, I'm not... shall I say, I'm not quite as high-ranked as you thought I was.'

'You're not?' Cutler stared at him. 'In heaven's name, what...?'

'I serve the Council,' the other broke in hastily. 'Only, I'm... if you must know, I'm a secretary.' He sighed. 'Did you think Skinner was on intimate terms with men higher than me?'

'Good God...' Cutler exhaled, and with an effort mastered himself. 'Then, I'm leaving to make report. You can question this man if you like, but I've done my part.'

And before the other could reply, he turned to open the door, stepped outside and looked about. There was nobody near, only a pair of gentlemen strolling some distance away, heads down in conversation. Picking up pace, he walked smartly to the front courtyard, to find Margaret in conversation with one of the horse-holders.

'Sir Amos, at last.' She was stroking the horse's neck while the boy stood by, seemingly in awe of her. 'Have you concluded your business?'

'I have, madam.' Summoning a casual air, Cutler offered his arm. 'Shall we walk?'

'If it please you.' She threw a smile at the horse-boy, who bobbed at once, and turned from him. Then the two of them were moving unhurriedly towards the gate, arm in arm. The gate-keeper opened it and bowed them out. Neither of them spoke until they were well on their way, along the road back to Shoreditch.

'I confess you frightened me, back there,' Margaret said at last.

'No one would have known it,' Cutler said. 'And once again, I'm in your debt.'

'What about our servant? What's he doing?'

'Christ alone knows... but I know one thing.' He stopped walking and faced her. 'I'm done with playing Sir Amos. When we get back, I'll relinquish the sword and these fine clothes, and become plain Matthew Cutler again – for good.'

'Well, that seems a pity,' Margaret said, after a moment. 'I haven't had such excitement in years... not since I saw you fence upon the stage, perhaps.'

She was looking intently at him. He met her gaze, and caught his breath. A moment passed, as she lifted her face to his... upon which they both started, as footsteps came hurrying towards them. Turning, they saw Barnabas, in shirt sleeves with his jerkin over his arm, making haste to catch them. Out of breath, he drew close and stopped.

'It wasn't wasted... far from it,' he said, nodding fiercely. 'You have your murderer, constable – and I have my spy!'

* * *

Half an hour later, after a day Cutler would never forget, he was seated at Margaret's table with a restorative drink before him. She was at the head, with Barnabas – they still knew him by no other name – sitting opposite him. Only now, after information had been shared, was there time for some reflection. For his part, as the reality of what had occurred sank in, Cutler was subdued. It was left to the lady of the house to break the silence.

'You believed Scamozzi, then?' She regarded Barnabas, who had recovered something of the confidence Cutler had first seen at Skinner's house. 'You're certain of it?'

He nodded. 'I played the madman, let him think I'd spike his eyes – blind him, unless he told me what I wanted to know. He chose the best course.'

He glanced at Cutler, who said nothing.

'Yet now, I cannot stay,' Barnabas went on. He had refused a drink himself, and was ready to leave. 'I'll go at once to my masters and tell of what I've done. But I'll keep your name out of it, constable. Along with yours of course, Mistress Fisher. You have my thanks for the aid you've rendered.'

'No... you're not going just yet.' Having found his voice, Cutler looked up sharply. 'You've said I have my murderer – and I want to know every detail.'

'By heaven, must you?' The other was impatient. 'You did your work, isn't that enough?' But when the constable merely held his gaze, he let out a sigh. 'It seems Scamozzi was dissatisfied with the bits of intelligence Brisco was bringing him – as well as the money he was spending. He thought he'd grown careless – a risk, and he didn't trust that rogue Burrell to deal with him. He went to see Brisco himself, by night. They quarrelled – Scamozzi's a vicious fellow, beneath the elegant exterior.' He shrugged. 'You know what he did.'

'So, he got Burrell to muddy the waters afterwards... throw accusations out,' Cutler said, to which Barnabas nodded quickly. 'And he told you all this, as willingly as that?'

'I've told you, I scared him enough to—'

'No.' Cutler shook his head slowly. 'I'll not believe it.' And when the other frowned: 'I'll wager you offered him something – what was it?' His mind was busy – as was Margaret's, he guessed. She too was looking intently at their bogus lackey who, Cutler had already told her, was no more than a secretary with soaring ambitions.

'I think you might explain yourself further, sir,' she said calmly. 'My servants are within call, and most devoted to my protection. Between them and Sir Amos here, I expect you could be detained easily enough.'

A moment followed... but it was no bluff, and Barnabas saw it. 'I told him he won't be arrested for murder,' he admitted.

'You did what?' Cutler sat up sharply.

'It's the only way,' the other went on, speaking quickly. 'I got the name of the Papist he talks to – the agent for Spain – but I won't reveal his name. It's a matter for the Council – and you can press me all you like,' he added, with a defiant look. 'Your part is finished – you could already face arrest, after what you've done. You can go back to your parish and calm people, tell them the murder is solved: a private matter, and no further threat. Let the dust settle.'

But Cutler's anger was rising anew. 'Let the dust settle?' he echoed. 'After all that righteous chaff Scamozzi spouted at Brisco's inquest... giving his poor countryman a burial – the man he himself had slain? I'll be damned if I'll let a murderer go free!'

'He will not be free,' Barnabas said testily. 'I lied to him – told him I'd give him the rest of the day to settle his affairs. In truth, he'll be captured and taken to the Tower within hours, to be interrogated at length. What happens then is beyond my knowledge – and far beyond your place to question. I've told you what you should do.'

'You have,' Cutler replied. 'And yet...'

But Barnabas stood up deliberately, pushing his stool aside. 'Think of your family, constable,' he said coolly. 'You can bring them home now, and have peace.'

A moment passed, as they regarded each other. Margaret remained silent – but it was all over, and Cutler saw it. Niccolo Scamozzi's crime of espionage was great – greater even than murder, in the eyes of the Crown. He would not be named as the slayer of the perfumer Brisco, and yet in the end, he would pay with his life, though the people of Bishopsgate would know nothing of that. The safety of the realm was at stake – and in time of war, secrecy was everything.

'I'll sing your praises to Alderman Skinner,' Barnabas said, with a nod to Cutler. 'He'll get a letter soon... but you must say nothing of what's happened. Believe me, it's for the best.'

They were his parting words: the last either of them would ever hear from him. With an elegant little bow to Margaret, the young man turned away. Cutler did not rise, but watched him go out the door in silence.

Finally, Margaret spoke.

'He is right, I suppose,' she murmured, with a sigh. 'You can recall Margery and your daughters, and live as a family again... master constable.'

He met her eye, but could find no words.

* * *

By the Sunday morning, the weather had changed again. Cutler awoke in his own bed in his own house, to the sound of rain on the thatch. For a moment, he lay still, as the events of the previous day came into focus... then he was up, and eager to act.

He dressed quickly, thinking of the day ahead with something closer to contentment than he had felt in many days. The previous evening, he had found the carter who had taken Margery and the girls away and engaged him again, doubling his fee on account of it being Sunday. The man had promised to leave as soon as the city gate was opened – he should already be on his way. Meanwhile, Cutler had much to do.

There was no food in the house for a breakfast, but he cared nothing for that. Within the half-hour, he was outside and walking down Bishopsgate Street in the rain, to tell John Willard that their troubles were over; he would skip the details. He found the gunsmith up and about, and informed him that their family would return sometime that afternoon. To Willard's questions, he gave only brief answers.

'You look like a different man, Matthew.' His father-in-law was looking him over in surprise. 'What in heaven's name has happened?'

'It'll wait,' Cutler said, already heading for the door. 'You must sup with us tonight. I have a tale for you – one that I scarcely believe myself.'

And he was out again among the folk of his parish, some of them making their way to St Leonard's church. His destination was closer: the house of the button-maker, Jean Meunier. Finding the shop door bolted, he knocked and waited... only to be distracted by a familiar voice, forcing him to turn impatiently.

'Master constable.' Henry Deans, cloaked and hatted, was regarding him frostily. 'Might I speak with you?' And on receiving a nod: 'You're to attend Master Skinner at your earliest convenience, if you'd be so kind.'

'I've a good deal to do,' Cutler told him. 'Perhaps tomorrow?'

'It's important,' Deans said. 'Or so I was told. Ward business.'

'Oh?' Cutler eyed him, thinking the man looked somewhat subdued, standing in the downpour. 'Are we both summoned, then?'

'It seems not.' Deans looked aside, water dripping from the brim of his hat. 'As it seems I've been reduced to the role of message-carrier today. Well, I've done my office.'

Cutler watched him stalk off up the street, wondering what Skinner wanted. But at the sound of a bolt being drawn, he turned about quickly. The door opened to reveal the button-maker standing stiffly before him. On recognising the constable, however, he relaxed somewhat.

'Might I come in, Master Meunier?' Cutler asked.

It was a short visit, barely longer than the one he had made to Willard. Standing in the shop, with its windows curtained, he told the button-maker that the murderer of Alessandro Brisco had been caught, and that the danger was passed. There was no campaign against the strangers, he said firmly, and never had been. It was a personal grudge, over Brisco's affair with a man's wife. The same man had arranged for the attack on Meunier, to sow confusion. He and his friends could now sleep easier, and put the matter behind them.

The tidings, however, were not received with as much warmth as he had hoped.

'I thank you, constable,' the artisan said. 'Yet some of those hereabout will not be reassured. They still meet and keep a watch on each other. Since Master Kett went away, there are few officers of the law here. As for the deputy alderman...' He shrugged. 'We put little faith in him.'

'I will be on the street again, starting from today,' Cutler said. 'I give you my word on it.'

Whereupon, Madame Meunier spoke. 'We heard there will be a burial tomorrow, for the watchman Bland,' she said. 'Will you attend, Master Cutler?'

'I will...' He found himself frowning; in the turmoil of recent days, he had almost forgotten about Stephen Bland. 'And more,

I'm to see Alderman Skinner soon. I will speak with him of what's passed here.'

The two of them regarded him in silence: an industrious and kindly couple. He was moved – not only to respect them, but with a wish to protect them. 'Will you tell your friends what I've told you?' he asked. 'I don't have the time to visit everyone.'

'We will, gladly.' Meunier nodded, and threw a glance at his wife. 'Yet, can you not tell the name of this villain who killed Monsieur Brisco? It would ease my mind to know it.'

'Alas, I cannot.' Cutler met his eye. 'I wasn't the one who captured him. But I swear to you that he's taken, and can do no more harm.'

To his relief, it seemed to satisfy them. After a farewell to Madame Meunier, he went to the door and was seen out by the button-maker. On the threshold, they paused.

'Bland was a good watchman,' Meunier said. 'And yet, I never felt truly at ease with him. Josiah Madge is, as we say, *un voyou*... a rough fellow. But I trust him – as I do you, Matthew Cutler. *A demain*... until the morrow?'

'Until the morrow,' Cutler said, and stepped out into the rain.

* * *

Fortunately, by the time he had arrived at the house of Thomas Skinner, the shower had tailed off, though the streets were awash. St Helen's parish was busy, bells clanging as people made their way to the church. After shaking the worst of the rainwater from his clothes, Cutler was admitted to the alderman's private chamber where he waited, standing before the fire. There were voices from without, as the man's family and servants made ready to leave. Master Skinner himself, however, would be following them later, as Cutler soon discovered.

'Constable.' The man greeted him on entering, dressed in a fine suit of black taffeta. 'I'll not stay you for long. Have you taken breakfast?'

'I have, alderman,' Cutler said, not wishing to prolong the visit. 'I had word from Deans...'

'I know.' The man was crossing the room to his table. 'Sit, will you?'

Cutler brought a stool and sat down facing him. On his way here, he had tried to order his thoughts, but without success. How much Skinner knew about his escapade with the young man who had called himself Barnabas, he could not know... He hoped it was nothing at all. But he stiffened when the man picked a paper up from his table, and remembered: *I'll sing your praises*, Barnabas had said. *He'll get a letter...*

'You've been a busy man, Cutler,' Skinner said, after a moment. 'Moreover, it seems you are to be thanked.'

'There's no need,' he began, whereupon the other lifted a hand.

'The thanks come not from me, but from the Privy Council... or at least, from one of its clerks.' He held up the letter. 'It was brought by hand early this morning. Though it's short on specifics, merely stating that you did good service. I wonder what they mean?'

His constable gave no reply.

'The man who was here... with whom I left you alone.' Skinner looked uncomfortable. 'What did he want of you?'

'It's... there's little to speak of,' Cutler answered, realising that he had rather dreaded a conversation of this nature. 'I told him all I knew, and he said he would act.'

'Well, there's more here,' the alderman said. 'For one thing, I'm told that the villain who murdered the perfumer is caught, and will be dealt with at the Queen's pleasure.' With a frown, he dropped the letter. 'I think that means I'm to forget about him – as I recall I urged you to do. Can you shed more light on that?'

'I cannot, Master Skinner.' Cutler kept his face free from expression.

The alderman paused, then: 'I'm also advised to offer you a post, subject to proper procedures being followed. The post of my deputy, that is, for the Ward of Bishopsgate Without. I expect that surprises you, for it certainly surprised me.' He waited, but when Cutler made no answer: 'Of course, it would depend on Henry Deans' willingness to stand down,' he added. 'However, that might not be insurmountable.' He cleared his throat and paused again; the man was more ill-at-ease than Cutler had ever seen him. Stuck for an answer, he averted his eyes and waited.

'In truth, words of discontent have been expressed,' the alderman resumed stiffly. 'I won't say more, although...' But he stopped as Cutler sat up abruptly. He had found his voice, and knew what he should do.

'I pray you, there's no need to say more, Master Skinner,' he said. 'I've no desire to have Deans' post.'

'No desire?' The other blinked. 'I thought...'

'Nor do I wish for anything other than to remain constable of my parish,' Cutler broke in. 'With your leave, that is.'

In near disbelief, Skinner stared at him. Matters of rank and status were everything to the man who hoped to become Lord Mayor. And here was his constable, this former player, refusing a chance to better himself... He swallowed.

'You are certain?'

'I'm certain,' Cutler said. 'And just now, I have much to do in Bishopsgate. The people have been afraid since the murder – a new constable should be found soon, for St Botolph's.'

'Well, indeed.' Skinner nodded – but Cutler hadn't finished.

'And the watchman Bland is to be buried tomorrow, at St Leonard's. Will you attend?'

'If I can.' Somewhat embarrassed, Skinner lowered his gaze. His constable's manner was altered, although he could not have said why he thought so. But the conversation was over... With relief, Cutler stood up.

'I'll leave you to take your family to church,' he said.

'Yes... I thank you,' came the uncertain reply.

But Cutler was already leaving the room, with a somewhat lighter step than when he had arrived.

He could hardly wait for the afternoon... As he left the house, he was even smiling.

19

Evening fell, and his family were home.

It had been only five days, yet it felt like an age, Margery said, as she embraced Cutler warmly. She and his daughters were tired and stiff after their journey, but it was not long before they began filling the house with chatter and bustle. Margery had brought a basket up from Surrey: a roasted goose, greens and a damson tart. The fire was lit, and supper would soon be on hand. But to their questions, Cutler was evasive: Brisco's murderer had been apprehended, and there was nothing more to fear.

'We'll talk further, someday,' he told Katherine, who it seemed had been restless while they were away. 'You should visit your friends, and put these troublesome days behind.'

'And what of Mistress Fisher, father?' she asked. 'Have you—'

'I've seen her about.' He turned quickly to Margery. 'John Willard will sup with us. He'll be mighty glad to see you returned.'

'Well, I shall be glad too.' She was eying him shrewdly. 'I spoke with the carter a little, on our homeward journey,' she added. 'He said you've not been at home much, of late. Can we truly be sure that all is put to rights?'

'You can,' he assured her. Whereupon, having remembered that there was nothing to drink with their supper, he announced that he would venture out in search of some ale. His daughters watched him go.

'He's been with Margaret,' Jane said, with a knowing look. 'How long will it be before he admits his feelings for her?'

Katherine chose not to answer.

And yet, when supper time came and the whole family were at table again, there was less speculation than Cutler had feared, and a deal more gossip. Their brief sojourn in Surrey had been uneventful, to his relief, while their own questions he answered only in vague terms. He was more ready to speak of the burial on the morrow, which most of Bishopsgate would surely attend. His hope was that, along with the body of Stephen Bland, the turbulent events following Brisco's death would be laid to rest too.

Only later, as he and John Willard took the air in Cutler's back yard, would he elaborate further about the events of the past days. The gunsmith, he knew, was a man who could keep his mouth firmly closed. It went with his trade, he had often said; customers who ordered firearms expected him to respect their confidences.

'By heaven, Matthew...' His father-in-law let out a sigh, gazing out to the distant fields. 'You've ploughed your furrow to the very end. I never knew a constable get so deep in matters beyond his office. Though it seems to me you've been somewhat lucky too.' He paused, then: 'Have you not had enough of it?'

'What... of my post, in this parish?' Cutler gave a shrug. 'What else would I do?'

'You'll not return to play-acting, then?'

'In truth, I think I've done enough of that lately.'

They were silent for a while, before Willard turned and clapped him on the shoulder. 'Let's inside then, and drink to the future,' he said. 'Or to the morrow, at least.'

Cutler nodded, and followed him into the house.

***

On the Monday morning, under a cloudy sky, Stephen Bland's burial was a sombre enough affair... or at least, so was that part of it that took place in the church. Once everyone had moved outside, the atmosphere changed considerably. The crowd, from the poor in their humble attire to the better dressed inhabitants of Bishopsgate Ward Without, proceeded to the grave in a straggle, already falling into conversation. Nearby, the sexton stood apart with his spade. Without too much ceremony, the body in its winding sheet was lowered into the ground, and the last part of the service delivered by the white-haired parson. Cutler looked towards the bench where he and Bland had sat that day: the last time he had seen the watchman alive. It seemed like an age ago.

He stood close to his daughters, along with Aunt Margery and John Willard, a short distance from the graveside. The only person related to the deceased was Bland's widow, swathed in black drugget, with head bowed. Others stood about: Henry Deans at his most officious, and Roger Farrant, who avoided Cutler's eye; once again, it seemed, Alderman Skinner was unable to attend. A small number of artisans had assembled, Meunier and his wife among them. There too, somewhat to his surprise, was Mary Martinhouse without her husband. He caught her eye, but she looked away. He had just noticed Josiah Madge standing a little way beyond her when his eye fell on Alice Leake, in an elegant gown of red and black, regarding him defiantly. For once, she was not accompanied by her tame giant. He returned her gaze... then stiffened. Margaret was on the edge of the crowd, and she too was looking his way. He raised a hand in greeting, and saw it returned; there were matters to be faced, which would not wait forever.

'I had a notion you'd be here, constable,' someone muttered. 'I thought I'd best come along too, see him put in the earth. Makes a kind of an ending, does it not?'

Recognising the voice at once, Cutler looked round: Ned Broad, in a scuffed leather jerkin, was at his elbow. The little scarecrow sniffed and drew a sleeve across his nose.

'Seems like all of Bishopsgate is here,' he went on. 'I never thought they cared enough... What say you?'

'I'd say they cared enough, Ned,' Cutler said.

'Aye... well, we're all God's creatures, some might say.' Ned threw him a crafty look. 'Even dyed-in-the wool sinners like me, eh?'

Whereupon he was gone, slipping into the crowd. Cutler caught a glimpse of his retreating figure, and turned back to his family. The funeral was over, and already people were drifting away. He watched them leave: the people of Bishopsgate, returning to their busy lives.

After all that had passed, he was still constable... and the keeper of their secrets.

* * *

MORE FROM JOHN PILKINGTON

The Ruffler's Child, the first instalment in John Pilkington's gripping Thomas the Falconer Mystery series, is available to order now here:

https://mybook.to/RufflersChildBackAd

ABOUT THE AUTHOR

John Pilkington has been a writer for over forty years, having written plays for radio and theatre, television scripts, children's series and numerous works of historical fiction, concentrating now on the Tudor and Stuart eras. He also ventured into speculative fiction with his biography of Shakespeare's famous jester, Yorick. John lives in Devon with his partner.

Download your exclusive bonus content from John Pilkington here:

Visit John's website: www.johnpilkington.co.uk

Follow John on social media here:

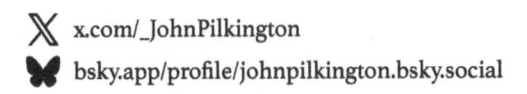

X x.com/_JohnPilkington
bsky.app/profile/johnpilkington.bsky.social

ALSO BY JOHN PILKINGTON

The Bishopsgate Ward Mysteries

Death of a Stranger

The Thomas the Falconer Mysteries

The Ruffler's Child

A Ruinous Wind

The Ramage Hawk

The Mapmaker's Secret

The Maiden Bell

The Jingler's Luck

The Muscovy Chain

POISON
& pens

POISON & PENS IS THE HOME OF
COZY MYSTERIES SO POUR YOURSELF
A CUP OF TEA & GET SLEUTHING!

DISCOVER PAGE-TURNING NOVELS FROM
YOUR FAVOURITE AUTHORS &
MEET NEW FRIENDS

JOIN OUR
FACEBOOK GROUP

BIT.LYPOISONANDPENSFB

SIGN UP TO OUR
NEWSLETTER

BIT.LY/POISONANDPENSNEWS

Boldwood

Boldwood Books is an award-winning fiction publishing company seeking out the best stories from around the world.

Find out more at www.boldwoodbooks.com

Join our reader community for brilliant books, competitions and offers!

Follow us
@BoldwoodBooks
@TheBoldBookClub

Sign up to our weekly deals newsletter

https://bit.ly/BoldwoodBNewsletter